Chelzy Stone's Mystical Quest in The Lost and Found Game

Chelzy Stone's
Mystical Quest
in The Lost and Found Game

Alex,
I hope you
enjoy this
magical adventure!

Lucille Procopio
Carin Shanley

LUCILLE PROCOPIO

Illustrated by Carin Shanley

RoseLamp

Publications, LLC

RoseLamp Publications, LLC, Wilkes-Barre 18705
©2013 by Lucille Procopio
Printed in the United States of America

ISBN: 978-0-9860607-0-0

Library of Congress Control Number: 2013917902

Edited by Brenda Judy
www.publishersplanet.com

Cover and Interior Illustrations by Carin Shanley
www.carinshanley.com

Cover and Interior Design by Carolyn Sheltraw
www.csheltraw.com

This book is a work of fiction. The characters, names, incidents, dialogue and plot are the products of the author's imagination or are used fictiously. Any resemblance to actual persons or events is purely coincidental.

∞ This paper meets the requirements of ANSI/NISO Z39.48-1992 (Permanence of Paper).

www.LucilleProcopio.com

For my husband, Frank, son, Steven, and daughter, Shelley,
who have surrounded me with more love than magic can ever bring.

Acknowledgments

Chelzy, Matthew and Tory, characters in *Chelzy Stone's Mystical Quest in The Lost and Found Game*, have been extremely anxious to leave their home in the hard drive of my computer, where they have been held captive for several years, and travel into the world in print and eBooks to share their adventure with young readers everywhere. Their escape has been made possible with the help of these special people:

To my husband, Frank, who has supported all my efforts, even when he wasn't sure where they were taking me;

To my son, Steve, who discussed mutated flies and robot-like creatures with me;

To my daughter, Shelley, my real-life Chelzy, who was at my side every step of the way, allowing me to seek her opinion on just about everything;

To my calico cat, aptly named Princess, who spent many an hour on my lap while I worked on the computer, not allowing me to move or stop typing;

To my great copy editor, Brenda Judy, who is not only a master at what she does, but who has guided me along, step by step;

To my illustrator, Carin Shanley, who worked so diligently to capture the essence of the adventure;

To my graphic designer, Carolyn Sheltraw, who magically put all the pieces together into my first book;

To Cody Januszko and Marissa Warnick, former students and new and upcoming authors, who kept me believing in the story and helped me make it better;

To Nicole Traeger, a very dear friend, who read the story and helped me see a future in it;

To Laura Rudloff, a special friend, who is assisting me in getting the word out about this magical story;

To Amy Walsh and the *Writing by the Word* writers' group, who helped me improve my writing early on;

To Madelyn Camasso, a gifted educator and friend, who is assisting me in my efforts to connect this magical adventure to learning in the classroom;

To J.D. Verazin, who had an enormous amount of patience, working with me to design my website;

To Dusty White, an author, who told me I could do it all.

To All of You, I Give My Profound Thanks

Prologue

An article from this month's edition of *The Paranormal Post* magazine:

The Disappearance
by Gary Grim

A section of the 200 block of Sycamore Street, Simonsville, located in northeastern Pennsylvania, is thought to be haunted as reported by some of the older residents. Peter Raven, a restaurant owner in the town, commented, "People, mainly teens, but a few adults also, have reported seeing ghosts walking through the playground at night. I'm not saying that I believe them, but the sightings have been numerous over the years and always in the vicinity of where an alleged abduction occurred decades ago."

The incident Mr. Raven refers to occurred early in the evening of November 18, 1982. Three children from the same family, two boys and a girl—ages 7, 8 and 10 respectively—disappeared while walking not far from their home on the 200 block of Sycamore Street. Police and detectives, including the FBI, have not been able to solve what they now consider to have been a kidnapping case.

Judith Takenette, a local resident, conveyed to our investigative team, "Many folks believe that deadly harm came to those poor children and that their spirits walk the streets at night, trying to find someone to help them. Of course, I am not saying that I believe this silly notion."

Several witnesses were interviewed by local law enforcement after the event in November 1982. One elderly man, who did not want his name printed, swore to police that he saw a black Cadillac drive up to the children, then two men got out of the car and forced the children into the backseat. According to him, the car drove away at a high rate of speed. Upon further investigation and reenactment of the apparent crime scene, it was found that the witness was suffering from cataracts in both eyes and, with the time being near sunset, he was unable to see much of anything from his porch where he was sitting. Hence, his account was dismissed as unreliable.

Another witness, Vanisha Plendergone, reported that she was walking in the same direction as the children, but on the opposite side of the street, and was about forty yards away when she saw a group of what appeared to be older children run out from a backyard. She wasn't sure, but she noted that it looked like the three young children followed them into another backyard. Unfortunately, she had broken her eyeglasses that same morning and, being nearsighted, she admitted everything appeared a little blurry.

The statement from the last witness was dismissed by law enforcement officials as mere speculation, so the official report stated just that. The last witness was John Avis Windsor, a local attorney. Mr. Windsor said that as he was driving his car slowly in the area where the children were walking, he observed three very large black birds swoop down near the children and then, after they flew away, he noticed the children were gone. Having taken up bird watching in his partial retirement, he told the police that he had never observed any species of birds that large in this area or, for that matter, anywhere else.

After talking with several older residents, *The Paranormal Post* reporters discovered that no one in law enforcement believed Mr. Windsor. Michael Dobbs, from Dobbs Emporium, explained, "I was told that John, I mean Attorney Windsor, swore to his story many times, even took a lie detector test, but eventually gave in and went for therapy to try to determine why his mind was playing such tricks on him. I am told that Attorney Windsor, now in his 80s, resides in a psychiatric hospital in the neighboring town of Bloomston. That was a sad, sad case. He was such a successful attorney, and look what happened to him."

Officials never closed the case but they had to cut back on the amount of time spent on it since all efforts proved unproductive. They have given very little attention to it in recent years. However, ten years ago, the citizens of Simonsville decided that these children should not be forgotten. So, the townspeople, working together, held several community fundraisers, including a 5K run. Participants who were not able to run the 3.1 miles were allowed to just walk the distance.

Students in the community also helped raise money by holding bake sales at school and car washes at the local gas station. They even did projects in art class and auctioned off paintings, drawings and sculptures to families and friends at an evening auction. "This was such a fun project to raise money. The auction was so cool because we couldn't wait to see how much people were going to pay for our projects," commented Samantha Artis, a fifth grade student at Simonsville Elementary.

Together, enough funds were raised to purchase a parcel of land near the location where the three children had been taken. It was easy to get the land because stories of the ghost of a young girl appearing in the area of the playground, as well as a number of people experiencing other strange phenomena, made it impossible to sell a few properties near the site. Volunteers from every walk of life and occupation throughout the town volunteered their time and materials, and prepared the playground site, installed equipment and mounted a dedication plaque with the names of the three children at its entrance.

Children in Simonsville have been using the playground regularly, and several families have organized a group of willing people to provide maintenance and upkeep of the play area. Brian Fright, a local historian, stated, "Some people have not heard of the stories associated with the abduction of the children or the ghostly apparitions that have occurred. Parents have tried to protect their children from these disturbing accounts and it has usually worked with the younger children, but teenagers have been found trespassing late at night, trying to scare each other by conjuring up ghosts of the children. Unfortunately for them, it has worked from time to time."

A high school student, interviewed by one of our reporters, stated, "Some of my friends say they have seen a young girl in a white dress floating about two feet from the ground, and moving in and out of the playground equipment. They say that her face is narrow but has no features, such as a mouth or eyes. She is not very tall, indicating to them that she is maybe 8 to 10 years old. I have an early curfew so I am not one of those eyewitnesses to the ghost. Of course, my friends' parents don't believe them; but I sort of do."

New information concerning this case can be reported to the Simonsville Police Department. As far as the ghostly sightings, are they true or made up? Were the children abducted or did something out of the ordinary happen to them? We may never know the answers to these questions; but, one thing is for certain, it remains an uncanny mystery that may never be solved.

CHAPTER 1

The Appearance of the Blue Unicorn

Chelzy Stone was not happy with her family's move to Simonsville last August. It meant she had to leave her friends behind, go to a new school and, worst of all, try to make new friends. Having just finished her first school year in the new town, she was thrilled that summer vacation had finally arrived. Even though she joined cheerleading and a few clubs at school, and made a couple of new friends, she was disappointed when she discovered that none of them lived close to her.

Her brother, Matthew, didn't mind the move as much. All that mattered to him was that his new school had a basketball team. Now, both were happy that it was the end of June and school was out, and they would finally have their first summer to investigate their new neighborhood.

Even though they missed their old friends, Chelzy and Matthew found their new neighborhood to be welcoming and kid-friendly.

The two-story houses stood tall and straight as they lined Sycamore Street. Even though similar in size and style, each house reflected a sense of nobility and charisma all its own. The sun-faded shutters and half-drawn shades made the windows look like eyes, and Chelzy imagined each house as a character in a fairy tale. The houses were built sometime back in the mid-twentieth century, and they had large front porches, perfect for hanging out with friends, and wide, welcoming walkways that easily accommodated bikes and skateboards. People jogging or just walking by always greeted the Stones with a smile or friendly hello.

The Stone's backyard was long and narrow. An area in the back of the yard was sectioned off for Mrs. Stone's vegetable garden and Mr. Stone used another area along the fence to stack wood for the winter. An alleyway, situated directly behind their fenced-in yard, led to a large, thick-wooded area that had nothing in it except bushes, rocks and trees. When Chelzy had asked her dad why no one ever cut down the trees to build houses, Mr. Stone replied, "I heard there were several people who owned the property but they could not agree on a selling price."

It seemed odd to Chelzy that this large wooded area was untouched by humans. She wondered if some type of spell or enchantment was put on it to preserve it for some other purpose.

* * * * * * * * *

As Chelzy and Matthew walked home from the bus stop on the last day of school, Chelzy decided to share her thoughts with her brother, "Bro, there is something very strange about the woods behind our house. I can feel it. It is almost like an incantation was put on it by someone so no one will touch it."

"SSSHHH, Chelz! There're kids behind us. They'll think we're crazy if they hear you."

Crazy or not, Chelzy and Matthew would eventually find out what made the mysterious wooded area behind their house so intriguing. But for now, they arrived home and flung their empty book bags on the nearest chair in the kitchen; and, in her loudest and happiest voice, Chelzy yelled, "Mom, we're home. School is out and today we begin summer! Yay!"

* * * * * * * * *

Over the last few weeks of school, Chelzy was thinking about her summer vacation. There were no kids her age living nearby, but this did not stop her from planning an exciting summer. She was just not sure how she could make it thrilling. Other than cheerleading camp, video games, going to the movies, meeting a few friends in the next block near the playground, gymnastic lessons and, of course, visits to grandpa and grandma's house, there was nothing out of the ordinary happening.

Going to Grandma and Grandpa Stone's house was always an adventure for Chelzy and Matthew. Grandpa Stone was the opposite of looking gaunt. He had a wide build, and a face with a white beard and bushy eyebrows. The only thing that kept him from being Santa Claus at Christmas was his lack of hair on his head. Chelzy had suggested that they buy him a wig so he could play Santa in the school Christmas play. Grooming his beard with his right hand, grandpa had said, "It is something to consider; and consider it, I will." But, of course, he never accepted their offer of a wig or the opportunity to be the main character in the school's holiday program.

Besides having fun plotting a way to convince him to be Santa Claus, Chelzy and Matthew especially enjoyed the supposedly make-believe stories Grandpa Stone would tell them about bizarre happenings from the past on Sycamore Street. "Don't believe those incredulous tales that grandpa tells you," their mother would warn. "He is getting older and his imagination is getting bigger all the time." Big imagination or not, the stories grandpa told were always mesmerizing, and Chelzy and Matthew could not get enough of them.

Thinking about Grandpa Stone made Chelzy wonder about the wooded area behind their house and the stories associated with it. Maybe Matthew would explore the Magic Woods with her. That's the name Grandpa Stone used in the stories he told them. She was, however, determined to find something intriguing and challenging so she would not have to succumb to a boring summer, which included required reading from their teachers. The last thing that she wanted to happen was to have to return to school and, when given the usual assignment to write about "what you did this summer that was fun," have nothing interesting to report.

That's what happened to a boy in her class last year, Timothy Tremont. Mrs. Moonster made each of the students stand up in front of the classroom and read their summer essay. Timothy simply wrote, "I went nowhere, I did nothing and I have nothing to tell." Mrs. Moonster made him rewrite the essay and find something to report.

Since it was their first afternoon free from worries about school or homework, Chelzy and Matthew ate lunch and then ran to their backyard. Matthew brought out Superman comic books to read while Chelzy lay in the grass looking at the clouds floating over her house. Suddenly, an ominous, thick black cloud materialized in the bright sky and hung directly over the wooded area behind the Stone's backyard.

Black hail fell from the cloud, piercing the rainbow that had appeared out of nowhere and bravely dared to cross the cloud's path. The bright colors changed to dismal shades of brown, gray and black as the rainbow shattered into pieces. The silhouette of a lady dressed in a black cloak, flying about like a witch without a broomstick, could be seen for only a few seconds as she captured the black cloud, put it into her pocket and disappeared downward into the tree tops.

"Why isn't that bird falling from the sky? He isn't flapping his wings," remarked Chelzy as she moved in the grass as if making a snow angel.

"He's just gliding in the air like a plane or a kite," responded Matthew, almost annoyed at his sister's ridiculous question. "And do not interrupt me again."

"Well, if you're so smart, Bro, why doesn't everything look sideways if I am lying on my back?" Quickly turning her head, she said, "Hey, what's that? I thought I saw something over there in the sky over the woods. It looked huge and black, like a bird or something,"

"I don't see anything, and stop asking those silly questions! I'm hungry and I'm going in the house to eat lunch. If you have any more questions, ask that tall maple tree next to you," Matthew replied sarcastically as he ran up the wooden porch steps, making it a point to skip over every other step leading to the kitchen door, "maybe it'll have an answer for you."

"Trees don't talk; and anyway, you just think I'm stupid," Chelzy yelled in her brother's direction. "Everyone just thinks I'm stupid because I'm the youngest in the neighborhood, youngest in my class, and worst, youngest in my family. Why can't I have a younger brother or sister? And why am I talking to a tree?"

Chelzy lay gazing into the sky, watching a very large black bird circle overhead. Just as she turned to get to her feet, she saw something that both startled and puzzled her.

"Matthew, Matthew, hurry! Come here quick! I—I just saw something strange and big and black in the sky!"

Matthew spun around quickly, almost hitting his head on the wooden post on the porch. "Chelzy, you're crazy. Don't be an idiot. There's nothing there. It was probably a black cloud changing its shape. Come on and eat lunch so we can check out the new neighbors moving in across the street." Matthew ignored his sister's screechy yelling and entered the kitchen.

"But, Matt, I really did see something strange. It was right over there. It was like big and black, and then it disappeared and then I saw something shaped like a lady wearing a black cloak. Oh, never mind. You never believe anything I say," muttered Chelzy, as she reached the steps to her back porch. As she stepped on each of the ten gray, worn steps, she stared at the sky where the illusive large black bird and lady had appeared and then disappeared. She felt a chill travel down her spine. The last time she felt this way was when her mom took her to the doctor's for a measles shot.

Just as Chelzy entered the kitchen and closed the screen door behind her, a blue unicorn landed on the back porch. A square piece of black cloth was hanging from its mouth. As it opened its mouth, the cloth floated down to the porch floor. The blue unicorn seemed pleased that she had accomplished her mission and soon took flight, disappearing into the sky.

CHAPTER 2

Tory the Adventurer

Chelzy's favorite sandwich was peanut butter and jelly. As she spread the peanut butter on a slice of bread, she would always make the design of an animal or flower, making sure that Matthew did not see what she was doing.

Matthew was the self-proclaimed artist in the family, and he liked to take credit for making the best clay models or drawing the best pictures. Of course, their mom would encourage him by always complimenting his work. Chelzy felt that she could never do things quite as well as her brother, even though her mom or dad would always say, "You'll get better at things as you get older, honey."

Matthew had a talent for solving riddles and puzzles, and for taking things apart and putting them back together. He also had a curiosity that would sometimes get him in real trouble. When he was in kindergarten, he decided that he would figure out just how a computer could play video games; so, he proceeded to take his father's desktop computer apart. As soon as Mr. Stone discovered the one hundred plus parts on the floor when he returned from work one day, Matthew was forbidden to touch anything electrical or mechanical in the same way ever again.

Chelzy knew that she wasn't as talented in an artistic way as her brother, but she still liked drawing and making sculptures of animals out of papier-mâché. When she was done forming a bird on the bread, she quietly admired it and then quickly covered it with jelly.

"Mmmm, I didn't think a bird could taste so good," Chelzy muttered as she slowly chewed the first bite of her sandwich.

Without hesitation, Matthew responded, "Now I know why I call you a birdbrain sometimes, Sis!"

Matthew liked cheese, a lot of cheese. He prepared a sandwich with four slices of cheese draped in mustard and ate it a lot quicker than Chelzy did hers.

"If I'm a birdbrain, then you're a cheesehead," Chelzy shouted. "It's disgusting to eat that much cheese at one time."

"All right you two, stop the name-calling, finish your lunches and go back outside to play. Remember, we're going to grandma and grandpa's house tonight right after dinner," ordered Mrs. Stone.

Most of Grandpa Stone's tales involved the disappearance of children from Simonsville and the wooded area behind Chelzy's house that became known as the Magic Woods. "There are other stories about bizarre incidents that date back to the 1800s, and they have been passed on from one generation to the next even though most of the citizens of the town have dismissed them as simply unexplainable occurrences," Grandpa Stone noted. Not only did Chelzy enjoy listening to Grandpa Stone's incredible stories but she especially liked the way both her grandma and grandpa made her feel so special and loved.

But, today was the day that she wanted to find out if the new neighbors had any kids her age with whom she could become friends. Since summer vacation had just started, they would have the entire summer to do things together. As Matthew swallowed the last bite of his cheese sandwich, he grabbed his sister's sleeve. He pulled her forward, walking through the dining room, living room and eventually out the door onto the front porch.

The new neighbors, the Herolds, were still unloading a few boxes from their SUV and bigger items from a U-Haul. They had moved in directly across the street from the Stones. "Tory, come and help me with the bags in the backseat of the car," yelled Mrs. Herold.

A young girl, maybe slightly older than Chelzy but younger than Matthew, appeared in the front doorway. Her long, blonde hair and blue eyes showed a resemblance to her father, who was using a dolly to move a TV set onto the front porch. Chelzy, on the other hand, resembled her mother because of her curly, black hair and brown eyes. As Grandma Stone always said, "Matthew is a spittin' image of his pa, having red hair, dark eyes and a light complexion; but Chelzy is her ma, no doubt about it."

Chelzy, being the outspoken one in the family, did not hesitate to yell across the street, "Can we help you? Ouch!" she grimaced as Matthew shoved his right elbow into her ribs. "Why did you do that?" she snarled at Matthew.

But, before Matthew even had a chance to answer, Chelzy had looked both ways and crossed the street in the direction of the new neighbors. "Hi, I'm Chelzy and this is my brother, Matthew, and we live across the street from you in the red-brick house with the white shutters."

By the time Chelzy's introduction was over, Matthew was at her side, quietly awaiting their reply. Mr. and Mrs. Herold introduced themselves, and informed the children that they would be welcomed at their house any time to hang out with Tory. As outspoken as Chelzy was, Tory was more reserved. Mrs. Herold had to coax Tory to come over to where they were and prompt her to introduce herself to Chelzy and Matthew, which she did.

"Can Tory come to our house and do something with us tomorrow?" asked Chelzy.

"I can't see why not," replied Mrs. Herold.

Tory nodded and smiled, and said shyly, "See ya tomorrow." She then ran into her house with a bag she had unloaded from the car.

Matthew ran back to the house while Chelzy stayed for a few minutes to chat with Tory's mom. Chelzy explained that she was ten years old and in fifth grade, and her brother was twelve years old and in seventh grade. Mrs. Herold said that Tory was eleven years old and in sixth grade, and she was very appreciative of Chelzy for having come over. She was afraid that Tory would not have any friends in the new neighborhood. Since they would all be going to the same school, Mrs. Herold felt much more at ease with the new school year coming.

She also described Tory as somewhat shy, yet adventurous and curious. "As soon as Tory gets to know someone, then her real personality emerges. She is very outgoing and she loves to try new experiences; and Mr. Herold likes to hike, so he would take Tory hiking in the woods all the time where we used to live. She would always want to try new trails. He would have a hard time keeping up with her," explained Mrs. Herold.

"There's a playground down the street with a basketball court. Would it be all right if Tory and I go there from time to time?"

"It sounds like fun. Tory is actually thinking of going out for basketball in her new school this year. So, that would be a great way for her to practice."

Chelzy enjoyed listening to Mrs. Herold because she spoke very dramatically. She was tall and thin, with long, black hair and dark eyes. Chelzy kept thinking that she would make a great witch for Halloween, not because she was scary or anything but because of her features. Mr. Herold, who was heavy set, had a light complexion and was stern-looking.

"She has a knack of going into places that she shouldn't, just because she is curious, or she's taking things apart, just to see how they work," sighed Mrs. Herold, who seemed tired, yet thought it was necessary to share that information with Chelzy.

"Sounds a little like Matthew," Chelzy thought to herself.

As Chelzy walked back to her house, she muttered, "Now they will both come in handy in the Magic Woods."

CHAPTER 3

The Glowing Black Cloth

Simonsville is a small town in the northeastern corner of Pennsylvania. This time of the year, early summer, welcomes many sunny warm days and cool evenings. After supper, Chelzy stepped out onto the back porch. She inspected the evening sky, looking for any traces of the fleeting black silhouette she saw earlier in the day. As she turned to go back into the house, she noticed a square piece of black cloth on the porch floor.

It was not an ordinary piece of cloth. She inquisitively picked it up. As she held it in front of her, gold specks leaped from the cloth. As she moved the cloth, the colors of the specks changed from gold to red to black and back to gold. The specks jumped high into the air from the cloth. It was like holding a Fourth of July sparkler. The specks kept changing colors and, once in the air, they danced with each other. Trembling, Chelzy wobbled backward and flung the cloth away from her.

"Matthew! Matthew!" shrieked Chelzy.

"I'm busy. I'm five points away from beating my record on the Speedway Racing game and I'm not moving," Matthew replied.

"But, Matthew, you have to see this," Chelzy shouted, almost frozen to the floor.

Just then, Mrs. Stone came from upstairs and gave orders for everyone to follow her out the front door. "But, Mom, I can't, I'm—" replied Chelzy, who was both mesmerized and frightened by the glowing colors radiating from the cloth and dancing in front of her.

"NOW!" interrupted Mrs. Stone in a very emphatic manner. Mrs. Stone could be very intimidating just based on her tall, broad stature alone. Her voice was something to be feared when she was angry. It was a cross between a lion and an elephant.

All of a sudden, the cloth stopped glowing. After deliberating a short time, Chelzy gently touched the cloth and, now that it seemed harmless, she put it in her pocket. At about the same time, Matthew put down the controller to his video game. Chelzy had decided that this find would remain her secret for the present. After all, who would believe her anyway?

Mr. Stone was already waiting for the rest of the family on the front porch. Grandma and Grandpa Stone lived a mere four blocks from their home. Since it was a dry, warm summer evening, everyone thought it would be fun to take a walk. During these walks, Chelzy and Matthew would always make up far-fetched stories of make-believe and afterwards, when they returned home, they would draw all the creatures they had made up in their story.

Green's Variety Store was located midway between their house and their grandparents'. If they did not leave too late, the Stones always stopped for ice-cream cones on the way home. Since Mrs. Green stocked twelve different flavors of ice cream, Chelzy made it a point to ask for a different flavor every visit. Sometimes they named their creatures in their made-up stories after their favorite flavors, like Chelzy's chocolate mutant marshmallow monster and Matthew's mad maple walnut werewolf. Mrs. Green's variety of ice cream flavors made this very easy to do.

Sometimes Chelzy walked ahead of everyone else. Tonight she walked with Matthew because she couldn't wait to get his full attention. When they were far enough ahead of their parents so they could not be heard or seen clearly, Chelzy darted out several steps in front of her brother and started walking backward.

"Matthew, you've got to see this," Chelzy whispered urgently.

"See what?" Matthew inquired.

Chelzy slowly withdrew the black cloth from her pocket and gently held it in front of her. She cautiously stared at it, not knowing what to expect. She knew she was taking a big chance in sharing her experience with her brother, especially if the cloth did not change colors. She hated being called silly and stupid.

"What am I supposed to see? It looks like a dumb piece of something torn off someone's coat. And why are you whispering?" Matthew asked.

Chelzy moved the black cloth in different directions. No gold, red or black specks shone from the cloth. Nor were there any colored specks leaping into the air and dancing together. To Chelzy's disappointment, it remained a plain, old, black cloth.

"But you don't understand, Matthew," Chelzy said in an irritated manner. "When I found it and held it, really cool colors were like jumpin' from it. No, really, it did happen. I can't explain why nothing is happening now. This is not one of my made-up stories!"

"Don't try explaining because I don't believe you. We make up stories all the time, so why should this one be different? How 'bout pickin' up the pace so we can get to hear grandpa's stories," Matthew responded.

"You never believe a thing I say; but that's okay because I know what I saw, and someday I'll prove it to you," said a very annoyed Chelzy.

After the disappointing experience with her brother, Chelzy decided not to show the black cloth to anyone else; at least, not for now. She gently put it back in her right pocket and continued walking; but this time, she walked behind her brother. She was angry with him for not believing her. All of a sudden, she felt something very warm. She looked down and saw her right pocket glowing red. She raced to catch up to Matthew. By the time she reached him, the warmness was gone, as was the glow. Chelzy softly whispered to herself, "Why even say anything to Matthew? He won't believe me anyway; but somehow, I will prove it to him. I really will."

CHAPTER 4

The Glittering Black Dust

Grandma and Grandpa Stone's house was quite unique, almost quaint. The façade was completely made of stones of different shapes and sizes and colors. It was Cape Cod in style and consisted of two upstairs bedrooms, both of which came in handy for Chelzy and Matthew's sleepovers. However, there was no bathroom on the second floor, which meant that every time anyone had to use the "facilities," they had to walk down to the main floor.

This was not normally a problem in an ordinary house, but the steps leading back down to the first floor creaked terribly. Every step's creak had a different tone and was so loud that it usually meant that someone would wake up to ask if everything was all right. Chelzy and Matthew learned not to drink a lot before bedtime. However, when that didn't work, Chelzy found a way to walk on the edges of each step, which lowered the tone of the creak. She shared the technique with Matthew.

Once the Stone family arrived, Grandpa Stone did not hesitate setting the tone for the stories to come. After dessert and some family conversation around a big wooden kitchen table, Chelzy and her brother walked from the kitchen to the den. Grandpa Stone asked Chelzy and Matthew, "Did you come upon any black dust on the road here?"

Situating himself comfortably in his big brown-leather recliner, he reached for his pipe. Hearing the tapping of the pipe on an ashtray from the kitchen, Grandma Stone scolded him, "Do not even think about smoking that awful pipe with the children in the house."

Grandma Stone did not like Grandpa Stone telling the children stories about strange happenings on their street and in the woods behind their house. So, grandpa would always wait until she was immersed in conversation before he started his storytelling.

"Grandpa, tell us more about the black dust. What is it?" questioned a very excited Matthew. "Where did it come from? Is it magic? Is it part of the weird things that you said have happened around here? Do you really think that there is still black dust on the streets?"

"No, no, no, I was only trying to get your attention; but, remember the story I told you awhile back about the old woman dressed in a black robe with an onyx tiara?" Grandpa Stone asked. "Well, there is more to the story than I told you, much more. Would you like to hear it?"

While nodding their heads, Chelzy and Matthew huddled close to the big brown-leather recliner as Grandpa Stone continued, "There is a story that has been told for generations about the wooded area behind Sycamore Street. It describes the appearance of an old woman dressed in a long black robe with a tiara made of onyx on her head. It is said that she could be seen walking down Sycamore Street, taking an onyx stone from her crown and holding it tightly in her hand. The stone would turn to black dust, which she would scatter in her path. The story continues that the first three children to step on the dust were taken by large black creatures and dropped in the wooded area, never to be seen again. Now remember, these are only stories made up by someone's overactive imagination, and you children should not believe them. I will have to admit, though, that these stories have surfaced again over the past few decades."

"Why do you think that happened, Grandpa? I mean, if they are just made-up stories, why do you think people are talking about them again?" Chelzy chimed in.

"Well, back in 1982, three children disappeared right down the street from where you live, you know, by the playground. No one has ever been able to solve the mystery of what happened to them. Most everyone thinks they were abducted by a stranger."

"Wow, Grandpa, what do you think really happened to them?" Chelzy inquired, anxiously waiting for his reply.

"Well now, there were a few witnesses, but most were determined to be unreliable. But there was one gentleman, now what was his name? Hmmm . . . let me think a moment. Oh, yes, yes, it was John Avis Windsor. As a matter of fact, he was, or I should say, is an attorney."

Matthew interjected quickly, "And what did he say?"

"Well, he thought he saw several things that were big and black come down from the sky. He said they looked maybe like birds, and when they were gone, so were the children. But you see, no one believed him, even to this day."

"What do you mean, Grandpa, is he still alive?" a very intrigued Chelzy inquired.

"As a matter of fact, yes, he is as far as I know. I believe he is a resident of a nursing home or a specialized hospital in Bloomston. He is quite old, somewhere in his eighties."

Chelzy's eyes grew large as she thought of the huge black bird she saw earlier in the day. She could feel her heart pounding in her chest and hear it echoing in her head. "Can you tell us more, Grandpa?"

"Well, people say that when the old woman dressed in a black robe with an onyx tiara on her head would appear, she would deposit black dust on the road. When older folk walked in the black dust, nothin' would happen to them; but for some reason, when young'uns walked in the stuff, black birds would appear and the children would then disappear. And they were never seen again. Well, that's what the story says. There were also some sightings of strange things in the sky. People would get a glimpse of something but it would disappear so quickly no one could describe what they saw."

"Do you think that's what happened to the three children that disappeared in 1982?" interrupted Matthew.

Just as Grandpa Stone moved to get yet more comfortable in his recliner to answer the question and continue his story, Mrs. Stone yelled from the kitchen, "It's getting late you two. Let's head for home."

Chelzy and Matthew were both very disappointed. Chelzy asked her grandpa, "Can we come back again soon? And next time, can we bring our new friend? Her name is Tory and I know she would really like to hear about the story, too."

"Why not? The more, the merrier. Now you two run along."

As they were walking out the door, Grandpa Stone placed four dollars in Chelzy's and Matthew's right hands. "Enjoy your ice cream on your way home."

Chelzy was almost ready to place the dollar bills in her right pocket but quickly put them in her left pocket instead. As Matthew and she walked down Sycamore Street, she had her eyes glued to the road, looking for any traces of the strange black dust in grandpa's story. They were both quiet as they walked. Rather than making up magical stories of their own, this time they were both focused on the story that Grandpa Stone had told them.

"Don't tell me that you are looking for some magic dust, Chelzy," Matthew commented as he walked a distance behind his sister this time. Mr. and Mrs. Stone strolled far behind both children and were not able to hear what they were saying. Matthew was very close to his sister but never passed up the opportunity to tease her. He also did not want to let on that he was really enthralled by his grandpa's stories. If she knew he was just as fascinated and captivated as she was, then he could not make fun of her as easily.

"Silly, silly, silly Chelzy; silly, silly, silly Chelzy," Matthew chanted.

"Oh, shut up, Matthew. You think you know it all. Even if I found the black dust, I would not show you. Better yet, I would push you in it! Then maybe some big black bird would come and take you away so that you would stop making fun of me."

"I think if you found black dust, it would be something like, maybe, oh yeah, let me think, dirt, Sis!"

With that, Chelzy angrily increased her pace to double that of Matthew's.

"Silly, silly, silly Chelzy. Sil—" Matthew abruptly stopped his chanting.

Something resembling black glitter appeared about two feet in front of him. He froze in his steps, trying to keep his balance so as not to step forward into the strange substance. His subconscious kept telling him it was probably some art glitter that some kid dropped. After regaining his balance, he looked closer. The glitter disappeared and only black dust remained. He looked up and realized that he was standing in front of the playground.

Matthew yelled for his sister, "Chelzy, Chelzy. Hurry, hurry, get over here quickly!"

Chelzy stopped, turned around and looked at her brother. He was standing in one place, his head bent forward, gazing at the ground.

"Now what, Bro? You gonna tell me ya actually found something? I know you are just fooling around, and you want me to come and see something that isn't even there, so you can laugh and make fun of me again. But this time I am not going to fall for your tricks," Chelzy yelled to Matthew.

By the time Matthew looked up in Chelzy's direction and then looked back down, the black dust was gone. In its place lay something very strange. Before anyone could see what he was doing, he picked up the object and put it in his left pocket. He decided that he could not show his sister what he had found. After making fun of her, he knew she would never believe him. He thought, "Is this even safe to have? Will it turn into something? Will giant black birds swoop down and take me away and make it look like I disappeared?"

Even though Matthew was scared, he knew that according to the story, as long as it didn't turn back into dust and he didn't step into it, he should be safe. When he arrived home, he would put it in a shoebox hidden under his bed where he kept all his special things.

CHAPTER 5

The Quivering Silver Feather

Chelzy had a hard time falling asleep the night they returned from Grandma and Grandpa Stone's house. She took the mysterious black cloth from her pocket and, after inspecting it carefully, placed it safely in her nightstand drawer. She wanted to hear more about the story, especially the part about the old woman with the black onyx tiara. She always thought that tiaras were crowns made with bright, shiny stones; but her Aunt Betsy once showed her an onyx ring that she bought for herself and the stone was black. She thought to herself, "Who would wear a crown made of black stones?"

She perched herself on a bench near her bedroom window and gazed out at the moonlit night. The full moon brightened the night sky immensely. The stars had just come out and she was trying to make out the constellations. She kept thinking about the black cloth and wondered why it sparkled only for her. Just as she glanced in the direction of the woods behind her backyard, a bright object began to streak across the sky.

At first she thought it was a shooting star. The object was following a path that would take it near her house. It was leaving a trail of light behind. All of a sudden, the object whizzed past her window at a high rate of speed. It was quivering and radiating a silvery white light; then it abruptly stopped and began floating gently down, very slowly, reminding her of the paper kite she made last summer. She would fly it in the backyard. When there was a good breeze, she would watch the wind roll off its surface and cause it to undulate, and then as the air currents subsided, it would gracefully fall from the sky.

Tonight the shimmering object did not look like the kite she made. Instead, it reminded her of a very large goose's feather. When her family went on vacation last summer, they stayed at a resort near a lake. She and Matthew fed crackers to geese that took up summer residence on the lake. Chelzy remembered feeding what seemed to be an entire flock of geese that would come and take crackers right out of her hand. Sometimes the geese would chase one another so that they could have more food for themselves. In doing so, they would at times pluck each other's feathers out. Chelzy kept one feather and brought it home as a souvenir.

Chelzy hurriedly ran to her nightstand and opened the drawer. She grabbed the feather, which was lying next to the black cloth, and held it up in front of her. By the time she returned to the window and looked up, she saw the shining object gently glide into the woods the same way her kite did when the wind died down.

Yawning and rubbing her eyes, Chelzy just sat at her window, staring at the sky above the woods. After about twenty minutes, Chelzy's eyelids began to feel heavy. She placed the feather back in her nightstand drawer. She then crawled into bed still thinking about the strange object she saw tonight. "Why am I the only one seeing these strange things? Or am I?" thought Chelzy. "It's time to start exploring the Magic Woods."

With thoughts of her, Matthew and Tory walking into the woods, Chelzy's eyes closed as she drifted into a sound sleep.

CHAPTER 6

The Lost and Found Game

The next morning, Chelzy woke up early and rushed to wash up, brush her teeth and get dressed. She kept thinking about the events of yesterday. She checked her nightstand drawer and, sure enough, the black cloth was still there. She then realized it was not just a dream she was having and she really was not crazy as Matthew thought she was. She ran downstairs and joined her brother at the kitchen table.

"Bro, can we go exploring in the woods?"

Matthew was engrossed in a *Fantastic Four* comic book and ignored his sister's question. As he went to turn a page, Chelzy slapped her hand on it. "I said, 'Can we go exploring in the woods today?' And can we ask Tory to come with us? Come on, Bro, I am really excited about everything grandpa told us and I want to see what's in those woods."

"Let me finish reading this story," replied Matthew. "And anyway, mom has chores for me to do first."

After some discussion, it was decided that Chelzy would also get her chores done quickly in the morning, and she and Matthew would ask Tory to get together with them right after lunch. Chelzy made her bed, watched some TV, helped her mom fold some clothes and then made her lunch.

She took her lunch on the back porch and sat on the bench of a red picnic table. As she ate, she stared at the woods, wondering where they should start to explore. She kept tapping both feet on the porch floor while curling her hair with her left hand as she imagined what they might discover. There was just so much to assimilate in her brain. She kept thinking about the three abducted children and the man who saw three very large birds at the same time the kids disappeared. Was it all a coincidence? Or was some type of outside force involved?

"Okay, I'm ready. Let's go," said Matthew as he walked through the kitchen door onto the back porch. Together they ran down the porch steps and around to the front of the house. Looking left, right and then left again, they ran across Sycamore Street and headed straight for the Herold's house. Chelzy ran up the front steps and rang the doorbell.

"Well, hello!" said Mrs. Herold cheerfully. "Make yourselves comfortable and I'll get Tory for you. She has been looking forward to you coming to get her since she got up this morning."

Chelzy was ecstatic to have another girl as a friend, especially one that lived so close. Several of her other girlfriends lived across town, and she always had to plan activities in advance when one of their parents was available to drive them to each other's house or to a movie. At least the playground and basketball court were nearby and sometimes they would meet there. It happened that her best friend, Sarah, was away on vacation for the next two weeks, so she was especially happy that Tory moved in across the street from her.

It seemed that there were a lot more boys in the neighborhood than girls and Matthew had no problem finding someone with whom to hang out. As Chelzy and Matthew sat in the Herold's living room, the first thing they noticed was a big-screen TV.

"Wow, Matthew! Look at the size of it!" commented Chelzy. "I think it has to be twice the size of ours."

"Yeah, maybe Tory's mom will let us play some of our video games on it," Matthew said. Mrs. Herold only had to call Tory once before she came running down the steps. Chelzy and Matthew both said "hi" in unison.

Tory replied with a very quiet, "Hi," and a slight wave of her hand.

"What are your plans for today?" asked Mrs. Herold.

"Well, we want to show Tory our new video game, the Speedway Racing game, and maybe go for a walk," replied Chelzy.

"Tory, why don't you take your board game over to their house; you know, the one Uncle Tony bought you. What's it called?" asked Mrs. Herold.

"The Lost and Found Game. It really looks like a cool game. It's like you're on a hike—you have to travel through different territories and you get lost in the forest, so you have to find your way home. I've asked my cousins to play it with me, but they think it is stupid to play with an old board game," said Tory.

"Yeah, bring it with you, Tory," said Matthew. "We'll take a look at it."

As Tory ran back upstairs to her bedroom to retrieve the game, Mrs. Herold explained more about it. "Actually, Tory's Uncle Tony likes to collect antiques; the older the things are, the better. When he was on a road trip in the country, he discovered this game that was for sale in an old barn that the owner turned into an antique store. Many of the old games that he has come upon, he had recognized from when he was younger, but he never saw anything like this game. As a matter of fact, when he tried to research it on the Internet to see how old it was, he couldn't even find it. So, it remains somewhat of a mystery. He decided to lend it to Tory because he knows how much she likes board games. Anyway, if you go for a walk, stay in the neighborhood. Don't wander off too far," warned Mrs. Herold.

With her game under her arm, Tory walked between Chelzy and Matthew as they crossed Sycamore Street. The sun became hidden behind dark clouds that began to overtake the afternoon sky. A bright sunny day suddenly became gloomy and dismal.

"Let's go exploring the Magic—" started Chelzy.

Matthew quickly interrupted, "Tory, can we play your game first? It looks like it's going to rain anyway."

Tory replied with a quick, "Sure. But we have to be careful. Since the game is so old, the cards are kinda fallin' apart and my Uncle Tony asked me to take good care of it. I don't think he wants it back, but I am not sure. He likes to collect old things, and wait until you see this game. It looks kind of dilapidated but still pretty cool."

"Sure, we'll try it, as long as it is not too complicated. Chelz has a hard time following games that don't have simple instructions."

"I do not!" snarled Chelzy. "I am a good game player, but you are just a sore loser, Bro."

Within a few minutes, Chelzy, Matthew and Tory were setting up the game on the living room floor. Just as Tory took the lid off the top of the box, a crash of thunder rattled the house. Everyone jumped at the unexpected sound, except Matthew, who said snidely, "Hey guys, it's just a storm. Ya know, we get them sometimes in the summer."

Chelzy carefully lifted the board and placed it on the floor then handed Tory the directions. As Tory was unfolding the worn, yellowing paper, Chelzy stared at the game board. There was something very familiar about it. Tory slowly read, "There are a total of four circular regions and an area in the middle. Each player moves by rolling a pair of dice. Each player has to choose one game piece and place it in the square marked 'start,' which is located in the center area.

"A forest is painted on the board in each of the regions, with trails leading to open areas. There are spaces on the open areas marked 'lost' or 'found.' Every time a piece lands on a certain open area, the player must pick up a card from either the lost or the found stack of cards. The card will then give the player directions as to how to proceed on the trails. The first player whose game piece travels through all four forest areas and reaches the space marked 'home' in the Candesia Land of Pines wins the game. In order for a piece to enter the home circle, the player must roll the exact number corresponding to the exact number of spaces to the home circle. The other players remain lost and never return home."

"That would be you, Chelz. Remember that time we were on vacation and dad took us hiking and you got—"

"Stop it, Bro. I am going to win this game just to show you that I am a good game player and I don't get lost."

"Hey, Sis, stop interrupting and let Tory read."

Before anyone could continue the argument, Tory continued, "In the center of the board is a patch of pine trees in an area where the start space is located." Chelzy thought it looked as if someone had planted a bunch of these trees when they were young and now the trees were all grown. It reminded Chelzy of the little evergreen trees that were distributed every year in school to celebrate Earth Day. She planted two in her backyard and they had grown to about a foot tall.

Mrs. Kim, her teacher, explained the difference between types of trees. She said that the trees, like the spruces and pines that the students were given, were called evergreen because they kept their leaves all year round. Other kinds of trees, like oak and maple, were called deciduous because they lose their leaves during part of the year. Chelzy especially remembered the lesson on trees because she had to collect different types of leaf specimens. She had made a scrapbook and labeled each leaf with its name and indicated whether it came from an evergreen tree or a deciduous tree. It was a fun project because it was like doing homework outside, which is where Chelzy always preferred to be.

Tory read, "Each player will have to travel from the start space and through the Candesia Land of Pines to the Bright Queen's Kingdom. From there, players will journey into another region called the Gelabar Land of Oaks where there are many tall oak trees. The third region is labeled the Sea of Weeping Willows with, obviously, large areas of weeping willow trees. The fourth and last region has different types of trees and has a picture of a large castle in the middle. This region is called the Dark Queen's Earth. Every player has to travel through this last forest area and through the Dark Queen's castle to get home. The first player to successfully reach the home space back in the Candesia Land of Pines wins the game.

"But, the Dark Queen's Earth is filled with danger and traps set by the Dark Queen who inhabits this region and travels relentlessly, trying to snare anyone who sets foot on her land. It is possible for a player to travel into the Dark Queen's Earth but never come out. There are also dangers lurking in the other lands that will keep a player from moving forward."

In the Candesia Land of Pines, where the home space was located, there was one tree that appeared taller than the rest. It was labeled the Black Willow Tree. Chelzy stared at the center of the board and started curling her hair with her left hand. It was as if she had seen all this before. She felt excited but somewhat apprehensive at the same time.

The Lost & Found Game

Nugget Cards

Lost Cards

Found Cards

Bright Queen's Kingdom

Calabar Land of Oaks

Candesia Land of Pines

Sea of Weeping Willows

Dark Queen's Earth

"This is a cinch," remarked Matthew. "Chelzy has no sense of direction."

Before Chelzy could respond to her brother's comment, she was distracted by the wind and rain that started to pound against the living room windows. Tory continued, "To help players find their way home, there is a stack of cards called 'nuggets.' These cards can either hinder or help a player get home. In order for a player to pick from this stack of cards, a player must land on a nugget space. Nugget cards can be played immediately or can be kept secret until a player wants to use the card."

"All right! Let's do it!" Matthew said. "This doesn't look too bad."

Each of the three players picked a game piece from a small, tattered, leather bag containing eight of them and put it on the start square. Tory picked a mountain lion, Matthew an eagle and Chelzy a deer. The remaining pieces were a squirrel, a bear, a beaver, a rabbit and a blue unicorn.

It was decided that since it was her game, Tory would go first. The wind continued to howl and the room darkened because of the lack of sunlight. Mrs. Stone turned a light on as she passed through the room. Using two dice, Tory rolled eight and moved eight spaces. Matthew then moved nine spaces. Finally, Chelzy rolled two ones and landed on a nugget space. She cautiously picked a card from the nugget stack. Just as she turned the card over, there was a flash of lightning and a loud crash of thunder. The light from the nearby lamp went out. However, the darkness in the room did not keep Chelzy from seeing what was on her card. She stood up, started curling her hair and stared out the window. "It can't be. It just can't be," she thought.

Each of the nugget cards gave a direction, and so did Chelzy's. She read silently, "This is a transport card. When your game piece is six or fewer spaces from home, you may move your piece directly into home. Or, if you are in the Dark Queen's Earth and are in danger, this card will protect you and light your way. You may use this card to escape and move to the first safe space." The name of her card was Glowing Black Cloth. As she moved the card, the picture of the cloth turned from black to gold to red and then back to black again.

Throwing the card into the air, Chelzy screamed, "I don't want to play this game anymore. Let's do something else."

"Why?" asked Matthew.

"Because I just don't want to," responded Chelzy. "I promise you, Tory, that we can play it again some other time. Can we please do something else?"

Chelzy picked up the black cloth card and, holding it tightly, she ran upstairs to her bedroom. By the time she reached her room, all the lights came back on. Each step she took toward her nightstand seemed to take hours as she furiously curled her hair. With her right hand, she opened the nightstand drawer. She moved the contents around and around but the black cloth was not there where she put it. "I know I put it here, but it's gone," thought Chelzy.

"Come on, Chelzy, it's your turn," yelled Matthew. "We're not letting you quit. We want to play."

Chelzy slowly turned around and began walking down the steps. "No one will believe me if I tell them that I found a cloth just like the one on the nugget card. I can't even prove it because it disappeared." She placed the nugget card face down on the floor next to her.

"Look, Chelz, Tory landed on a lost space and the card sent her back three spaces. I landed on a found space and the card sent me forward six spaces. I should say fly forward. After all, my piece is an eagle," said Matthew. "Come on, please, Chelzy, this game isn't all that bad. Let's keep playing."

Reluctantly, Chelzy returned to her space on the carpet to resume the game. She decided that she was more inquisitive than frightened, so she decided to continue the game. After all, she didn't want her brother calling her a coward, afraid to lose the game.

"Why did you want to quit?" asked Tory.

"Because she is afraid that she'll lose," replied Matthew.

"No, I am not!" said Chelzy. "I just saw something strange, but I don't want to talk about it. Is it my turn?"

"Yep. Roll the dice. I wish I knew what your nugget card says, but I guess you just want to keep us in suspense," said Matthew.

Giving no reply, Chelzy rolled the dice. She continued her uneventful journey through the Candesia Land of Pines. They each kept taking their turns, first Tory, then Matthew and finally Chelzy. Nothing unusual happened, other than being sent forward and back from time to time until Matthew was in Gelabar Land of Oaks. He landed on a nugget space. He picked up a nugget card and stared at it for what seemed like hours to him but it was actually just a few seconds.

Matthew silently read to himself what was on the card, "If you are adventurous, and want to get home more quickly and have a better chance of winning this game, throw this card into the air. If it lands with the black dust facing up, the black dust will make you invisible as you travel through danger. This means for the next three turns, you will be able to only move forward, not backward. It also means that you can look at every nugget card in the stack and decide whether you want to keep it or trade it for another nugget card. You can use the card now, keep this card and use it during another turn, or trade it for another nugget card." Matthew kept the card.

"This is amazing. No, this is crazy. It just can't be," said Matthew.

"What, Bro? What are you talking about? What is so amazing? Show us."

"I—I don't want to. Not right now." Matthew could not believe what he was seeing and he was not ready to show his sister the Glittering Black Dust card yet. He wasn't sure if it was just coincidence but he didn't want to get into a discussion about the black dust in grandpa's story. He knew that the Dark Queen's Earth was the last region that a player had to travel through before reaching home, and he also knew that this area had many dangerous spaces in it. He decided that he would wait to collect more nugget cards that might help him safely travel through that region. There was also a space within the Dark Queen's Earth that sent the player directly to the Dark Queen's castle. The castle looked dark and foreboding and eerie. He decided that he would hold on to his card because he was not quite ready for that journey. Not yet anyway.

But, Tory was.

CHAPTER 7

Tory Meets Grandpa Stone

Having received permission from their mom to place the game in a safe place to finish it later, Chelzy and Matthew, with Tory's help, carefully placed the board and all the pieces in place on a nearby card table. Before Tory left for the day, Chelzy and Matthew repeated the stories that Grandpa Stone had told them about Simonsville, Sycamore Street and the Magic Woods. They filled Tory in on all the details that they had learned to date. They especially made sure that they didn't leave out any information relating to the disappearance of the three children back in 1982.

"When can I meet your grandpa? He sounds really cool. I want to hear more about the stories. Can I come with you the next time you visit him?" asked Tory.

"Can't see why not. We'll ask our mom, plan a day and let you know tomorrow," Matthew responded.

Chelzy was taking gymnastic lessons and Matthew promised his friends that he would spend time with them practicing basketball at a nearby park. The week went by quickly. From time to time, Chelzy would check her nightstand drawer but, to her disappointment, there was no black cloth. Intrigued by the black dust card, Matthew made it a point of passing The Lost and Found Game every time he walked through the living room and quickly scanning it for anything unusual.

Mrs. Stone had told Grandpa Stone that Chelzy and Matthew wanted to introduce their new friend to him, so she decided to invite him for a visit on Friday. This was a good day for Grandpa Stone because that was the day that Grandma Stone always had a few errands for him to do anyway, so he figured he would make it one trip, stopping at stores on the way home.

It was a mild July evening with clear skies and warm breezes gently blowing. Walkers and joggers could be seen throughout the neighborhood along with children on bikes happily peddling and acting carefree. Mr. Crumbly was walking his Chihuahua on a leash. "They say that many pet owners look like their pets. Well, this is a case of the direct opposite," thought Chelzy. Mr. Crumbly, whose name did not fit him either, was big and burly while his pet Chihuahua was quite small and compact. Grandpa Stone arrived, carrying two large pizza boxes.

"Come and get it! Let's eat here on the front porch. Bring paper plates and napkins, Chelzy," requested Grandpa Stone.

The Stone's front porch was very large. It held an oversized green wooden swing attached to the roof of the porch and a white rocking chair. There were small tables scattered throughout the porch. Mrs. Stone had a very green thumb and managed to keep a variety of plants alive in pots on these tables. It was cozy and welcoming and a great place to hang out with friends. Chelzy thought it would be a perfect place to play Tory's Lost and Found Game when the weather was good. But after experiencing the game so far, she wasn't sure any place would be a great place for that game. She kept dismissing what happened as just an "unexplained phenomenon" as Mrs. Kim would sometimes say in science class.

Chelzy and Tory handed out paper plates and napkins, while Matthew began placing slices of pizza on the plates. Mrs. Stone brought out lemonade for everyone and placed the plastic tumblers on small round tables, after placing her potted plants on the porch floor. Chelzy, Matthew and Tory sat on the swing, and Grandpa Stone sat on the rocker. Tory sat between Chelzy and Matthew.

Matthew introduced Tory to grandpa while, in the same breath, asking, "Grandpa, can you tell us more stories about the town and the Magic Woods? We've already explained to Tory about the old woman with the black dust and the big black birds carrying children away."

"Oh, hold on young'uns. You know your grandma frowns upon me sharing such stories with ya," remarked Grandpa Stone.

"Young'uns?" whispered Tory to Chelzy, "What are young'uns?"

"That's what our grandpa calls young kids," Chelzy whispered back. "He likes the word and thinks it's funny because his grandpa used to call him a young'un, so he wanted to make it a 'tradition' thing. You'll get used to some of his special words."

"Oh, we know they are just stories and we promise that we'll remember what you say about not believing them. Please, please, Grandpa, they are just so much fun to listen to," pleaded Chelzy.

"Well, all right. Here goes. The last thing I told you was about strange things happening at the same time that the young'uns were disappearing," started Grandpa Stone. As Chelzy, Matthew and Tory were eating their pizza, they were also rocking back and forth on the hanging porch swing. Just as Grandpa Stone started to tell his story, they stopped swinging and sat up straight. Having finished her pizza, Chelzy started to curl her hair. The traffic on Sycamore Street seemed to disappear as did the joggers, runners, bikers and Mr. Crumbly with his dog. The surrounding neighborhood became silent, noticeably silent.

Grandpa Stone began, "After the old woman with the black onyx tiara left, her black dust remained in the street. Three huge black clouds appeared in the same area. It was said that each of these clouds hovered over the place where the old woman scattered the dust until three young'uns started walking in the area. Each black cloud took the shape of a large black bird. When the three young'uns stepped into the black dust, they became invisible to the human eye. But, as the story goes, what actually happened was that each black bird swooped down and picked up one of the young'uns as they stepped onto the black dust and then carried them off into the wooded area behind Sycamore Street; but as soon as the birds grasped the children, they also became invisible. And, after searching the wooded area, no one was able to locate the children. I mean young'uns. At least that's how the story has been told."

"So that's why no one actually saw the birds fly off with the children," Chelzy commented. "They disappeared. The black dust had the power to make them invisible."

"And that is why poor Mr. Windsor was said to be crazy, because no one believed him that it had to be the birds who took them," added Matthew.

Tory's eyes got bigger as she asked, "What happened to them? And who is Mr. Windsor?"

"Nobody really knows for sure what happened to the children. The story has it that this happened several times many years ago, and that some children returned and some did not," said Grandpa Stone.

"But, of course, the children in 1982 did not return. It is very sad. I did not know them, but heard they were very nice young'uns. After about a dozen years, the parents moved away, but they still keep in touch with law enforcement, hoping their children will be found."

"Wow, a mystery! I love mysteries," said Tory. "Is there more, Grandpa Stone? And who is Mr. Windsor?"

Grandpa Stone went on to explain who John Avis Windsor was and his role in all of this. Then he went on to add, "There is one more thing. In one of the stories, it was said that one of the children that did return home held a long silver feather from a silver eagle. The child couldn't say where he was taken, only that someone or something gave him a silver feather before his return home. He could not remember anything else and, of course, no one believed him because it sounded sort of strange."

"Silver feather? I wonder," Chelzy thought, "could that have anything to do with what I saw last night that was silver and floating?"

"All right! Enough about stories and magic. Tell me, Tory, do you like living on Sycamore Street?" asked Grandpa Stone.

"Well, I've only been here a week, but it's cool. I really want to go exploring the woods behind Chelzy and Matthew's house. I think it will be fun," said Tory, "especially after hearing about all the strange things that have been happening around here."

"Our dad took us there once last fall right after we moved into our house. It's great and it has all kinds of trees back there. There are paths and trails, and it makes you feel that you are in a different world. That's where I saw them," Chelzy said after a brief but thoughtful pause.

"Saw what?" asked Matthew.

"All the different trees in the game. The Magic Woo—I mean the woods behind our house has all those kinds of trees like the ones in

The Lost and Found Game," explained Chelzy. "You may say it is just coincidence, but I think there may be more to it."

"What game are you talking about?" asked Grandpa Stone.

Chelzy, Matthew and Tory described The Lost and Found Game in detail to Grandpa Stone. Chelzy did not mention the magic cloth nor did Matthew reveal the fact that he found black dust on Sycamore Street. Neither thought that Grandpa Stone, or anybody else for that matter, would believe them and they didn't want anyone to take their treasures away from them.

"Well, young'uns, all woods have trees in them, so it probably is just a coincidence that they all resemble Tory's game. Who knows? Maybe someone heard the story and made a game about it. But, I have to say that in all my years, I have not ever heard of a game like that before. You just never know where it may take you; well, I mean, in a fun sort of way."

Grandpa Stone's comments did not satisfy Chelzy's curiosity. As a matter of fact, it made it worse, especially when he said that you never know where it will take you. Now, more than ever, she had to explore the Magic Woods. As she curled her hair with more speed than usual, she began imagining what she would discover as she, Matthew and Tory walked through the woods. She thought, "Why does the game remind me of the Magic Woods so much? And how did the black cloth I discovered become part of the game? Or was it always there? How could it have lights jumping from it? And why hasn't anyone heard of the game before, not even Grandpa Stone who is old and has lived a long time? And wouldn't it be interesting if we could interview John Avis Windsor about what he saw that night?"

At the same time, Tory began imagining what it would be like to walk through the Magic Woods and perhaps travel through some of the wooded areas like those in the game. She wondered, "Will there be trails we can follow? Will we get lost just like in the game? Will there be real dangers in the woods?"

Matthew, on the other hand, kept thinking about what he discovered while walking home from his grandparents' house on Sycamore Street. He kept questioning himself, "I saw black dust on the road and then I picked up a black dust card from the game. That can't be a coincidence. Can it? And if we explore the Magic Woods, will we get lost like in the game? And how can magic dust transform into—"

"Well, I'm off. Your grandma is going to think that I got lost. Hope you enjoyed the pizza," said Grandpa Stone as he slowly rose from the white rocking chair.

"Wait, Grandpa, can we talk more?" Chelzy quickly inquired. Everyone wanted to tell Grandpa Stone what they were thinking but knew that would not be in their best interests. They felt that everyone would then think that they were crazy taking his stories so seriously. Grandma would then probably make him stop describing the tales to them.

"No, young'uns, your grandmother will be sending out a search party for me if I don't get home. Anyway, I still have to stop at the store for her and pick up a few groceries."

Chelzy, Matthew and Tory thanked Grandpa Stone for the pizza and walked him to his car. When they arrived at his car, Chelzy asked, "Grandpa, can you take us to meet John Avis Windsor? There are a lot of questions that I have for him."

"That would be great! Can you? Can you, Grandpa?" Matthew chimed in.

"Oh, wait one minute. Your grandmother would skin me alive and hang my hide out to dry if I did that."

"But, Grandpa, we are always given assignments where we have to write essays and do reports on national, state and local interests.

This would make a great paper if we wrote on the topic of the disappearance of the three children in 1982. See, it would be school related and very educational. And it would be about our town," argued Chelzy.

"Just call it research, Grandpa," Matthew added. "The best kind; you know, personal interviews."

The children all took turns saying "please, please, please" until Grandpa Stone finally said, "Let me sleep on it. First I have to find out where Mr. Windsor is living and then if he is allowed visitors and, of course, if he wants visitors. I also don't want to upset him, so I would have to ask someone in charge at the facility."

Surprising herself, the shy Tory shouted, "You're the best," and gave grandpa a big hug.

"All right, Chelzy, I will call you on your cell phone and let you know what I decide. In the meantime, I suggest you do not talk about this proposed visit anymore before we all get in trouble."

After Grandpa Stone left, Chelzy, Matthew and Tory started to plan their first venture into the Magic Woods. They hoped that Grandpa Stone would take them to talk with Mr. Windsor first so they could learn more about the children's abduction. Then they would set out to explore the woods and search for clues about what really happened to the children. They decided that each of them would write down questions for the interview. They felt like real detectives and decided that this summer might not turn out boring after all.

That evening, Chelzy decided to go to bed early but, when she did, she tossed and turned and could not fall asleep. She put paper and a pen on her nightstand in the event she would think of a good question. In a short period of time, she came up with what she felt were two important ones. The first being, what exactly did Mr. Windsor see; and the second one, just how big were the birds? She figured they had to be pretty huge to lift a child and fly away with him. And, if that was the case, then magic had to play a role in this somehow.

As Chelzy contemplated other questions to ask, she stared out her bedroom window at the beautiful, flamboyantly colored sunset. The clear blue daytime sky had given way to a sunset swathed in pink streaks on yellow light across the darkening horizon. Several tall trees against the sunset took on different shapes. One looked like a butterfly with wings spread out; another reminded Chelzy of crystals that she saw on display at a recent school science fair. Some of the colors were striking and others were shaded softly, but none danced about like those from her seemingly magic black cloth.

Just the thought that the Magic Woods might resemble Tory's Lost and Found Game caused Chelzy to lie in bed, curling her hair with her left hand. She imagined finding black dust and a silver feather that Grandpa Stone told them about. She figured that the black cloth she had found must play a significant part in the game and, maybe, in the mystery.

She also wondered what the Bright Queen in the game would look like and if she would really be a good queen; and, of course, she worried about the Dark Queen. It was too frightening to think about how bad she could be, and the thought of the big black birds frightened her. Were they sent by the Dark Queen? But then she was getting tired and decided that Grandpa Stone was probably right. It was just a story. Or was it? Chelzy decided that it was time to find out.

CHAPTER 8

Determined Detectives

As days came and went, everyone became busy. Chelzy went to the movies with her school friends, Matthew had soccer practices and Tory had to help her mom finish unpacking. Of course, there were summer reading assignments that needed to be started along with regular chores. But, even with the hodgepodge of activities, Chelzy, Matthew and Tory still found time to meet early one afternoon to formulate a plan for their first adventure into the mysterious wooded area called the Magic Woods. And then it happened: Grandpa Stone called Chelzy.

"Hello, my dear. How are you?"

"Fine, Grandpa. It is so good to hear your voice. I thought maybe you weren't going to call me."

"Oh, my dear Chelzy, I would never do that. If I say I am getting back to you, that means I will definitely get back to you. Now, I have spoken to your mom and dad, and asked them if I can help you do some historical research at the town library, and they said yes."

"The library? But I thought we were going to go talk to Mr. Windsor."

"Well, you see, I think first we should all go to the library and find the newspaper article about the children's abduction and read it. Then we will take a ride to Bloomston to meet John Avis Windsor. He will be part of our research."

"That will be great, Grandpa. I'll tell Matthew and Tory. When are we going?"

"Tomorrow, right after lunch. I'll pick everyone up at one o'clock. First, you and Matthew will have to talk to Tory's parents and ask if it is all right with them if we take her along."

"Okay, Grandpa, we'll see you tomorrow. Matthew and Tory will be really excited, too. See you then."

Chelzy could not run fast enough to Matthew's room where he was watching a movie. "Bro! Bro! Guess what?"

"Let me guess, Chelz, you broke your record on Farm and Zoo Animal Brigade."

"No, nothing like that. Something better! Grandpa called and he is taking us to talk to Mr. Windsor tomorrow at one."

"Really? All right! Now we're talking. Is Tory coming?"

"If her parents say it's all right. We have to go ask them. Can you come with me now?"

Before Chelzy could finish her sentence, Matthew was halfway down the steps. Chelzy decided that she better do the talking since grandpa asked her to do the asking. And anyway, Matthew did not know they had to do research at the library first. Matthew was not much of a reader, not like Chelzy anyway. So, he probably would like to skip that part of the research. Whenever they were given summer reading assignments at their former school, Chelzy would have hers done by the middle of July. Matthew, on the other hand, usually procrastinated and would not start his until the middle of August. What really annoyed Chelzy was that Matthew would always get higher grades on his reports.

Chelzy ran up to the Herold's door and rang the doorbell. Mrs. Herold answered, "Hi, Chelzy, what can I do for you? I don't know if she told you but Tory is spending the day with her cousins in Dalesville."

"Oh, no, we are not here to see Tory. We are actually here to talk to you."

"Well then, come right in and have a seat."

"No, thanks, this will not take long. Can Tory come with Matthew and me and our grandpa to the library tomorrow to do research; you know, like on historical stuff?"

Matthew immediately gave his sister an incredulous glance. He was basically thinking that she was either joking or making it up so that Mrs. Herold would let Tory go with them. Matthew would not be found dead in a library in the summer. What if one of his friends from school saw him going in or out of the library? He could not even use the excuse that he was taking out a library book to read because he would not be carrying a book.

"What kind of research would you be doing during the summer when there's no school?" asked Mrs. Herold.

"Well, you see, every year we usually have to do some type of report on our town for school; so, since our grandpa is available to help us, we thought we would get a head start on it. He is picking us up tomorrow at one, and we should only be a few hours."

"Well, Chelzy, if it is all right with your parents, then it is fine with me. I'll tell Tory to be ready. I'd like to meet your grandpa tomorrow before you leave."

"Thank you, thank you, Mrs. Herold. I'll ask our grandpa to stop here first."

The next day, Grandpa Stone was at the house promptly at 1:00 p.m. Chelzy asked him to visit Mrs. Herold first because she wanted to meet him. As soon as Mrs. Herold answered the door, Tory ran out of the house and joined Chelzy and Matthew on their front porch. Grandpa Stone explained that they were first going to the library and then out to Bloomston to talk to John Avis Windsor who knew a lot about the history of the town.

"I think it will be a good experience for the children to meet a gentleman who has lived a long life in this town. I am sure Tory will fill her dad and me in on everything that she learns from him and at the library, Mr. Stone."

"Oh, I am sure she will. Nice meeting you."

And with that, Grandpa Stone, Chelzy, Matthew and Tory set out on their adventure to learn more about that infamous day in the history of the town of Simonsville.

It was only a short drive to the Simonsville Public Library and everyone was quite chatty in the car on the way. Chelzy and Tory sat in the backseat while Matthew sat in front with Grandpa Stone. Chelzy explained why it was important to look back at old newspaper articles about the children's abduction. "That's what real detectives would do first," she assured everyone. "Anyway, it sounds more educational than just talking to Mr. Windsor. It will certainly be more convincing to our parents."

"Grandpa, I have one question. Why couldn't we have just researched the article online at home?" a curious Matthew asked. "Why do we have to go to the library?"

"Well, Matthew, it's like this. At one time, when I was growing up and schools and homes did not have computers and all the fancy technology that there is today, the only way that you could read an article from years past was to go to the local library and look it up on microfiche."

"What is microfiche?" asked Tory.

"Well, I guess now I can tell you all that my real motive for taking you to the library is to actually teach you something about how libraries work. I think with all the computers that you use for research, you may have no appreciation for how all this technology evolved."

"But, it is the summer. Do we really have to learn something?" Matthew said reluctantly.

"Oh, don't be a lazybones, Bro. You might actually discover something really cool if you take your head out of those comic books for a change."

Grandpa Stone continued, "I don't know how far back the library has kept the actual newspapers; but 1982 was years ago, so I guess we probably will not be able to view the authentic newspapers from that date. If that is the case, they will either have it on microfiche or on a CD, or we can probably use their computers to check their digital repository if their newspapers have been converted to digital data."

"Wow, Grandpa Stone, you really know your libraries," noted Tory.

Chelzy whispered with her hand cupped over Matthew's ear, "Bro, I am really impressed with grandpa's knowledge of technology. I just thought most older people didn't know this kind of stuff."

"Well, you see, Tory, I actually volunteered at the library years ago and I have tried to keep up with current services in recent years. It is really a great place and they offer many activities for children your ages, like board game night every Tuesday and a scavenger hunt on the last Thursday of every month."

"Really? I thought it was just a place to go and read," Matthew commented.

"Getting back to your question, Tory, about microfiche. Storage of newspapers and magazines became a problem for libraries, so they began using photographic film to take pictures of articles to store them in a very small size. The images require the use of a machine called a reader, which uses a magnifying lens and a light to project the images onto a screen. The person using the reader and reading the image can scroll, enlarge and even print the images.

"Microfiche was used to store a lot of old newspaper copies, because newspapers disintegrate over time. The film was rolled and put in small containers, taking a lot less space than the actual newspapers. Today, of course, copies of old newspapers are put in a digital database that anyone with a computer and the Internet can access. We have come such a long way since I was your age."

"So what you're saying, Grandpa, is that we could have done the research at home, but we will learn more about the history of research at the library," Matthew contributed.

"I am impressed, Bro. You actually figured out something on your own!"

"Actually, Sis, I wanted to make sure that *you* know why we're going to the library."

Grandpa Stone's car pulled up to a meter about fifteen yards from the library entrance. They entered the library and were immediately greeted by a friend of Grandpa Stone who introduced herself as Miss Giddy. Miss Giddy was in charge of the reference section so, at Grandpa's request, she showed and explained to the children all the ways they could do research. She gave them a tour of a large room that contained some old newspapers and magazines; then she demonstrated the use of microfiche. Finally, she directed them to a room where there were four long tables holding computers. After she explained how to log on and access the databases, she left them to their work.

Everyone, except grandpa, used a computer, and Chelzy located the article first. After a few minutes, both Matthew and Tory were successful also. The article, taken from the *Simonsville Daily Courier* on November 19, 1982 read:

Children Disappear Near Their Home

Three children from the same family, two boys and a girl, ages 7, 8 and 10, disappeared while walking not far from their home in the 200 block of Sycamore Street early yesterday evening. Police and other law enforcement officials were reluctant to comment on the case, and only indicated that evidence is being gathered and the investigation has just begun. Several witnesses have been questioned but officials have not been able to arrive at any conclusions yet.

The children's mother, Patricia Owens, was overcome with emotion and could not comment. The children's father, Lieutenant Leonard Owens, is currently serving overseas in the Navy and has been notified. The family expects him to be granted leave to join his wife within the next few days.

"Wow! They used the word, 'disappeared,' like they vanished."

"Chelz, I think they used that word because they could not explain what happened to them or where they were taken," offered Matthew.

After looking through newspapers for the days and weeks that followed the disappearance, and finding nothing of noteworthy interest, they decided that their research at the library was finished. They did, however, print a copy of the initial article to take with them. Grandpa Stone agreed that they had done a good job and that the library visit did teach them some important information about how research was done in the past. At least each of them had something valuable to report to their parents. They would also now be prepared if they were assigned a report to do in class about their town or about how to investigate a topic in a library.

Feeling like true detectives, Chelzy, Matthew and Tory were ready to conduct their second interview. Grandpa Stone would actually count as their first, since he was a wealth of information and they credited him with being a reliable source. Excited as they were to speak to Mr. Windsor and gather more information about the so-called abduction, each felt that they were slowly being drawn into the story by some strange force, a force that would soon be made very clear to them.

CHAPTER 9

Mr. Windsor's Story

The determined detectives were on their way to see John Avis Windsor in Bloomston, which was about a half-hour drive from the library. Grandpa Stone had contacted the staff at the psychiatric hospital, who in turn phoned Mr. Windsor's family to get permission for him to be interviewed by the children. His family thought it would actually help him to get young visitors.

Grandpa Stone explained everything to Chelzy, Matthew and Tory on the way. He told them that Mr. Windsor was once a very reputable attorney in town and he was well-spoken. But after the disappearance of the children and his insistence that three very large black birds took them, he stopped practicing law because the state of his mind was viewed as questionable. In his eighties now, he was hard of hearing and sometimes had trouble understanding conversations.

When they arrived at the facility, Grandpa Stone checked them in at the front desk. Mr. Windsor was in a less restricted section, more like a nursing home where individuals with dementia were housed.

The receptionist gave them directions to Mr. Windsor's room. As excited as they were, Matthew, Chelzy and Tory became somewhat intimidated by the elderly residents walking through the hall, some using canes, some in wheelchairs and others just holding on to the railing attached to the wall. A few were carrying on conversations as if there was someone next to them, but there wasn't.

As they were trying to locate room number 138, a nurse's aide stopped them and asked if they needed assistance. When Grandpa Stone asked for John Avis Windsor's room, the aide laughed and said, "My goodness, it is so nice to see someone visiting John. He doesn't get many visitors, you know. Young people are just too busy to care about their relatives that grow old. Oh my, John is quite a character. He tells a lot of stories to the other residents about his life experiences but they don't believe him most of the time. He sort of makes up things and exaggerates, if you know what I mean." Giving them a small wink, she pointed to his room across the hall.

Mr. Windsor's room was very neat and sterile. It contained a bed immaculately made, a nightstand with a small lamp on it and a small dresser. There were two plain white doilies on the dresser that held a comb and a small mirror on one side, a book on the other and a small round ornate container in the center. The container had what appeared to be rhinestones of round and diamond shapes covering it. Small silver beads encircled the stone-like pieces. On the top was one round stone that resembled an eye. The background was black. It immediately caught Chelzy's attention and she concluded that it must be of great importance to Mr. Windsor because of its prominent location on the dresser and because nothing was placed close to it. A small TV was situated on an octagonal shaped table between the dresser and the door. There was a black-leather recliner in the corner of the room. In it sat John Avis Windsor.

When it came to talking, Grandpa Stone took the initiative and spoke loud enough to be heard by Mr. Windsor. "Good afternoon, John, my name is Sam Stone from Simonsville. These two young'uns are my grandchildren, Chelzy and Matthew, and this is their friend, Tory. Thank you for allowing us to visit you." John put out his hand and shook Grandpa Stone's. Then he gave the children a small wave and the children waved back.

"My father used to use the word 'young'uns' and I haven't heard that word since I was a pint-sized boy. It is kind of refreshing because it brings back memories . . . good memories," Mr. Windsor noted.

"John, the children are doing a little research about events that have happened in our town, and they were wondering if they could ask you a few questions."

"Yes, of course. I lived in Simonsville my entire life until I came here. I practiced my profession for many years, and now they tell me that I am not thinking straight so I am not allowed to go into the law office any more. Can you believe that?" a very annoyed Mr. Windsor said.

"I am very sorry to hear that, John. Do you remember back in 1982 when the three Owens children were abducted in front of their home?" asked Grandpa Stone.

"I certainly do. Tragic. Very tragic. I don't know where those frightful birds came from, but the fact is they came from the sky and then the children were gone. And that's the truth. You see, no one ever believed what I saw. But I know what I saw and I wasn't imagining it or having hallucinations as some people said. I am sticking to my story until the day I die."

"Mr. Windsor, what exactly did you see before the birds appeared?" Chelzy inquired.

"What's that child? Speak up, please speak up for me."

"Oh, I'm sorry, Mr. Windsor," Chelzy said in a louder and more clear voice. "What exactly did you see before the birds appeared?"

"Well, it was a mostly sunny day and the early evening remained cloudless. Nothing in the sky, just unblemished blueness as far as one could see. I was in court on that day, so when I arrived home, I decided I wanted to get some exercise, which greatly helped me key down from an eventful and stressful day. I walked for a short time and then I remembered that I promised my wife that I'd pick up the dry cleaning, so I went back home, got in my car and started driving.

"Now for some reason, something told me to use Sycamore Street to get to the cleaners instead of Main Street, which is my usual route. Sycamore Street is not a shortcut so, to this day, I don't know why I used it.

"Anyway, as I was driving down the street, I got a call on my car phone. I decided to pull over to take the call. You know that is the safest thing to do and that was always my practice. Back then we didn't have cell phones, only car phones. They had just come out and were pretty popular if you could afford one. By the way, they won't even allow me to drive anymore. They took my car away from me. They say it's my eyes but I have 20/20 vision, so I think that is just an excuse. It is terrible how old folk are treated these days. There is no appreciation for—"

"Excuse me, Mr. Windsor, the abduction?" Chelzy interrupted.

"Oh, yes, yes, yes. Well you see, I pulled over and answered my phone. It was a wrong number. That was strange because I never received a wrong number before on my car phone. Back then, you know, there were no cell phones. Car phones were the big thing. Anyway, as I was putting my phone down, I heard laughing and giggling. I looked up and the three children were passing me, walking on the opposite side of the street. All of a sudden and out of nowhere, three huge birds flew down from the sky and appeared to grab the children, but then the children disappeared and I only saw the birds fly back into the sky. These birds each looked as big as a small private jet. And then, the birds also disappeared."

Matthew quickly asked, "Did you notice anything on the road where the children were walking?"

"No, not at first. You see, after they were gone, I ran onto the road and looked around to see if they darted behind a house or something, but they were nowhere to be found. When I did arrive back to where they disappeared, I found something unusual."

"What, Mr. Windsor, what did you find?" Tory asked with great excitement.

"First, I called the police to report what I saw. They came within ten minutes and questioned me. I didn't know who the children were, so they had to go door to door to find out if any children were missing. When they inquired at the Owens' residence, their mom, Patricia, said that her three children, two sons and a daughter, had left only about ten minutes ago to walk to Green's Store for an ice cream. The police found two other witnesses who saw the children also, but their reports were determined to be unreliable. My report, on the other hand, was found to be totally ridiculous. They even went so far as to have me take a blood alcohol test to determine if I had been drinking. But I saw what I saw and I am sticking to my story. I know it happened that way, even though I cannot explain it."

"You said you found something unusual where the children were walking, what was it?" Tory asked again.

John Avis Windsor lifted his right hand and, with his finger shaking, he pointed to his dresser. More specifically, he pointed to the ornate case on the dresser. For a moment, there was complete silence in the room. Chelzy thought perhaps he found a black cloth like the one she had discovered on her back porch. Tory had no idea what could be in the container unless it had to do with one of Grandpa Stone's stories and the black dust he described. Matthew, on the other hand, immediately thought that maybe Mr. Windsor found exactly what he had discovered when the black dust had disappeared from the road on the way home from Grandpa's house.

"Bring me the case," directed Mr. Windsor. Chelzy was closest to the dresser so she started walking over to it, but Matthew stopped her.

"Please, Sis, can I get it?"

"Sure, go ahead. You never say please."

Matthew slowly proceeded over to the dresser and gently picked up the ornate chest. He then handed it to Mr. Windsor while asking, "Is this what you found?"

"No, no, I did not find the chest. I found what is in the chest. Matthew, would you like to open it?"

"Yeah, I sure would." Matthew took the case from Mr. Windsor's hand, placed it in his own left hand and slowly lifted its lid with his right hand. Lying on the black, velvet interior was something that was very familiar to him. He stepped back and made a gasping noise.

"Matthew, are you all right?" asked Grandpa Stone.

Matthew looked at Chelzy, then Tory, and said. "I'm fine, I think."

"Take it out and show it to everyone," shouted Chelzy.

Matthew then lifted a shiny, irregularly shaped onyx stone and held it up for everyone to see. "It's an onyx stone, Grandpa, just like in your stories, just like the one I—"

"You what?" Chelzy interrupted.

"Never mind," Matthew replied as he quickly placed the stone back in its case and carefully placed it on the dresser in the exact location from which he took it.

Mr. Windsor just sat in his chair, staring out the window and mumbling, "No one would believe me, no one would believe me, no one would believe me."

With that, Grandpa Stone attempted to thank John for their visit but he kept saying the same words over and over again. The children each gave a small wave goodbye. Everyone walked back to grandpa's vehicle without saying a word.

Finally, when everyone was in the car, grandpa said, "Okay, young'uns, it is possible that Mr. Windsor heard the stories and then his mind played tricks on him and he thought he saw the birds."

"But, Grandpa, then what about the black onyx stone? That's real. Where do you think he got that from?" asked Chelzy.

"That I am not sure of. He could have already had it or maybe he bought it; it's too hard to tell what exactly happened."

"Or maybe he found it where the children were and he is not crazy at all," added Matthew.

"Well, let's go home. And don't forget to tell your parents about all the things you learned at the library. And, uh, maybe you can leave out the conversation with Mr. Windsor. We don't want to spread rumors about him still having mental problems."

Matthew turned around and looked at Chelzy and Tory as he said, "I don't think he is crazy at all."

CHAPTER 10

The Vote

Chelzy and Matthew each concluded on their own that Mr. Windsor was not crazy, because if he was, so were they. Chelzy had wanted to share her encounter with the unusual black cloth with Mr. Windsor and Matthew had a hard time not shouting out the fact that he, too, found an onyx stone where black dust had disappeared, but they both kept silent during their visit and on the ride home. Each knew they needed more proof before they could share their findings with anyone.

The day came on Tuesday of the following week. Chelzy's mom couldn't figure out why Chelzy got out of bed earlier than usual and was even more surprised to find Matthew already finishing breakfast by the time she came down to the kitchen. "We must have something really special planned today," commented Mrs. Stone to Matthew as he slurped the last drops of milk from his cereal bowl.

"I'm not really sure. We may play more of Tory's game or just walk around the neighborhood today," responded Matthew.

Chelzy and Matthew finished breakfast at different times, but managed to get beds made and dressed in record breaking time. They had told Tory that they would come get her at 10:00 a.m. and were walking out the door at 9:55 a.m.

It was a typical summer morning. Glistening dew was still present on the tips of blades of grass as the sun shined brightly. Squirrels could be seen hiding their prized finds of nuts and seeds in caches. Robins and sparrows adorned the oak trees that lined the street as they chirped happily away. The weather forecast called for clear skies with little or no chance of rain. The breezes were light and refreshing. It was a great day for an adventure.

As Chelzy and Matthew crossed Sycamore Street, their eyes peered in different directions. Chelzy's eyes looked to the sky, searching for a faint glimpse of any dark objects, while Matthew's eyes roamed all parts of the macadam road, looking for anything that sparkled. Of course, neither told the other what was on their minds.

Just as Chelzy walked up to the Herold's front door and lifted her hand to ring the doorbell, the door quickly opened. "I thought you'd never get here," said Tory. "This is so exciting that I couldn't even sleep last night. I kept waking up, looking at the clock and hoping it was morning."

As the threesome crossed Sycamore Street, they continued to plan their day. "Maybe we should play more of the game," Chelzy said.

"Why? Don't we want to explore the woods and see if we can find any evidence of black dust, silver feathers or what happened to the kids that disappeared?" Tory questioned.

"Yep, I agree with Tory, let's go. The Magic Woods await us," said Matthew.

They walked through the Stone's front yard, around back and out a gate that led to an alley behind their house. The alley was adjacent to the wooded area. The expanse of trees was thick and luscious with tall branches full of leaves and small animal life. Different types of birds could be seen perched atop branches but none were in flight. Shadows of varying sizes and shapes were scattered along trails, and there was an abnormal absence of sound.

A few narrow trails led into the woods, each inviting visitors to explore the unknown. Chelzy, Matthew and Tory stood facing the woods in the alley, trying to decide which path to take into the area. Not wanting to appear afraid, yet feeling a need to share her concerns about entering the woods, Chelzy said, "This place looks really creepy to me."

"It doesn't look that strange, so which way should we go in?" asked Tory.

"Well, it looks like there are a couple of ways to get in, so why don't we just take the one closest to us," Matthew remarked.

"Who wants to go first?" asked Chelzy.

"Oh, I'm not afraid. Just follow me," said Tory.

"Wait! I forgot something," said Chelzy.

"So did I," added Matthew.

"We'll be right back. We're just going to run back to the house for something. Stay right here. We'll just be a minute," said Chelzy.

Reluctantly, Tory stood waiting while Chelzy and Matthew ran back to the house. Neither Chelzy nor Matthew had a clue as to what each other was running to retrieve, but neither one wanted to ask the other. They knew that if they had to explain what it was that they were going back home for, the other would not believe them. So, each ran quickly but silently. Chelzy was hoping she would find the black cloth in her nightstand drawer, even though it had strangely vanished.

Tory became very restless and she started pacing back and forth for a couple of minutes, then she decided to start exploring on her own. Slowly and cautiously, she took the path into the woods. As she looked around, she noticed the tall evergreen trees. They immediately reminded her of last year when her family went to a tree farm to cut down a Christmas tree for their home. All these trees looked exactly alike, so identical and perfectly formed as if someone made them out of plastic, enchanted them and then brought them to life. "Very strange. There are so many of them. Chelzy didn't mention anything about this area being a tree farm," Tory thought to herself.

As Tory continued to walk around and discover more about her surroundings, Matthew ran to his bedroom, crawled under his bed and gently removed the shoebox. As he held it in his hands, a black light began glowing from the box. He slowly opened it and gently picked up the onyx stone. For some reason, it did not frighten him. It made him feel better knowing that Mr. Windsor also had an onyx stone just like his. He returned the box to its hiding place and placed the stone in his pocket.

In the meantime, Chelzy ran into her bedroom but quickly stopped in her tracks. Her nightstand drawer was emitting gold, red and black light. She immediately knew that her treasure had reappeared where she had originally placed it. By the time she opened the drawer, the black cloth had stopped glowing. She retrieved the black cloth and ran from her room. By that time, Matthew was already out the back door and on the porch waiting for her.

"What took you so long, Sis?"

"Never mind, let's run and catch up to Tory," Chelzy responded.

Chelzy and Matthew ran back to the alley. Since Tory was nowhere in sight, they decided to walk down the same path they decided on earlier.

All of a sudden, as Tory was inspecting the evergreen trees, there was a loud swish through the trees as if a plane flew very low overhead, but there was no sound of a motor. When Tory looked up, she saw a glimpse of something very large, silvery and bright; but within seconds, it was gone. Unexpectedly, it felt as if someone had tapped her on her left shoulder. Hoping that it was either Chelzy or Matthew, she jumped and turned around quickly at the same time. She looked all around and saw nothing. She felt goosebumps from her head to her toes. She was ready to run, but when she looked down, she could not believe her eyes. She wanted to move but her feet felt glued to the ground. And then it happened.

A very large shining silver feather had landed at her feet and then began to glide upward toward her face. Based on its size, she could not even imagine what kind of bird lost it. It was gigantic, the size of a car. Tory stood motionless. The feather suddenly stopped and was suspended in mid-air. At that moment, Tory heard Chelzy and Matthew in the distance. She turned her head and opened her mouth to yell but couldn't. It was as if her vocal chords were paralyzed. No sound came out of her mouth. When she turned back to the feather, it had become small and white and just ordinary, and even though she didn't remember grabbing it, the feather was in her right hand.

"Tory, I thought you were going to wait for us out there near the alley," said Chelzy. "What's in your hand?"

Tory raised her right hand and slowly opened it. The white feather lay motionless.

"Where'd you find that?" asked Matthew.

"I . . . I don't know. I didn't find it. It found me. I mean, it just floated down from some huge silver bird or something. No, I mean it, it was silver and glowing and . . .," stammered Tory.

"It looks like an ordinary feather to me, Tory," Matthew said.

"I believe her," said Chelzy.

"What do you mean you believe her?"

"There have been some very strange things happening around here lately, and if Tory says it came from a huge silver bird and it was shining, then I believe her," Chelzy responded.

"All right, let's start walking," Matthew said.

Matthew stopped abruptly in his tracks. "Did you say that it was silver and shining, Tory?"

"Yes, but I was afraid to say it again 'cause I thought you would think that I was crazy or just imagining things."

"Are you thinking what I'm thinking, Tory?" said Matthew.

At that point, Chelzy spurted out, "Remember grandpa's story? He said one of the children returned with a long silver feather from a silver eagle. And what about the black cloth card in the game?"

"Now this is really getting interesting. What black cloth card, Chelz?"

"I didn't want to say anything either because I thought you'd think I was crazy, too, but one day I found a glowing black cloth on the back porch, and every time I moved it, it would turn colors. It looked the same as the nugget card that I picked up in the game. I hid the black cloth in my nightstand drawer, but then it disappeared. But then it reappeared. It's so strange I didn't think anyone would believe me. Here, I'll show you."

Chelzy slowly put her hand in her right pocket. Gently, as if holding the Hope diamond, she lifted it out and held it between Matthew and Tory.

"But it won't glow anymore."

"Okay, this is getting weirder by the minute," Tory said.

"No, it's actually about to get even stranger," Matthew said.

"What do you mean?" asked Chelzy.

Matthew took a deep breath. Chelzy started curling her hair faster than she ever had before. Tory held her left hand over her mouth.

"Did you find something? Show us before I die of suspense," Chelzy demanded.

Matthew put his right hand in his pocket. After hearing about Chelzy's and Tory's finds, he was sure that they would now believe him.

"All right, listen. When we were walking home from grandma and grandpa's house, I saw something like black glitter on the road."

In unison, both girls responded, "Black dust? You found black dust?"

"Well, yes and no. I mean it looked like black dust, but when I went to touch it, it changed," Matthew said.

"Into what?" Tory asked.

Slowly, Matthew withdrew his hand, in the form of a fist, from his pocket. He held it up for both girls to see.

"You're not going to believe this," Matthew said as his voice quivered.

"Open your hand! Open your hand!" Chelzy demanded.

After another deep breath, Matthew slowly opened his hand.

"It must be a black onyx stone from the tiara of the old woman in the story grandpa told us," Chelzy said.

"And it looks exactly like the onyx stone that Mr. Windsor showed us," Matthew added.

"There's more. I thought I might need this so I borrowed it from the game," said Matthew as he put his other hand in his left pocket and withdrew a card, and held it out for both Chelzy and Tory to see.

"This is the black dust card that I picked up in the game," Matthew continued. Somehow this stone changes to black dust and takes you right to the Dark Queen's Earth in the game. And the black dust is supposed to make you invisible as you travel from one place to another through her kingdom. It allows you to choose nugget cards that help the player travel safely through the Dark Queen's Earth."

"I am sure glad we are not playing the game right now," said Tory.

"Okay, we are not playing the game, but look at these paths. What do they remind you of?" Chelzy questioned.

"I was afraid you'd ask that," remarked Tory.

"All right, let's think. We are walking along paths with three weird items and a card from The Lost and Found Game in the Magic Woods," Matthew reported. "It's all pretty creepy to me. What should we do, keep going or go back? Let's take a vote. If you want to keep going, raise your hand."

The vote was taken. It was unanimous.

CHAPTER 11

The Large Tree Stump

Chelzy, Matthew and Tory started walking along the path through the evergreen trees. The suspense was intense and the silence was deafening. Chelzy was curling her hair relentlessly with her left hand while clutching the black cloth in her right hand. Matthew secured the onyx stone in his right hand while Tory held the silver feather in both hands, making sure it would not float away.

The trees were so tall that their tops shaded the path from sunlight, leaving it dim and sullen. The path curved to the left, then the right. Tory set the pace since she was leading the group. All of a sudden, she stopped and gasped as she let go of the feather with one hand and pointed to an area that the path had taken them. An enormous tree stump stood in the center of an open area.

"What is that?" exclaimed Chelzy.

"Wow, it's humungous!" added Matthew.

Without saying a word, Tory ran to the stump. As she stood next to it, it was more than twice her height. What was more astounding was its abnormally enormous girth. She rubbed her hand against the bark, unsure of what it was that she was feeling.

Finally, Tory said, "Let's climb up and see what it is."

Matthew just stood by, staring at the stump and sizing up the whole situation. "It looks like part of a tree; and if this is its stump, the tree must have been gigantic. But where's the rest of it? And if someone cut it down, he'd have to be a giant."

"A tree stump? Wait a minute. That means we can figure out how old it is by counting its rings," added Chelzy.

Besides teaching her students about evergreen and deciduous trees, Mrs. Kim also taught her students that a person can determine the age of a tree by counting its growth rings. Chelzy especially remembered this lesson because her dad took her to a family friend's farm and together they counted rings on stumps of trees that their friend had cut down.

"And how do you propose we are going to climb up there?" asked Matthew.

"My dad has a ladder," Tory said. "He used it yesterday to clean out the gutters on our house. Let's go back and get it. We have to find out more about this stump. Nobody will believe us, so don't say a word about our discovery to anybody."

With Chelzy leading this time, they ran back through the woods and out into the alley. They decided that they would put their special finds in their pockets and not share what they had or what they found with anyone. "Matthew, you have the black dust card from the Lost and Found Game. I want to get the black cloth card and, Tory, you should see if there's a silver feather card. We may need them in the Magic Woods," Chelzy explained.

"Good idea. Let's do it. No telling what we are going to find on that stump when we climb on it," Matthew said.

They ran into the Stone's backyard, up the back steps and onto the porch. As Chelzy was ready to open the back screen door, Mrs. Stone greeted them. "I was hoping that I would see you soon. How about some lunch? And I have to tell you about an accident I had with your game, Tory."

"Accident with my game?"

"No! No! No! It's fine. I didn't damage it; but when I was dusting the furniture, I accidentally bumped it and all the pieces fell. I figured you would all have to start a new game, so I put it all back in the box."

"Phew, that's okay, Mrs. Stone," Tory said with a sigh of relief.

Chelzy asked her mom if she would make some sandwiches for them; but, before they ate, they wanted to check the game to make sure all the pieces were put away properly. They ran into the living room. Tory picked up the box. They all stared at it as if it had a direct connection to the Magic Woods. At least, that is what they were all thinking to themselves.

Tory gently placed the box on the coffee table. Matthew slowly lifted the lid and placed it on the floor. Tory picked up the nugget cards and began looking for the black cloth and silver feather cards. Matthew opened the folded playing board and placed it on the table. Tory looked at the board and threw the nugget cards into the air in disbelief. Chelzy stood up and screamed as if she had just seen a ghost. Matthew lurched away from the table and landed on the nearby sofa.

"Look at the middle of the board! The willow tree is gone. Oh wow, there's a huge tree stump in its place!" yelled Chelzy.

"Oh no, wait, look at the nugget cards on the floor!" Matthew added, taking a slow, large gulp.

All the cards landed face down except three cards. Although they didn't know it, these three cards would decide the fate of the adventurous threesome.

CHAPTER 12

All Aboard

Matthew realized that his black dust card had disappeared from his pocket and appeared on the floor with the other two cards. Without even saying a word, Chelzy picked up the Glowing Black Cloth card. Tory grabbed the Quivering Silver Feather card and Matthew, in disbelief, retrieved the Glittering Black Dust card from the floor. Each placed their card in a pocket, and all three rushed out of the room just as Mrs. Stone entered.

"Wait one minute. Before you go off to wherever it is you are going, put the game away and have some lunch. Whatever you three are up to, you will need energy, so come on the back porch and eat the sandwiches I made for you," said Mrs. Stone.

"Mom's right, guys. Let's have a quick bite to eat and then we can go for that walk that we were talking about," Matthew responded.

Picking up the game from the floor would normally take only a minute but this was no ordinary game. Chelzy held the game board tightly with both hands as she stared at what once was a black willow tree and now appeared as a huge tree stump. Matthew picked up the game pieces, including his eagle, Chelzy's deer and Tory's mountain lion, and gently placed them back in the game box while Tory gathered all the remaining nugget cards from the floor.

"Do you think we should see what the other nugget cards say?" Tory asked as she neatly stacked them face down.

"I don't know about you, but I've seen enough for now," Matthew replied. "Maybe we better just take our three cards and leave the rest here with the game."

"This time I agree with you, Bro. I'm too scared to read them. Let's just keep them face down and put them back in the box," remarked Chelzy.

After the game parts were carefully placed back in their worn container, the game was placed on a nearby end table. Then the three ran through the kitchen and out onto the back porch.

"Thank you for lunch, Mrs. Stone," said Tory.

"Hey, slow down, you three. Eating fast is not good for digestion. What's so important that you are all in such a rush anyway?" asked Mrs. Stone.

"Ah . . . oh . . . umm . . . we are just going to take a short hike through the Mag—oh, I mean the woods behind our house, Mom." But a quick kick under the table from Matthew stopped Chelzy from revealing the fact that Grandpa Stone's stories had a profound effect on them.

"You know, dad said it would be okay if we wanted to explore the wooded area this summer, and it is officially summer now. Actually, there is a nice picnic area there, so why don't we take our sandwiches and finish them there?" asked Chelzy.

"All right, but do not go too far into the woods, and I want you to check in with me in one hour," Mrs. Stone ordered. "And I don't mean a call from a cell phone, I mean in person. Understood?"

"No problem, Mom, see you then," Matthew said as the three grabbed their sandwiches and drinks and headed for the woods.

"The ladder, we need the ladder," shouted Tory as they walked and munched at the same time.

By the time they were at Tory's house, they were too excited to finish their lunches. They deposited what was left in a nearby trash can. They walked around to the back of the house toward the garage. "There it is. Do you think it is tall enough?" asked Tory.

"Sure, it looks like the kind that my dad used to have," Matthew remarked, "where you sort of extend it to make it taller. We'll figure it out. Let's grab it and move quickly. One hour is not a lot of time. And anyway, if anyone sees us with this ladder, they will want to know what we are going to do with it, and no one would believe us if we told them."

With Matthew taking the lead, Chelzy in the center and Tory on the end, they lifted the ladder, carefully crossed Sycamore Street and proceeded to the Magic Woods. They entered through the same path that they had chosen the first time. "Bro, slow down. Your legs are longer than Tory's and mine, and we're tripping over our feet trying to keep up with you," yelled Chelzy as she held tightly on to the ladder.

Disregarding his sister's plea, Matthew kept his fast pace as the two girls kept up with him, but with some difficulty. They finally reached the huge stump. They leaned the ladder against it, extended it to the top, stood back for a moment and looked at each other. "Okay, who wants to go up the ladder first?" asked Chelzy.

"You know what they say, 'Ladies first,'" Matthew replied. "And anyway, someone should hold the ladder, and that should be my job."

"I'll go first," Tory quickly interrupted. "I'm not afraid. It's only a dumb old tree stump."

Matthew held the ladder tightly while Tory climbed and Chelzy watched. "You know, Tory, I'm not afraid. I just happen to be the oldest and strongest, and I don't want you to fall," Matthew yelled.

With hands on her hips, Chelzy retorted, "Yeah, sure, Bro, you have got to be joking if you think for a moment we believe that."

Tory slowly made her way up the tall ladder, inspecting the stump carefully as she stepped onto each rung. Chelzy then added, "Maybe we shouldn't let her go up alone. We don't even know what is up there."

Matthew quickly responded, "There's not enough room for two of us to walk up the ladder together. Anyway, she doesn't seem a bit scared. It's probably just a big, old tree stump."

"But this is not a normal tree stump. I don't think the great sequoia trees out west are anywhere near half this size. Aren't you frightened to think who or what put it here or grew such a huge tree and why?" Chelzy rambled in a fashion that did not allow Matthew to intervene. "And someone or something would have had to use a really big saw to cut it down, don't you think, Bro? And that someone or something could be lurking behind a tree and watching us right now. And anyway, it must be pretty important since it appeared in The Lost and Found Game."

"Sis, it's probably just some anomaly of nature," Matthew responded.

"Wow!" exclaimed Tory, having reached the top of the tree stump.

"What do you see? What do you see?" shouted Chelzy. Then turning to Matthew, she said, "Anomaly of nature? Where did that come from?" She then refocused her attention back on Tory.

"There are hundreds of rings. I have never seen anything like this, ever!" shouted Tory so that those on the ground could hear her.

"You've never seen what? What are you talking about? We can't hear everything you're saying," Matthew shouted back annoyingly.

"Just come up here and see for yourselves," responded Tory.

At that point, it became a race to see who could reach the top of the ladder first. Matthew tried to jump on the ladder but could not reach the first rung faster than Chelzy, whose gymnastic abilities helped her leap onto the third rung of the ladder. With Chelzy in the lead, they each reached the top of the stump within seconds of each other.

"There are a ton of growth rings, and they are all different colors," Chelzy said in astonishment. "They are beautiful but I don't understand. This tree must have been hundreds of years old but the rings look like someone painted them."

All of a sudden, an amazing sight appeared before their eyes. "Look, the rings are changing colors and they are like strobe lights. What do we do?" asked Tory.

"Hey, my pocket is getting really warm," exclaimed Matthew. He then removed the onyx stone from his left pocket and held it securely in his hand. It was warm to the touch but not too warm to hold. Tory's feather floated out of her pocket. She quickly grabbed it and held it tightly. Chelzy's right pocket started to glow brightly. She removed the black cloth, which was glowing gold, red and black colors alternately. She held it snugly with both hands.

Just at that moment, beams of colored lights began radiating from the stump and shooting high into the sky. The center of the stump opened up and the beams formed three glowing slides heading down a vast abyss. They each fell onto a differently colored slide that traveled at a high rate of speed toward a deep chasm. Each of the slides twisted around the other two, forming a triple helix configuration similar to a very loose hair braid. Lights were coming and going from all directions. Chelzy, Matthew and Tory began a journey that would take them to a far off place well beyond the most bizarre imagination.

CHAPTER 13

The Inhabitants of Candesia Land of Pines

Chelzy rode on a yellow slide, Matthew on an orange slide and Tory on a red slide. As the slides twisted around each other, Matthew, Chelzy and Tory exchanged quick glances. At one point, Chelzy tried yelling something to Matthew, but she could not even hear her own voice. It seemed the colors were bellowing sounds unlike anything she had ever heard.

Chelzy's yellow slide seemed to make melodic sounds that involved acoustic enhancement almost like what you would hear at an opera. The orange from Matthew's slide appeared to be whistling sounds resembling a fratesdys during fireworks, while music resembling swing jazz emanated from Tory's red slide. Together, they made a deafening, yet somewhat pleasant sound as they blended harmoniously. Flashes of light were in synchronism with the blended sounds.

All of a sudden, they felt themselves slowing down. The twisted helix untwisted itself and they were now traveling side by side. Chelzy remembered that she had removed the black cloth from her pocket right before they had begun falling. "The black cloth," she shouted, "it's gone." She no sooner finished her sentence when she felt something very warm in her right pocket. She put her hand in her pocket, and was relieved to find the cloth snug and safe.

"Where are we going?" Matthew yelled loudly. The colors had stopped making sounds so Chelzy and Tory were able to hear him.

As Tory slowed down to almost a snail's pace, she hollered, "Look! Look at the trees! They're all different colors." All three came to a stop at the end of their slide.

"Why thank you, little lady. It's so kind of you to pay me such a compliment before we have been properly introduced."

Eyes and mouth wide open, Tory froze as a blue pine tree gently lifted her from the slide and placed her feet down on the ground. A red pine tree lifted Matthew from the slide and placed him on a nearby boulder while a copper pine tree placed Chelzy on a log.

"Allow me to do the introductions. I am Eulb and I am the official greeter in the Candesia Land of Pines; and these are my helpers, Der and Reppoc."

"But pine trees are not supposed to be colored like you are, and they don't talk. Are you some special mutation or something?" Chelzy asked as she balanced herself on the log. She learned about mutations when her class visited a seventh grade life science class and the seventh grade students had to teach her class about a new concept. "Aren't you supposed to be green and quiet?"

"Yes, yes, yes," laughed Reppoc, "but only in your world." Here in the Candesia Land of Pines, nothing is black or brown. Everything is brilliantly colored because that's how the Bright Queen likes it; and being radiantly colored is a good thing and lifts one's spirits, do you not think so?"

"Yes, I do, but who, or I mean, what Queen did you just refer to?" said Matthew.

"Why, the Bright Queen. You know, she who sent for you," said Der.

"The Bright Queen and the Candesia Land of Pines, these are all things from my game. Are we actually in the game?" Tory asked hesitantly, almost afraid to hear the answer.

Eulb went on to explain. "You see, the Bright Queen arranged that Tory's Uncle Tony would find The Lost and Found Game and give it to Tory so that you would have the three powerful cards and treasures in your possession."

Reppoc added, "You can sort of say that you are not in a game but part of a game. You should know that the Dark Queen lives in her castle in the——"

"Dark Queen's Earth, right?" Matthew finished Reppoc's sentence, having anticipated the answer.

"Yes, that is correct," said Der.

"I still don't understand. Why were we brought here?" inquired Chelzy.

In unison, the three trees responded. "That is for us to know and for you to find out."

As Chelzy began curling her hair, Matthew slid off the boulder and Tory, who was sitting on the ground, jumped to her feet. Before anyone had an opportunity to ask the pine trees more questions, a blue unicorn flew past them, then returned and circled overhead before landing smoothly on the ground in front of them.

Matthew quickly asked, "What is that?"

Quite shocked by the question, the blue unicorn answered, "Pleased to meet you also, young man. Where are your manners? I am a blue unicorn."

"Sorry, I didn't mean to be impolite. I—I just never saw anything like you before."

"Apology accepted."

Using her mouth, the blue unicorn took out a scroll from her saddle and threw it into the air. It magically unrolled and situated itself directly in front of the unicorn. She then read, "'The Bright Queen summons Miss Chelzy, Miss Tory and Master Matthew immediately to her castle in the Bright Queen's Kingdom.' All right, young ones, jump up on me. We must be on our way. The Bright Queen is anxious to meet you, and I like to make my deliveries on time." The scroll then rolled itself back up and disappeared in a puff of smoke.

The blue unicorn knelt down and motioned for all three to climb onboard quickly, which they did. "Hold on, there seems to be a cross wind today. It does terrible things to my mane."

After nodding three times, the blue unicorn took off like a jetliner with all three children holding on tightly. Chelzy rode in front, Tory in the middle and Matthew in the back. The saddle was quite large with plenty of room for the three of them. The unicorn's wings extended far from its body as it effortlessly glided through the air. Chelzy was not fond of heights so she decided not to look down. Since Matthew had made a model airplane that would not stay airborne after studying basic aerodynamics in science class, he was trying to figure out how the unicorn was flying. They held on tightly to each other.

"My name is Melzabod," said the blue unicorn as she glided above the colorful pines in Candesia Land. "I am the Bright Queen's chief unicorn. My friends call me Melzy, so I would normally invite you to call me that too, but it sounds a lot like your name, Chelzy. So, in order to avoid any confusion in calling out our names, I think it best if you call me Melzabod."

"You mean there are more like you?" replied Chelzy.

"Oh, yes. There are quite a few of us and we serve the Bright Queen in the Candesia Land of Pines. You do know that she has been waiting for you. Well, not just one of you; but yes, you, the three of you. She has been referring to you as The Trio."

"This is all so confusing. Can you tell us why we were brought here? And will we ever be able to get back home?" inquired Chelzy as she held securely on to Melzabod's reigns and shouted toward her ears.

Matthew kept asking Tory what Chelzy and Melzabod were talking about, but with the wind rushing past their heads, it was difficult for either to hear the conversation. Melzabod then flew above the clouds. "This is amazing! Can I put my hand out and touch a cloud, Melzy—I mean, Melzabod?"

"Only if you are sure you will not fall off. I am not the best at retrieving falling passengers."

"Never mind, I think I will just hold on with two hands," shouted Chelzy.

Before Chelzy could ask Melzabod how much farther to the Bright Queen's Kingdom, the blue unicorn slowly glided, as if she was a passenger jet, to a smooth landing in an area where there was a large clearing. As she gently placed all four hooves on what appeared to be a sea of bright yellow grass, she gently lowered herself close to the ground so her three passengers could easily jump down.

"You'll walk from here. It is not far to the Bright Queen's castle," said Melzabod.

"We're going to a castle to meet the Bright Queen? Are you kidding? This can't be happening, can it?" asked Matthew.

"Hurry along, children. You must not keep the Bright Queen waiting. She has much to tell you and you have much to accomplish, and I have an appointment in the royal stables," said Melzabod. Before anyone could ask any questions, Melzabod took flight.

"Why is the grass bright yellow?" asked Tory.

"Well, let's see. Pine trees come in blue, red and copper, and they talk," Chelzy chimed in. "So, why wouldn't the grass be bright yellow? And look at the landscape in general. It's all vividly colored as if an artist spilled paints all over a canvas. The colors are so intense; I wish I had brought a pair of sunglasses."

As The Trio stood taking in a panoramic view of their surroundings, a flock of silver colored birds flew by right above their heads. An abnormally large, white butterfly landed on Chelzy's shoulder. "Moths are white but you're a butterfly, and a big one at that. Where did you come from?" asked Chelzy, not expecting an answer.

"I live here. Where did *you* come from?" But before Chelzy could answer, the butterfly flew away, joining a rabble already in flight.

"And how are we to know which direction the Bright Queen's castle is in?" asked Matthew.

Just as Matthew had finished his question, some of the yellow grass began changing to a crimson color, forming a path into the woods. As the trail grew, the trees and shrubs seemed to move out of its way, forming a walkway. "Unless someone has a better idea, I think we need to follow this path," said Chelzy.

"I have to agree with you on this one, Sis. It's like an invitation or something; and Melzabod did bring us here, so I think we should take the path. Anyway, I really don't have a better idea."

"Okay, let's go. I don't think I want to keep a queen waiting, and I am really excited about seeing her castle," remarked Tory.

The three children, now better known as The Trio, walked on the crimson path until they came to a fork in the road. They stopped and exchanged glances.

"Okay, now what?" asked Matthew, looking back and forth at both paths.

"Let me guess, let me guess, you are lost and you are looking for directions," shouted a nearby voice.

"Who was that?" Chelzy said as she quickly turned around, startled by the loud voice.

"Who are you and where are you going? Wait, oh wait, that's right. The Bright Queen has summoned the three of you—I mean, The Trio," said a silver squirrel emerging from a patch of tall, crimson grass. "I know I read that news somewhere. Forgive my annoyance but I am busy making repairs in the crimson cave, and I am on a deadline, on a deadline."

"You are a silver squirrel and you can talk like the trees," said Chelzy, "and, as I would now expect, you are larger than a normal squirrel. Why doesn't any of this surprise me anymore?"

"I am insulted by your tone of voice. I believe *I* am the normal one here. All of us have to be silver before we turn to gold. You have to deserve and earn gold, you know, so I consider myself quite attractive and fortunate being silver."

"No, I didn't mean to insult you. I—I think you look wonderful in silver; but you mean you are going to turn gold, real gold?" asked Chelzy.

"Oh my, oh my, I guess I have to explain everything to you, don't I? You see, all animals start off white. There are no dark colored animals, or dark anything for that matter, in the Bright Queen's Kingdom. Then as we grow and complete certain tasks, the animals turn bronze. Then in time, if we earn our way, we turn silver, we turn silver. And then we are given a challenge by the Bright Queen, and if we succeed, we turn to gold; and it is, of course, real gold, which is a big honor in the Candesia Land of Pines.

"We are then able to serve the Bright Queen in her castle, in her castle. I am up for my initial review in only three days; so you see, I have to get back to what I was doing. Can't waste time, can't waste time. Take the middle path. That path will take you directly to the Bright Queen's castle. Away with you. Now, hurry along, hurry along; I have work to do, I have work to do. By the way, my name is Skeemor. Put in a good word with the Bright Queen for me when you see her. Tell her I helped you on your journey to meet with her," said Skeemor.

"Wait, Skeemor, what is your challenge?" asked Chelzy.

"The Bright Queen has not assigned it to me yet, but soon, real soon," replied Skeemor. "I am getting a little nervous, but one thing at a time, one thing at a time, and I must finish my job. You are holding me up. I will never finish at this rate. No time for chitchat. Now, get along, get along."

"Oh, it was nice to meet you; and yes, we will tell the queen how you helped us," said Chelzy. "But there is no middle path, only a fork in the road, leading right and left."

"Good luck turning gold and thanks for your help," added Tory.

When The Trio turned around to decide which path to take, Matthew announced, "Look, that middle path wasn't there before! Here we go again. This is really strange. Do you think we are all just dreaming?"

Chelzy quickly turned around and pinched Matthew on the hand. "OW! You didn't have to do that. I would have just taken your word for it, Sis. All right, let's get moving. The queen is waiting for us," Matthew said as he took the lead, rubbing his hand and heading for the middle path as directed by Skeemor.

As they walked along the crimson trail, they came upon deer, rabbits and more squirrels. All were white, bronze or silver. The green landscape was not green, except a few plants that were neon green in color. All the grass, trees, shrubs and flowers appeared as though they were painted in a kaleidoscope of colors.

Even though a sun was not present in the sky, it was as bright a day as any clear, sunny day at home. Everything exuded peace and happiness. It was as if the plants emanated a feeling of contentment and joy. Petals from nearby flowers danced on a tranquil pond. Birds sang soft melodies that saturated the air just enough to be pleasant and calming. As they reached the top of a hill, they looked up to see a palatial edifice peeking through some low hanging, puffy clouds in the distance. These clouds appeared to be gently hugging the Bright Queen's castle.

"Wow, it's huge," Matthew remarked.

"And it's emitting all kinds of colors," Chelzy said, "which makes a lot of sense around here."

As they looked down at the path, the crimson color disappeared. In its place appeared a path that had all the colors of the rainbow.

"Oh wow! It's ROY G. BIV," exclaimed Chelzy.

"Who?" asked Matthew.

"Not who! What! Don't you pay attention in school, Bro? You had Mrs. Kim for a teacher, so I know she also taught you an easy way to remember the colors of a rainbow. Just remember the name ROY G. BIV. She said it was a mnemonic because each letter stands for a color and they are in order. See! Look at the path. The colors are red, orange, yellow, green, blue, indigo and violet. ROY G. BIV! It's like we are walking on a rainbow. Do I have to explain everything to you?"

"I must have been absent for that class. Anyway, this is getting really exciting, so let's skip the science lesson and pick up the pace."

"I don't know about you guys, but I'm running," Tory announced. "I can't wait to see the castle up close and meet the Bright Queen."

"Wait. Everyone stop. Does everyone have their special cards and treasures?" Matthew asked. "Let's call them treasures because I have a feeling they are going to be pretty important to us; and let's not trust anyone with them. Right now, we don't know who is good and who isn't. Keep them hidden for now."

Chelzy put her hands in her pockets and withdrew the black cloth from her right pocket and the black cloth card from her left pocket. "Got 'em both," she replied.

Tory removed both the silver feather and the silver feather card from her left pocket. "Have them," she responded.

Matthew removed his treasured onyx stone from his left pocket and the black dust card from his right pocket. "Phew, me too. We're ready to meet the Bright Queen."

"No, wait," interjected Chelzy. "Let's all do the same thing. Put your treasure in your right pocket and your card in your left; just in case we have to pull them out quickly, we'll know where everything is."

"Not a bad idea. I agree, Chelzy, let's do it," Tory responded. As the Trio decided to put their treasured objects in their right pockets and their cards in their left pockets, they started their journey down the rainbow path. A journey they would never forget.

CHAPTER 14

The Bright Queen's Kingdom

All the grass, trees and shrubs on both sides of the rainbow path were also richly colored and exquisitely sculptured. It was a picture-perfect day with a cool, but slight breeze, and bright light shining, the source of which was undeterminable. The temperature was very comfortable and it reminded Chelzy of her Uncle Pete's car, which had dual controls, enabling the driver and passenger to set their own desired temperature. The landscape looked as if someone with great artistic ability took a palette of dazzling colors and painted the most beautiful scenery.

Tory took the lead with a brisk pace, followed by Matthew. Chelzy, on the other hand, concentrated on the colors of the rainbow and her surroundings.

"What's wrong, Chelz?" asked Matthew.

"Something is happening to these colors. They are bright, but then they get dull for a few seconds, then they get bright again. Don't you see that?"

"No, not really. Doesn't that happen in a real rainbow? Let's hurry. Tory is getting a big lead on us."

Matthew's explanation didn't convince Chelzy. She kept her eyes on the colors as they seemed to radiate degrees of brightness. Chelzy and Matthew then caught up with Tory, who was jumping from one color to the next on the path.

"This is so cool," said Tory. "I wish we had a rainbow track like this in our school playground. And it would be a great way to teach the little kids their colors. You know, I want to be a teacher someday and teach kids in kindergarten."

"See, I learned something new about you today, Tory. Do you think we could ask Principal Thomas to put in a colored track when we get back? If we get back," Chelzy remarked.

Matthew and Tory stopped in their tracks and turned to Chelzy, who also had stopped to consider her remark. Even though all three were thinking the same thing, it was rather frightening to hear someone say it aloud.

"What do you mean *if* we get back?" asked Tory.

"Hey, you two, stop it. Of course we'll get back home. If the Bright Queen had the power to get us here, then I am sure she has the power to get us back home," Matthew said in a somewhat authoritative voice, which actually surprised him.

"If she is a good queen, she will; but we don't know that yet," Chelzy said.

"Well then, let's not stand around and waste time. Let's go meet her," said Matthew.

And with that comment, The Trio picked up their pace. With the castle in sight, they traveled down one hill and started up the next. The majestic Bright Queen's castle stood atop the second hill. The castle's keep, or main tower, appeared to soar into some low-hanging clouds. It was made of stone, and each piece was emitting shards of colored light. The windows were bright as if the daytime light was on the inside shining out. There were several balconies, each adorned with what appeared to be ruby railings. There was a flag atop a slender steeple rhythmically waving in a slight breeze. The flag appeared to have pictures of something on it, but they were undistinguishable from a distance. The castle was surrounded by a tall gate made of pearls, each perfectly situated in a gold setting.

"Wow! Have you ever seen anything like that? It's beautiful!" a somewhat stunned Chelzy called out.

"She must be a very rich queen to own all those jewels. There are so many of them," Tory contemplated.

"Could you imagine building this castle with all the different kinds of precious stones? They must have used special tools," a mesmerized Matthew added. "I bet there are mines nearby with different gems in each."

"I never saw so many colors and shades of colors in one place in my whole life," added Chelzy. "There are colors that I have never seen before, and I don't think I will find them in my crayon box."

As they approached the yett, or silver gate, at the entrance to the castle, there stood a huge bear. It was a mammoth grizzly bear, colored gold instead of brown. The Trio was awestruck by his magnificence, yet intimidated by his size. They weren't sure whether they should run or talk to him. Based on their experience with Skeemor and the fact they were on the grounds of the Bright Queen's castle, they decided to approach the bear, but with great caution.

"Halt. Do not come any closer," said the bear in a grizzly, but non-threatening voice.

"Wow, I have never seen a gold bear before. We're just kinda afraid of you—I mean, are you friendly? Is it safe to come closer? Do you work for the Bright Queen?" Chelzy asked.

"I ask the questions here, young lady. And no, I am not going to attack you unless, of course, you pose a danger. Who are you and what is your business in the Bright Queen's castle?"

"Of course, the bear talks too," whispered Matthew to his sister.

As Tory and Matthew stared upward at the impressive looking bear, Chelzy replied, "I'm Chelzy and this is my brother, Matthew, and our friend, Tory."

"What is your name?" asked Chelzy.

"I am Greeter, and I do not *work* for the Bright Queen. It is an honor to *serve* her, and I have one of the most prestigious positions in the kingdom," replied Greeter, who appeared to grow right in front of their eyes as he stood tall and proud.

"Sorry, we just didn't know. We have never been here before. This is all very different to us; but, at the same time, it is very cool. Now, can we see the Bright Queen?" asked Tory.

"I think not until you have shown me your treasures."

"Treasures? What treasures?" Matthew asked cautiously.

"I am referring to those valuable items and cards the Bright Queen sent you in order for you to travel here and to complete your quest, the one called Master Matthew," said Greeter.

"Quest? What kind of quest?" Chelzy asked with alacrity.

"Only the Bright Queen can explain the quest to you and your friends, the one called Miss Chelzy," replied Greeter.

"Listen. Let's stop wasting time and show Greeter what we have in our pockets so we can meet the Bright Queen," said Tory impatiently.

"All right," Matthew said, giving off a nervous sigh, "everyone, let's show Greeter what we have."

Chelzy, Matthew and Tory slowly took their treasures from their right pockets and the cards from their left pockets, and held them in their opened hands. Greeter, delighted to see them, immediately clapped his paws twice. A large silver key instantly appeared in his paws. He unlocked the yett and said, "Enter, the one called Miss Chelzy. Enter, the one called Master Matthew. Enter, the one called Miss Tory." The tall ornate gate slowly opened.

"Everything here is enormous; first Skeemor, then Greeter and now this gate. I bet it is as tall as a *Tyrannosaurus rex*!" noted Chelzy.

"Not only are they big, but they also talk and they are colored, except, of course, for the gate. It can't talk. Well, at least I don't think so," Tory rambled on. "I feel as though I am in a fairy tale. Are you guys sure we are awake and we are not just dreaming?"

"Yes, Tory, we're awake. Remember, Chelz pinched me when we were walking on the path just to make sure. I still have a red mark and I am sore to prove it. And, Sis, how would you know just how tall a Tyrannosaurus rex is?" Matthew chimed in.

"I pay attention in school, Bro. You know, I don't take power naps during class like you do. Anyway, I know it is believed that they were forty feet tall."

After replacing their treasures and cards in their pockets, Chelzy led the way, followed by Matthew and Tory. As they walked past Greeter and into the courtyard of the castle, the silver gate closed loudly behind them. As they turned around, they noticed that Greeter was gone.

The rainbow path was no longer in front of them. In its place was a path of rubies, which led up to a huge door with an oval diamond in the center. As they approached the door, it automatically opened. "I do hope you enjoyed walking on our ruby path," said a shrilly voice. "You do know that rubies are stones of nobility, which is one of our many traits in this kingdom. Their intense, vivid color gives everyone a sense of bliss; and here, they also have healing powers. But enough of all this, come. Come. Do not keep the Bright Queen waiting."

"Who is that? Where are you? We can't see you," Tory said nervously.

By this time, Chelzy was curling her hair with her left hand and holding tightly on to her brother's sleeve with her right hand. The room they had entered was large and very ornate with brightly colored walls lined with jewels.

"Why, I am Pelamar, your escort," a voice replied.

Chelzy looked around the room and then gasped as she looked down, "Oh wow, you were not here a second ago. You're a beaver, and of course, a gold beaver; and of course, a bigger than normal gold beaver that, of course, talks."

"Excuse me! I like to think I am very normal; and well, of course, I am gold. And it took me a long time to earn it. But I do apologize. I am quite overdue for a buffing, especially on my tail. Oh dear, we mustn't hesitate. Follow me at once."

As Pelamar led the way, he explained to The Trio that emeralds are symbols of immortality and they also have healing powers in the kingdom. He also described emeralds as being related to communication, as they used to be associated with Mercury, the messenger of the gods; and lastly, he connected rubies with love and the goddess Venus.

Chelzy curled her hair even more feverishly as they followed Pelamar down a long emerald path. This time Tory led the way as Matthew followed and Chelzy took her time looking at all the brightly colored stones in the hall.

On both sides of the emerald path were walls of gold, which held portraits that were enclosed in gem-lined frames. The portraits appeared to be of all the animals in the Candesia Land of Pines that had achieved the golden state, and their facial expressions displayed pride for what they had achieved. Chelzy recognized Greeter and Pelamar.

There were a variety of animals and even some creatures that she could not recognize.

Chelzy wondered why all the animals were much larger than normal and also wondered what these animals had to accomplish in order to turn gold. She eventually came to a portrait of a blue unicorn that she immediately recognized as Melzabod. "How did a blue unicorn merit a place on this wall of achievement? And why is Melzabod blue and not gold?" Chelzy said softly so that no one else could hear her. She hoped that, in time, she would have answers to her questions. Patience was not one of Chelzy's strong qualities, but she knew that right now there were more important things that she did not understand and to which she needed answers. She also wondered if Skeemor would appear on the wall someday. Chelzy then ran to catch up with Pelamar.

"Pelamar, wait up. I have an important question for you," Chelzy yelled.

Chelzy ran past Matthew, then Tory, as she caught up to Pelamar. Even though the emerald path was very long, the beaver had no trouble keeping a distance in front of The Trio as he used his tail to catapult himself ahead periodically.

"Pelamar, we met a squirrel named Skeemor in the woods, and he said that he had to participate in a challenge and be successful before he could turn gold. Do you know him? Do you know what his challenge is?" Chelzy asked.

"Well, perhaps, but that is for me to know and not to tell. Let's just say that you will come to meet the silver squirrel again soon," replied Pelamar.

"So, you do know him; but what about his challenge? He was really nice to us and maybe we can help him," Chelzy persisted. "And what about Melzabod? Her picture is on the wall of gold, but she is not gold, she's blue."

"You ask too many questions and all this talking is slowing me down. The Bright Queen is expecting you and I don't want to keep her waiting. Keep moving. No babbling allowed," Pelamar responded.

Once again, Chelzy noticed something peculiar. The stones began pulsating. As they went from bright to dim, she felt her heart throbbing like the colors as she wondered what lay ahead.

All of a sudden, they came to the end of the emerald path and the wall of pictures. A uniquely decorated tall door stood before them. It began illuminating a bright blue color. In the center appeared a small pulsating rainbow. The rainbow descended to about three feet from the floor. Pelamar reached up and touched it. The rainbow began getting larger and larger until it spanned from one end of the tall door to the other. Then the colors of the rainbow became very vivid and began glowing. Pelamar stood on his hind legs and stretched out his front legs. The door immediately started to open from the center and, as it did, the rainbow was divided in half. From the end of each rainbow flowed snowflakes of colors that filled the air.

"Wow, look at these snowflakes; but they can't be snowflakes, they're colored," Chelzy said as she gently grabbed one in each hand. "And they are warm not cold like real snowflakes." But when she opened her hands, they were gone.

"They're beautiful," exclaimed Tory.

Matthew, on the other hand, was peering past the snowflakes, the rainbow and the door. All of a sudden, he put both hands over his eyes, stepped backward and fell to his knees.

"Bro, are you all right?" Chelzy asked as she ran to his side.

"The light—it's too bright. Don't look in the room, Chelz. Don't look!" shouted Matthew. "Tory, put your head down! Cover your eyes! Quick!"

Disregarding Matthew's warnings, both Chelzy and Tory turned and looked directly past the opened door and into the room. Chelzy gasped and immediately turned her head away.

CHAPTER 15

The Beautiful Bright Queen

The extraordinary brilliant light, which caused Chelzy and Matthew to stop in their tracks and cover their eyes, had become dimmer. When Chelzy opened her eyes, she saw Tory staring down at her shoes. "What happened to my sneakers? They're gone. And what are these?" remarked Tory. On her feet were a pair of bright red slippers, soft and cushioned. They felt like they were the perfect size, fitting not too snugly, nor too roomy. They were probably the most comfortable slippers that Tory had ever worn.

"I feel like Cinderella," Chelzy said as she bent down to feel her glittering yellow slippers. "I have never felt anything like this before. They are beyond soft. I feel as though my toes are hugging cotton balls."

"Wait a minute. I want my sneakers back. I am not wearing any orange girly slippers," Matthew said. "I don't care how soft or comfortable they are!" Matthew sat down to take off his left slipper, but could not. No matter how hard he pulled and tugged, it would not budge. "What? Are they glued on?"

"I think they look kind of cute on you, Bro," Chelzy said with a smirk on her face.

"I am not wearing these!" said a frustrated Matthew emphatically.

"Oh, I think indeed you are!" said a voice even more forcefully.

"Who said that?" asked Chelzy.

Her attention quickly turned to a large silver rabbit with gold ears and a gold tail that seemed to appear out of nowhere.

"Hey, you're not all gold," Matthew remarked.

"I beg your pardon. You don't need to be insulting. I am transitioning and I should be completely gold in a few days. Now then, my name is Tibbit and I will accompany you to the Bright Queen. You are about to walk on Her Majesty's most precious pearls. Hence, you are to wear the castle slippers so as to protect her gems. You would not want to mar them in any way and upset the Bright Queen now, would you? After all, she does hold your futures in her hands. Now, Master Matthew, do you have a problem with that?"

"No, ah, no, no, not at all. I really didn't like that brand of sneakers anyway," responded Matthew, smiling in an attempt to appease Tibbit.

"By royal decree, you shall all wear them and be careful with Her Majesty's pearls," warned Tibbit. "You should know that Her Majesty's pearls emit a deep inner glow, which gives them a magnificent luster. Each is perfectly round and has no blemishes. According to Persian mythology, pearls are the tears of the gods; and, in this kingdom, they have—"

"Let me guess, healing powers," Matthew interjected.

"You are correct, Matthew, and it is satisfying to see that you are also learning about our precious gems," remarked Tibbit.

The path that led to the Bright Queen's throne was adorned with highly polished pearls. Chelzy then understood the reason for the slippers. She had never seen pearls so large and round and perfect. She remembered when her mom showed her a pair of pearl earrings that was given to her by Chelzy's grandma. "These will be yours someday, Chelzy. They have been in the family for many generations, so treasure them always," her mother had told her. Chelzy felt they were beautiful, but the pearls in the earrings could not compare in any way to the pearls she was going to be walking on.

Tibbit insisted that Chelzy lead the way, followed by Tory and then Matthew. As they stepped onto a pearl, it changed into a bright color and sang a note. As Tibbit and The Trio walked toward the Bright Queen, her gems made melodious tunes similar to the slides that brought them to the Candesia Land of Pines. As they stepped off each pearl, it changed back to a brilliant white.

As Tibbit stopped walking, a glowing, but not blinding light began to shine in front of them. As they stared into the light, which was almost hypnotic, it slowly began to diminish. What was left was like something out of a fairy tale or even out of a fantasy fiction book. Each member of The Trio stopped and gazed at the striking sight. All three became speechless, a trait uncharacteristic of them.

"I present to you, Your Majesty Bright Queen, those that you sent for," said Tibbit, extending one paw toward The Trio and the other toward the Bright Queen while, at the same time, bowing respectfully.

A beautiful lady dressed in glowing white stood before them. On her head was an elegant tiara with stones that appeared to be diamonds. Her long white dress was lined with diamond-beaded organza and lace. Her long blonde curls, which gently lay on her dress, were adorned with threads made of diamond droplets. Her dress's long sleeves ended in lace intertwined in pearls. The hem of her long dress was lined with more diamonds of various shapes, each catching and reflecting light as it sparkled.

"Children, come closer. I will not harm you. I am very happy to finally meet you," the Bright Queen said as she greeted Chelzy, Matthew and Tory.

Chelzy and Tory instinctively curtsied while Matthew, taking Tibbit's lead, bowed before the queen. Chelzy first noticed her smile, which was warm and welcoming. The Bright Queen extended her arms out to them in an almost motherly way. She not only radiated light but also a sense of peace and happiness. It was no wonder all the inhabitants in her kingdom wanted to serve her.

"You must be hungry. Come, you will eat and rest before you begin your journey," said the Bright Queen. She then turned and proceeded to lead The Trio to another room.

"But, Your Majesty," started Chelzy, "journey, what journey?"

"No questions yet. There will be time for us to talk and I will give you all the details of your quest at that time."

Chelzy, Matthew and Tory exchanged glances as they followed the Bright Queen to an enormous room. In its center was a very long turquoise wooden table surrounded by wooden rainbow colored chairs with high backs. There were many bowls and dishes on the table filled with different types of colorful foods.

The Bright Queen sat at one end. The Trio, unsure of where they should sit, took their places about halfway down the length of the table on either side of the queen. Chelzy sat on one side, and Matthew and Tory on the other. The Bright Queen gently raised her right hand and, turning her palm upward, commanded, "Friends, you may now serve our guests."

Immediately, the bowls and dishes, serving spoons and forks rose into the air and, in a clockwise motion, began moving around the table, stopping so that each guest and the Bright Queen could put food on their plates. A pitcher of milk began filling the goblets. More bowls of food, suspended in midair, began to follow the milk pitcher around the table as each of the children placed portions on their plates. Each bowl, dish, goblet and serving utensil was brightly colored, and the color matched their contents. The food was also vibrantly colored and had a pleasant aroma, which made it all very appetizing.

"This stuff is really good," remarked Matthew. "What is it?"

"These are many delicacies that are, of course, grown right here in the kingdom, and they are all very tasty and nutritious. I am happy that you are enjoying them. Please, eat as much as you want." As soon as someone's plate was empty of one type of food, a serving bowl would immediately float to near that person's plate, offering a refill.

The Bright Queen refused to talk about their quest while they were eating. Instead, she discussed the structure of the castle and the special tasks that each of the animals have in her kingdom. "All our inhabitants are very familiar with every kind of gem that adorns our kingdom. It is important that they know what purpose they serve and how to care for them."

"Why are the animals so much larger than normal here?" asked Tory.

"As you all can see, we have so much more light here, so everything absorbs special abilities from the various colors of light to grow beyond their normal capacities. Now, children, do you have bright lights where you come from?" asked the Bright Queen.

"Well sort of, we have colors and the sun, but nothing like this," Matthew replied. "I don't recall seeing a sun. Do you have a sun here?"

"No, Matthew, our light comes from our gems."

"If we lived here, would we grow to be giants?" asked Chelzy.

"It is a little different with humans, but yes, I do believe that you would grow slightly taller than usual."

When their meal was finished, the Bright Queen invited The Trio to join her in her sitting room. Each wall was painted a different color as was each piece of furniture. The Bright Queen sat in a large purple chair that began glowing as soon as she sat down. Chelzy was drawn to a yellow chair, Matthew to an orange chair and Tory to a red chair. "Why did I sit in this orange chair," asked a perplexed Matthew. "I don't even like the color orange."

"Matthew, think of the slide that brought you here and look down at your slippers," replied Tory.

Once seated, Chelzy also finally realized something strange. Turning to Matthew and Tory, Chelzy whispered, "We are each sitting on the same colors as the slides that brought us here."

"No kiddin', Sis. Tory was thinking ahead of both of us on this one."

They each looked down at their slippers and then turned to each other. "Okay, we're being drawn to the same color all the time. I better not start turning orange," remarked Matthew.

"No, no, children, that will not happen. Let us just say that each of you has been given a lucky color."

"If I get home, I will make orange my lucky color even though I really don't like it," remarked Matthew.

"Oh, my dear children," the Bright Queen began, "colors are very important in the Candesia Land of Pines and in my kingdom. You see, all the plants and animals in this land have special powers. Because they are very content and happy, their happiness emits a glowing light, which fuels all the diamonds, rubies, pearls, sapphires and other gems in the kingdom as well as all the bright colors. The light from the gems, in turn, keeps everything living and healthy. We call it the Cycle of Well-Being. The sun no longer exists in our world, so the warmth and light in the kingdom comes from our gems; but without happiness, our gems would turn dark as would our kingdom and the entire Candesia Land of Pines. We only regard the gems in our world for their beauty and their light, not for any other value. We also cherish happiness and peace; because without them, our gems would grow dark and so would our world."

Before Chelzy could begin asking the Bright Queen questions, all the gems and colors in the room grew dim for a few seconds. Once the light returned to its fullest, Chelzy realized it was the same strange phenomena that she had been observing ever since they first arrived at the Candesia Land of Pines.

"Now I see what you were talking about, Sis."

"Bright Queen, what just happened?" Chelzy asked as she looked around the room while curling her hair. "I have observed this happening ever since we came here."

"Remember the story that Grandpa Stone told you about the children who had disappeared?" asked the Bright Queen.

"You know our grandpa?" shouted Chelzy.

"Yes, I know of him."

"We know the story, and he said some children returned home and some did not," explained Chelzy. "In 1982, three children were abducted from our street and never found. Do you know about them, Bright Queen?"

"Yes, I am very aware of the three children," the Bright Queen continued. "The Dark Queen has captured those children for her own selfish purposes. More importantly, by keeping the children, they have been deprived of returning to their families. They have become her servants, or more like her slaves, cleaning and working in her kingdom. These children are very sad and cry a great deal. Their sadness travels to the Candesia Land of Pines and dims the light in the Bright Kingdom as well as the other lands. This is why, from time to time, the light in my kingdom grows dim for a few moments.

"In my kingdom and the Candesia Land of Pines," she resumed, "the plants and animals are very content and happy, and their happiness gives our gems the power to light our land; just like in the Dark Queen's Earth, the children's sadness enables her onyx stones to give off light for her land. Listen carefully. The captured children's sadness drains power from our gems, and the joy and happiness in my kingdom drains the power from the onyx stones and causes them to turn to dust. So you see, this is why our land is slowly growing dark. If our land turns dark, the Dark Queen's onyx stones can exist forever, and everyone in the Bright Kingdom will become the Dark Queen's slaves or will die."

"Did you say onyx stones?" inquired Matthew.

"Yes, onyx stones, my dear Matthew. These stones also give off just enough light to dimly illuminate the Dark Queen's Earth. That is the way she wants it, because too much light will harm her and her creatures. The sadness of the children is keeping the stones lit and from turning completely to dust."

"If an onyx stone turned to dust and took children away from their families into the Dark Queen's Earth, why haven't we disappeared from being in its presence?" Matthew asked.

"You have remained safe because I have put a magic spell on your stone, Matthew. Your stone has a certain power as does Chelzy's black cloth and Tory's silver feather," replied the Bright Queen.

Chelzy began curling her hair nervously and stood up from her chair while yelling, "A magic power, what magic power does my black cloth have?"

"And my silver feather, what magic power did you give it?" asked Tory.

"My dear children, try to calm yourselves and listen carefully. I have brought you here for a special purpose. If the captured children are not rescued soon, their sadness will darken our Bright Kingdom forever. All the animals and creatures in our kingdom will become weak, and either be captured or die. The Dark Queen will seize the gems and transform them into onyx stones, and these jewels will fuel her evil ways for eternity. If that happens, these children will never be reunited with their families, and they will always remain the age that they were when they were abducted by the Dark Queen's evil birds."

"Just imagine being a child slave forever. That is all so sad," Chelzy commented. "Can we do anything to help?"

"Oh, I think the Bright Queen already has plans for us," Matthew responded.

"Plans, what plans? What can we do? We are only kids too, just like those captured by the Dark Queen," remarked Tory.

"No, you are very special children. I chose you because of your adventurous spirit and because you believe in magic," the Bright Queen responded.

Chelzy, Matthew and Tory looked at each other. They sat motionless for a few minutes, just trying to absorb everything the Bright Queen had said. Frantically curling her hair, Chelzy asked, "Bright Queen, what does The Lost and Found Game have to do with all of this?"

"Tory's Uncle Tony did not know it, but he bought her a very old, magical game. It is not one that conjures up witches or wizards or potions in cauldrons; instead, it gave you three magic cards that you will need on your quest. It also served as a map of the adventure you are about to embark upon. Without that game, the three of you would not be here now."

"I knew there was something very peculiar about that game," remarked Chelzy. "It just gave me an eerie feeling when we were playing it. The things that I thought were strange kind of make sense now."

"Bright Queen, you said our treasures have magic powers. Can you tell us more about them?" asked Matthew.

"Indeed, I can. Listen carefully. You will each need to hold your treasures in a certain way and say the magic words in order for them to work."

"Magic words? Do all our treasures need magic words to work?" Chelzy asked.

"Yes, they do. Chelzy, your black cloth can glow brightly, light your way in the Dark Queen's Earth, and form a protective shield around you and anyone else holding on to you, either directly or indirectly; but this power will only last for a short time, about five of your minutes. You must hold the black cloth in your right hand and the card in your left hand. You must outstretch your arms upwards while grasping them tightly in your hands. You must then say, 'Oh cloth, so colorful and bright, glow and protect us with all your might.' The powers of this cloth will only work three times, and you must save one time to help you return home. And remember, Chelzy, these magic words will only work for you."

"Dark Queen's Earth? You mean we have to travel through the Dark Queen's Earth?" asked Chelzy. "It looked pretty spooky and dangerous in the game."

"Well, how else are we supposed to rescue the children that were captured?" asked Tory. "They must be with you-know-who in you-know-whose kingdom."

"What was I thinking?" Chelzy said. "Of course we have to travel to the Dark Queen's Earth. That is the only way we can get back here to the Candesia Land of Pines and your kingdom. I remember that the home space in the game was in the Candesia Land of Pines. That means we also have to travel through the Gelabar Land of Oaks and the Sea of Weeping Willows."

"Yeah, but if you recall, in the game, there were dangers in those lands too," added Matthew.

"He's right. If I can only use my treasure two times before using it to get home, will we have any other special powers to help us get though these lands alive?" Chelzy asked.

"Let's get back to my onyx stone," Matthew interrupted. "Bright Queen, you said you put a special spell on my stone. What can it do?"

"Your treasure, the onyx stone, will allow you to become invisible for a short time; again, about five of your minutes, perhaps more. It will depend upon the amount of energy you are using at the time, Matthew. The more energy you are using, the shorter the time the invisibility will last. You and those holding on to you, or touching the person holding on to you, will then be able to move around the Dark Queen's Earth or other threatening places, and her evil creatures will not see you. But first, you must hold the onyx stone tightly in your right hand and the black dust card in your left hand. Bring both hands together and hold them close to your heart as you say these words, 'Black stone, so dark as night, make us invisible with all your might.' As I told Chelzy, Matthew, these magic words will only work for you."

"Will I be able to use it in the Gelabar Land of Oaks and the Sea of Weeping Willows?" Matthew asked.

"You may, but every time you use the stone, it will lose some of its power. Also remember, the dangers will be the greatest in the Dark Queen's Earth. The stone can effectively be used only three times, and you must save one of those times to return home. After the third time, it is powerless."

"And you spoke of creatures? What creatures?" Matthew asked.

Before the Bright Queen could respond to Matthew's question, Tory interrupted, "What about my silver feather? Can it do anything special?"

"Indeed, it can, Tory. The silver feather has the ability of transporting you from one place to another."

Tory interrupted, "My feather isn't big enough to climb onto, so does it need magic words in order to work?"

"Yes, it does. Tory, I will explain further about your silver feather; but first, I need to remind you that each treasure can be used only three times, and you must save one power from each treasure to get home. Now listen carefully. Tory, you must hold the silver feather in your right hand and the silver feather card in your left hand. Close your eyes and slowly bring the feather and the card together so they are touching. You must say, 'Silver feather, bright and light, transport us to a safe place with all your might.'"

"Bright Queen, you just said 'transport us.' Does that mean we can all use the feather at the same time?" asked Tory.

"It means that whoever is connected to you when you say these words will also be transported to a place that you, Tory, are thinking of as you say the words; but the silver feather's magic will only work for you. After you say these words, the feather will grow in size large enough to hold all of you as well as the captured children, and it will take you to the place you wish to be.

"Tory, in order for it to work, you must concentrate very hard on where it is that you want to be transported; but its range is limited and will only transport you to a nearby adjacent region. For example, it does not have the power to transport you from the Sea of Weeping Willows to my kingdom. And one last thing, children, the power of these treasures will only work if you think you are in grave danger. So, use them wisely."

"Wow, that's awesome," remarked Tory as she removed the feather from her pocket and stared at it.

"Bright Queen, I also think we really need to know about the creatures in the Dark Queen's Earth. Can they hurt us? What do they look like? Will we be able to defeat them?" Matthew asked again.

"As you travel through the Gelabar Land of Oaks, the Sea of Weeping Willows, and finally, the Dark Queen's Earth, you will come upon dangers. That is why I have given you these treasures. They will help keep you safe, and your companions will also help you survive and be successful. But, yes, these creatures are very capable of causing you harm, and they do have the power to kill," explained the Bright Queen.

"The power to kill? This is like mortal combat," Matthew remarked, "but I'd rather be playing a video game."

"What companions?" asked Chelzy.

"I will send Melzabod with you on your journey; but keep in mind that outside of the Bright Kingdom, she will not have the strength to carry you. Her task will be as a lookout to warn you of impending danger and traps as she flies above you. Skeemor will also accompany you and serve as your guide. He has an acute sense of direction. Skeemor has the ability to climb tall trees and locate landforms while assessing the area so as to warn you of what is ahead. This is important because he will be able to identify creatures that may be lurking in the region. He can also grab things with his needle-sharp claws. However, when peril arises, he may have to hide and leave you to your own ingenuity to survive," explained the Bright Queen.

"Skeemor helped us find our way here to you, Bright Queen. Is this the challenge that he must meet in order to turn to gold?" asked Chelzy.

"Yes, it is. Skeemor will be very instrumental in helping you find the captured children," explained the Bright Queen. "However, in order for him to achieve a gold state, you all must succeed in rescuing the three children and returning them to their homes."

"I guess he's like the GPS system that my dad has," said Matthew.

"Oh, much better," the Bright Queen responded, "he will be able to locate all the hidden caves, crevices and other hiding places that you may need to use throughout your journey. There is something else you need to know. Tibbit and Pelamar have asked to accompany you on your quest. They are in no need of accomplishing a challenge, for each of them has already attained their golden state. If I allow them to go with you, they will be in great danger because their brilliant gold color will make them very visible in the Dark Queen's Earth. However, they can serve you well."

The Bright Queen continued, "Tibbit, being a rabbit, has a heightened sense of smell; hence, sensing approaching creatures. He can also jump, or in the case of all rabbits, hop, tall heights. In gratitude for his loyal service to my throne, I have bestowed a special enchantment on Pelamar. His tail now serves as a radar device, which enables him to detect anything in flight in the area, and it also enables him to catapult himself well beyond where he is sitting. I have not made my decision as to whether they may leave the Bright Kingdom and take this perilous journey with you."

Chelzy, Matthew and Tory looked at each other. "Are you both thinking what I am thinking?" asked Tory. They nodded.

"Bright Queen, we can't ask you to put Tibbit and Pelamar in danger. It is our quest, not theirs," Chelzy said. "We would feel terrible if something happened to them because of us."

"I understand your concerns, dear children, but it's a decision that only I can make."

In a softer tone, the Bright Queen continued, "There are two other matters to discuss. I have placed your game piece in each of your pockets that holds your treasured card. You will have the ability to transform into your game piece, but only once. You will discover when the best time is to use this power. Just hold it tightly, clenched between both your hands, and concentrate on the abilities of the animal. You must remove all other thoughts from your mind or it will not work. Remember, concentrate very hard. Use this power wisely and only when you are in grave danger. You will remain that animal for only a short time.

"Finally, each of you can transport one rescued child and yourself home, but only if you have one power left from your treasures. That is why it is extremely important to use the power of your treasures wisely. It is not only your futures at stake here, but also those of the abducted children."

All of this information was very overwhelming for The Trio. They sat in their chairs speechless as each of them began visualizing in their minds what the Dark Queen's Earth would be like and what kind of creatures they might encounter. Chelzy kept thinking that if she were one of the captured children, she would want to be rescued by someone. Matthew thought how exciting it would be to use the magic in his onyx stone to find the children, and Tory—well, Tory just thought this was going to be the best adventure of her life. Of course, all three then realized that the dangers were real, and fear started to invade their minds.

"There is something of paramount importance that I want you to keep in mind," the Bright Queen began. "Your success or failure will depend upon your determination and on how much you believe in yourselves. True courage and strength come from within, not from magical treasures or weapons; and you, Miss Chelzy, can release great power. You hold the force of compassion and empathy for others as well as the virtue of good judgment. There are three children who need your help. Draw from your inner gifts that make you special, and always follow that voice within you—it will guide you on your path. Matthew and Tory, both of you must place your trust in Chelzy."

Matthew and Tory exchanged glances as Chelzy sat in awe at what the Bright Queen had just said. She never thought of herself as special and she certainly didn't believe that she was courageous or strong. She was the one who wanted to quit playing The Lost and Found Game because she was frightened, and she wouldn't climb the great stump first. She was the one who always complained about being the youngest and always felt stupid. She wasn't sure she had the ability to do what the Bright Queen asked.

"But, Bright Queen, I am not brave or strong, or even very smart. How am I supposed to rescue the children?"

"Miss Chelzy, believe in yourself, believe in who you are. Trust the voice within you. Listen to what it is telling you. The power to save the children lies within you. But remember, the three of you have to work as a team. Only then can you succeed."

Matthew and Tory were quite surprised with the Bright Queen's comments to Chelzy. Matthew always thought of himself as the older and smarter one, and Tory thought of herself as the adventurer. After some thought, Matthew exclaimed, "We can do it. We can work together as a team."

"It is now time for you to decide if you accept the quest to rescue the children. One of three things will happen. If you accept the quest, you may fail and be captured by the Dark Queen, and remain with her as her servants. That is if her creatures do not inflict fatal harm upon you first. Or, you may decide not to participate in the quest; in which case, you may use your treasures to return home. Or, you may accept the quest, travel to the Dark Queen's Earth and free the children. You will then return to your homes while, at the same time, saving the Candesia

Land of Pines, Gelabar Land of Oaks, Sea of Weeping Willows and my kingdom. The children you have rescued will return to their families in the time they lived. What, dearest children, is your decision?"

"I have two more questions, Bright Queen. What will happen to the Dark Queen and her kingdom if we are successful in rescuing the children? And where did light in the Dark Queen's Earth come from before the children were abducted?" asked Chelzy.

"The Dark Queen seized the children because her onyx stones were losing their natural ability to give off light. She discovered through a book of spells and incantations that the tears of innocent children have the ability to revitalize the onyx stones. Once they are rescued, the captured children's sadness will be gone, and the onyx stones will once again lose their power to illuminate her kingdom. The Dark Queen and her evil ways will cease to exist, and children will no longer be threatened by her."

Straightening her stature even more than before and taking a deep breath, the Bright Queen added, "If you are successful in your quest, you will also be accomplishing one more great deed. The Dark Queen has placed a spirit to roam and haunt children in the playground on Sycamore Street at night. You see, she does not like to see children happy, only sad or frightened. If you are successful in defeating her, this spirit will cease to exist as well."

Chelzy, Matthew and Tory huddled together for a few minutes. During that time, Chelzy continually curled her hair and periodically looked up at the Bright Queen. Matthew kept pulling his sister back into the group and the discussion. When they had come to a decision, they took their seats. After glancing over at each other, Chelzy stood up, put her hands at her sides and took a long, deep breath, which ended in a shallow sigh. The decision had been made.

CHAPTER 16

The Journey Begins

The Bright Queen was very pleased to hear The Trio's decision. She wished them well as she left them with Skeemor, who was in charge of the preparations for the journey. He led them through another room in the castle, which was different than all the other rooms through which they had traveled. The Meeting Hall, as it was named, contained many tall shelves of books.

As one could imagine, the books were of various bright colors; and more impressive were the radiantly colored letters that made up the words on the spine of the book. Chelzy learned in library class that the spine is the part of the book that holds it together and makes it strong. It made sense to her since a person's spine or backbone gives the body strength to stand erect. When she looked directly at a book, colored letters jumped off the spine, danced in the air and then settled back in their place. Chelzy wondered what would happen if she actually opened a book and tried to read it.

They then followed Skeemor into another room. The four walls were all mint green, and held paintings, spanning from the floor to the ceiling, of beautiful landscapes in the Bright Queen's Kingdom. The paintings themselves were so colorful and realistic that it was difficult to assimilate their indescribable beauty and not to gaze at them for long periods of time. In the middle of the room was a throne-like chair surrounded by many round tables. Each round table had chairs of different sizes, shapes and colors around it. The tables were of varying heights as were the accompanying chairs.

"What is this room used for?" Tory asked. "I have never seen so many different kinds of tables and chairs. They are actually funny looking because I can't imagine anyone being able to sit in most of them."

"This is the Grand Meeting Room where the Great Council Members of Decisions meet," responded Skeemor in an annoying tone.

"Who are they?" Chelzy interrupted.

Before Skeemor had an opportunity to explain, Pelamar entered the room and proceeded to walk into a scene of one of the paintings on the wall. This particular landscape depicted a tall waterfall feeding into a stream that flowed through luscious, colorful, thick woods. The moment Pelamar entered it, everything in the picture came alive and in motion. Droplets of water from the waterfall invaded the dry, still air in the room and could be felt where The Trio was standing, which was a distance from the canvas, then it settled back down into being a regular painting.

"What just happened? Where did Pelamar go?" demanded a stunned Chelzy.

"You are the inquisitive one, are you not, Miss Chelzy? First, these paintings allow us to move more quickly through the kingdom. It's a very efficient way to travel, especially when we have tasks to accomplish on a schedule, on a schedule.

"Next, to answer your first question, some animals that have reached the golden state are asked to serve on this very prestigious council. They make recommendations to the Bright Queen as to who should be given the golden state, the golden state. Of course, the Bright Queen sits on the royal throne and she makes the final decision. I hope to be granted that honor someday, someday. I have my chair all picked out, all picked out. But first, I have to become gold, and I can't do that until you have been successful in your quest. So, less talk and more action, less talk and more action. Come find a comfortable chair and listen to my instructions," directed Skeemor as he seated himself in a bright orange chair just his size.

After looking around the room and sitting in different chairs, The Trio found the chairs to be either too small or too big; and therefore, uncomfortable. They decided to sit on the fiercely colored red carpet in front of Skeemor, who, with a tug on his tail, grabbed a white scroll that appeared out of thin air. He held on to it gently between his two front paws. After expelling a long sigh, he unrolled it.

Once he had cleared his throat, Skeemor began reading, "Let it be known that Miss Chelzy, Miss Tory and Master Matthew are hereby granted permission to leave the Bright Kingdom. The Bright Queen wishes The Trio a safe journey as they enter the Gelabar Land of Oaks, travel through the Sea of Weeping Willows and finally reach the Dark Queen's Earth.

"Each child needs to heed the warnings of those that accompany them, but they are to be wary of inhabitants that may appear to be offering help. Not all creatures have kind hearts. Some are in service to the Dark Queen, herself, and may try to capture the children. They are to trust their instincts and use their treasures only when they believe there is no way out of danger. Though they can use them anytime, they should try to save the powers of the treasures until they reach the Dark Queen's Earth. This proclamation has been sealed, signed and delivered on this day by the Bright Queen of the Bright Queen's Kingdom."

Skeemor let go of the scroll, which, in turn, rolled itself back up, became very small and, with a puff of purple smoke, disappeared back into thin air. There was a moment of silence. Skeemor sat quietly and upright in his chair, front paws resting on his lap, and awaited a response. Chelzy, Matthew and Tory looked at each other, all thinking the same thing.

"I think I'm kinda scared," Chelzy whispered to her brother.

"No, I know I am scared," Matthew added in a much louder tone of voice.

"Look guys, we can do this. After all, we have our treasures, and I don't think that the Bright Queen would have sent for us if she didn't think that we could handle the challenge," said Tory.

"Challenge? Challenge? I am never going to turn gold at this rate. Let's get going. Time's a wasting, time's a wasting."

Skeemor quickly stood up and motioned for them to follow him out of the Grand Meeting Room. They walked down a long, narrow, green passageway and sidled through a door that was only half as tall as Matthew. At one point, each had to bend over and crawl out the exit. They then walked through a postern, or gate, that led them out of the castle.

"Why was that such a short door, Skeemor?" asked Matthew. "Skeemor, Skeemor, where are you?"

"He's gone," said Tory.

"But he was just in front of us," added Chelzy.

"He is not the only thing that disappeared. I think you both better turn around and look behind you," Matthew suggested.

"Where did everything go? A huge castle can't just disappear, can it?" Tory asked.

"Yep, I think it can, and it did. Anything is possible around here," Chelzy muttered.

The Trio just stared at each other. Everything was gone—the Bright Queen's castle, the yellow grass, the paths made of gems, and Skeemor. All had disappeared. When they turned back around, it was obvious where they were. They were standing in a region full of very tall oak trees, and saw a winding path ahead. "We're in the Gelabar Land of Oaks. But how did we get here, and where is everything and everybody?" asked a nervous Chelzy. "This is so bizarre."

No one had answers to her questions. After a short, silent pause, Chelzy took a deep breath and, while curling her hair, led Matthew and Tory down the trail, not knowing what dangers they might encounter. Hoping that they would rendezvous with at least Skeemor again and not wanting to reveal the panicky gnawing in her stomach, Chelzy faced forward and marched like a commander leading her troops off to battle. Aware of the fears that surrounded all of them and still determined to succeed, she raised her right hand in the air and loudly announced, "One for all, and all for one! Together we will succeed!"

CHAPTER 17

The Cumba Trees

The Gelabar Land of Oaks was a dismal region; because the oak trees grew tall and thick, the light that traveled from the gems of Candesia Land of Pines had a hard time reaching the ground there. Therefore, the area nearest the earth was void of any grass or small plants. All the small animals traveled to the Candesia Land of Pines for food and shelter. Only taller animals made the Gelabar Land of Oaks their home.

"Grandpa Stone has three very tall oak trees in his yard," said Chelzy. "When I was there one afternoon, he told me about the powers that oak trees hold. You weren't there with us that day, Bro, but I will never forget it because I thought it was a cool story. He went on to explain that oaks are powerful wand woods. Wizards look for wands made of oak because they make good magic, especially magic involving time and countering. Of course, grandpa said these were just stories that he had heard as a child; but he also said that an oak tree is a tree of protection, and it inspires people to be brave and good leaders."

"I certainly hope that he was right, because we need protection right about now," Matthew commented.

"Feeling a little braver wouldn't hurt either," added Tory.

Chelzy, Tory and Matthew walked briskly down a narrow path through the trees. They decided to stay on the main trail even though there were narrower passageways that veered off in different directions. The atmosphere was ominous and eerie because of the lack of light and animals. Chelzy kept thinking what a beautiful forest this would be if only there was a sun. However, she was also feeling a sense of dread, not knowing what was ahead. She was experiencing a queasy feeling in her stomach because she felt someone or something following them. She did not want to alarm Matthew or Tory, so she decided to keep that feeling to herself for the present time.

"How do we know that we are going in the right direction?" Tory asked.

"Think of where the spaces were on the game. The Gelabar Land of Oaks was connected to the Candesia Land of Pines, but also connected to the Sea of Weeping Willows," Matthew pointed out. "My guess is that the main paths represent the spaces on the game board; and if we follow this main path, it should lead us to the Sea of Weeping Willows. Sis, what do you think? Remember, the Bright Queen told us to use your judgment, so we can really use it now."

"I agree, Chelzy, maybe she gave you some special powers to make good decisions or something; and right now, we can really use your help," remarked Tory.

"So, wait a minute. Neither one of you think I have my own ability to lead us through dangers. You think the Bright Queen bestowed some special powers on me. Is that it?" Chelzy said in a somewhat annoyed but more disappointed fashion.

"Chelz, no, we don't think that at all. Honest. And I know the Bright Queen didn't mean that either. Anyway, if we really felt that way, I think we would be doomed to failure. You're my sister and I know you pretty well, and I don't think you need any enchantment to make you smart."

"Thanks, Bro. I was beginning not to believe in myself, but I know I can't do that. Not now."

"I'm sorry, Chelzy. You're pretty cool and I know you're smart all on your own," Tory added.

"All right, guys, we have to get back to figuring out if we are walking in the right direction. So, Sis, what do you think?"

Chelzy decided that for now they should keep on the main trail and not take any smaller paths into the woods. She continued to sense a presence near them, and decided that it was time to warn Matthew and Tory. "I don't think we are alone. I can feel something either following us or watching us from above. I can't explain it, but I think we need to be extra careful. Maybe Skeemor can help us. Where is Skeemor anyway? Isn't he supposed to be our guide?" Chelzy asked as she apprehensively curled her hair.

"I don't see Melzy—I mean, Melzabod—either," Tory added. "I keep forgetting she asked us to call her by her full name. Anyway, I think we are all alone and no one is here to help us, and I'm really getting worried."

All of a sudden, the earth shook and The Trio stopped abruptly in their tracks. Not realizing that it was in motion, Chelzy grabbed a low-hanging tree limb.

"Hey, let go. What do you think I am? And you are getting in my way. Move aside before the three of you get trampled on."

"I'm—I'm so sorry. I didn't mean to be rude, but who are you? And why, or rather, how are you walking?" Chelzy asked meekly as she stared up at the huge oak tree.

"I am Quercus, and I am the chief oak tree in the Gelabar Land of Oaks. I am on my way to a conference with tribal representatives. We have much to discuss with all the problems going on; and you are not helping matters by getting in our way."

"What problems?" asked Chelzy.

"Our land is also growing darker and colder, and many of the trees are growing weak. We need light in order to live, and we are once again plotting a way to try to overthrow the Dark Queen and rescue the children; but we do not have a way to send them back home. According to Melzy, that will be your job."

"Did you try to free the children before?" Tory asked.

"Yes, we did try several times, but we always failed," explained Quercus. "The Dark Queen is evil, and so are her creatures. Her powers have always thwarted our efforts. We have lost several good friends in the battle with her."

"Who are the tribal representatives that you spoke of?" Matthew asked.

At that point, the earth started to shake more violently. Without something to hang on to, Chelzy just outstretched her arms as if she was on a balance beam in gymnastics.

As Quercus continued his pace through the woods, he yelled back, "You better get out of the way. My friends are about to come through. One more thing: we oaks are not all friendly. Watch for the Cumba Tribe of trees. They're notorious for squeezing nourishment out of living things with their roots and then absorbing it into their barks when they are hungry. It is a very painful process, so you need to vacate this area *now*."

"I thought trees make their own food," Tory commented.

"Mrs. Kim taught us that plants need light to make their own food." Chelzy continued, "If the light is disappearing, that means the trees are not able to carry on photosynthesis like they should, which means they are not making enough food for themselves. And that must mean that the trees are—"

"Hungry, and that means we are in danger. Let's pick up the pace; let's start running now!" Matthew yelled.

Chelzy, Matthew and Tory had just cleared the area when a group of tall oaks walked by briskly in an attempt to catch up with Quercus. "That was too close for me. We almost got trampled on by Quercus's friends," Matthew said.

"I am in panic mode because there is no end to these trees," Tory shouted. "How do we know what direction to go in now? Somehow we ran off the main trail, and I don't even see it!"

"I'm more worried about which one of these trees is going to eat us," Chelzy yelled as she kept up the pace with Matthew and Tory, "but I have to stop. I can't run anymore. I'm getting tired."

The Trio slowed down their pace to a brisk walk when, suddenly, they heard a voice coming from the top of a nearby sleeping oak. "Quickly, turn right. Take that narrow path through the woods. There are Cumba oak trees heading right toward you. They are dangerous. Run quickly! Run quickly!"

"Skeemor, is that you?" yelled Chelzy.

"No time for conversation. Just run! Just run!"

Chelzy led the way in the direction that their friend had advised them to go. As they were running, they felt the earth begin to shake again beneath their feet. Tory was behind Chelzy, and Matthew behind her. A group of four Cumba oak trees was gaining on The Trio, and they were now able to see them. "Don't look back, just keep running!" Matthew screamed.

"Look my friends, dinner awaits us. Let's get them!"

All of a sudden, a large tree branch came swooping down on Matthew, barely missing him. When he turned around to look at the tree, he stumbled on a large rock that lay across the path and tumbled to the ground. The earth was shaking so violently that Tory lost her balance and fell. Chelzy, terrified that they may be scooped up at any moment, stopped in her tracks when she realized that Tory and Matthew were no longer behind her. The terrain kept quaking with each step that the huge Cumba trees took.

Matthew had managed to get to his feet and ran over to Tory, who was now standing but disoriented. Chelzy reached Tory at about the same time. All four Cumba trees were stretching their limbs in an effort to grab The Trio; but, because they were so big, the trees' movements were slow. This gave The Trio opportunities to evade their attacks, but once surrounded by the trees, there was no way for them to escape their predators.

"Quick, everyone, hold on to me and don't let go no matter what!" yelled Matthew.

Tory, who had fallen once again, reached up and grabbed Matthew's shirt as Chelzy shouted, "Tory, grab my hand." Chelzy, using all her gymnastic abilities to keep her balance, held out her hand to Tory, who, after several repeated attempts, grabbed it and stood up. The trees were purposely moving about so that the ground would continue to shake, which made it very difficult for The Trio to hold on to each other.

All of sudden, Tory lost her balance and fell backward, losing her grasp on Matthew's shirt and Chelzy's hand. At that moment, a Cumba tree began to lower its branch as it extended it towards Tory. It opened up its end branches and, like an outstretched hand, it was ready to scoop her up and make her its next meal.

At that moment, Matthew grabbed Chelzy by the hand and, together, they both jumped in Tory's direction. He then gripped Tory's arm. He quickly shouted, "Grab my shirt, NOW!" As Matthew let go of Chelzy and Tory, each of them grabbed on to him. Matthew then withdrew the black dust card from his left pocket and the onyx stone from his right pocket. He held them tightly in his hands close to his heart as he recited, "Black stone, so dark as night, make us invisible with all your might."

Just as roots began crashing down to the ground, each of the Cumba trees extended their long arms as they opened their claw-like branches and began to grab each of the children. The tree that was about to snatch Tory was only seconds away from having her in his grasp. He chuckled, "Delightful, they will provide nourishment for many meals to come, and this one looks especially appetizing."

Tory began screaming in fear as Matthew held tightly on to the onyx stone, concentrating on the words he had just spoken. Chelzy closed her eyes in fear of what was about to transpire. Just as the claw-like limbs of the Cumba trees closed around Chelzy, Matthew and Tory, something happened: The Trio disappeared and the Cumba trees, no longer seeing them, loosened their grips.

"Matthew, where are you? Tory, I can't see you either," a frightened, yet relieved Chelzy said in a hushed tone.

"I'm here, right next to you!"

"Everyone, move quickly!" Matthew whispered.

"I'm with you, Bro; let's get out of here, fast!" The Trio, holding on to each other, ran right before the Cumba trees could react to what just happened. Their branches grabbed only empty air. The Trio was invisible and gone.

"Didn't the Bright Queen say that the invisibility power would only last for a few minutes?" Chelzy uttered in a low tone. "That means we better get out of here before we become visible again. I prefer not being someone's dinner tonight."

The Cumba trees were surprised when they drew their branches inward toward their trunks and discovered they were empty. "It was your fault. You let them get away."

"No, I didn't. It was your fault. I know I almost had one of them trapped in my branch," another Cumba tree responded. "You must have done something wrong!"

Yet, a third Cumba tree said, "It's both your faults. You are too clumsy and make the worst possible hunters ever. Anyway, where did they go, and how did they move so fast? They could not have gone that far. Maybe we should separate and go in different directions. Maybe one of us can find them."

As the Cumba trees continued to argue, Matthew placed the onyx stone back in his right pocket and the black dust card in his left one. The ground had stopped shaking because the Cumba trees were still trying to figure out what happened to The Trio; and they just stood still, blaming each other for letting them escape.

"What direction do we go in now?" Tory asked quietly.

"Well, I think I know the direction that Skeemor originally showed us. Chelzy, keep holding on to me, and, Tory, you grab on to Chelz, and I'll lead the way," Matthew said. "Let's get out of here fast!"

"Wait, Bro! Maybe he was just trying to help us get away from the Cumba trees, which, of course, didn't work. I think we should turn left in the direction that we first started. The Bright Queen said that I should believe in myself and listen to my instincts, so I say that we continue in the direction where the oak trees are shorter," said Chelzy.

"All right, let's follow Chelzy. If the Bright Queen believes in her, that's good enough for me. Matthew, hold on to me while I am grasping Chelzy's shirt," Tory said.

"Thanks, Tory. Bro, what about you?"

"I'm going to trust your judgment, Sis. Lead the way."

Curling her hair nervously, Chelzy led them down the narrow footpath in hopes that the only trees that they would run into would be harmless and definitely not hungry.

CHAPTER 18

The Young Oaks

As The Trio continued along the path, they each turned visible again. The ground no longer shook. The oak trees that lined the path were either sleeping or they were part of a friendly tribe like the one that Quercus belonged to, and were talking among themselves. These trees paid no attention to the young travelers, at least not right now.

"Oh, no, the light is getting dim again and pulsating just like it did in the Candesia Land of Pines; but now it seems even darker. You know what that means, don't you?" remarked Chelzy.

"It means the Bright Queen's gems are losing their power because of the captured children's sadness. We better speed up our pace or we may be too late," Matthew said.

"How much farther do you think it is to the Sea of Weeping Willows?" Tory asked.

"It depends upon which way you go," a voice interrupted.

"Who said that?" asked Chelzy.

"It's me, Winston," the voice replied.

"Wow, you are short—I mean, compared to all the other oak trees we have encountered so far," Matthew noted.

"Hey, who are you calling short, carrot top?"

"Carrot top? I haven't been called that since I was in second grade."

"Enough, children!" Chelzy interrupted. "That's what our mom says all the time. Enough name calling!"

"For your information, my name is Winston."

"Listen, Winston, I wasn't trying to be rude or disrespectful. I just think that you are smaller. I guess you are just younger than the rest, kinda like if you were to compare us to our parents," Matthew surmised.

"No kiddin', carrot top; I am only ten years old, but I hope to be as tall as my great-great-great-grandfather someday. He's eighty feet tall," Winston proudly said.

"It's nice to meet you, Winston, and I'm sorry for calling you short," Matthew said meekly.

"Uh, ooh . . . I think you better leave now. There is a gang of oaks our age that are not as hospitable coming down the trail, and they would probably want to capture you to make themselves look cool in this part of the Gelabar Land of Oaks. Then they would turn you over to their parents for you know what," warned Winston as he ran off to avoid seeing The Trio having a confrontation with other oaks.

Before The Trio had time to react to Winston's advice, a group of young oaks approached them as they were talking to one another. "Look, what do we have here? Yum, yum, just what the chef ordered. How about we have a little fun first before we tie you up and bring you to our parents?"

"No, I don't think that we are interested in playing any games right now. You see, we have to go. We are on a mission, and we can't be late," Chelzy explained, anticipating the worst.

"Mission? What mission?"

"Nothing that would interest you. Really, it's nothing. Please, just let us go," Matthew pleaded.

The young oaks encircled The Trio and began intertwining their branches. Chelzy, Matthew and Tory stood back to back, looking at their captors. "What do we do now?" whispered Chelzy.

"It's okay, Chelz, it'll be all right. We'll think of something," Matthew whispered back, trying to reassure his sister.

"You had better not do anything to us. We have magical powers and we can stop you," Tory blurted out.

"Magical powers? What magical powers? Show us. Do you have a magic wand or something? Are you witches and a wizard? Wow! Wouldn't that be something if we captured magical creatures! I wonder how they will taste? Yummm . . . Our parents are going to be really pleased with us. How about emptying your pockets."

"No, we can't do that because we don't have anything in our pockets. Just let us go," Matthew pleaded.

"Can't do that! Let's get them, boys."

The young oaks began closing in on The Trio. There appeared to be no way to escape. Just as Matthew began to put his hands in his pockets to retrieve his magic treasures, a voice called out from above, "Look out, hit the ground." Recognizing the voice, Chelzy, Matthew and Tory immediately fell to the ground. The unicorn swooped very low over the young oaks, almost hitting them. The quick rush of air and the threatening motion of the unicorn broke the chain of branches that encompassed The Trio, creating spaces for them to escape.

"Run! Run as fast as you can! Follow me! Don't look back! Just keep running!" Matthew shouted.

Chelzy, Matthew and Tory quickly rose to their feet and took off at lightning speeds. Their hearts were pounding in their chests so hard and loudly that the sound reverberated in their ears as their feet moved faster than they ever had before. They were breathing so rapidly that words were unable to escape their mouths. When they were at a safe distance from the young oaks, the blue unicorn slowed down and gracefully landed near The Trio. Everyone stopped running.

"Melzabod, you saved us. I didn't think that we were going to get out of that trap," said Chelzy, bending over and panting out of breath.

"My pleasure. Now, children, the only safe way out of the Gelabar Land of Oaks is through a dark cave that lies ahead. It will take you directly to the Sea of Weeping Willows."

"A nice quiet cave, now that sounds a lot better. Let's get out of here," Matthew said as his chest kept rising and falling in an attempt to return its heart to a normal beat.

Melzabod continued, "Not so fast, children. The cave is long and dark. You will have to use your resources to get through it. Once you enter it, you may not turn back. If you do, you will never be able to enter it again and, therefore, you will never be able to escape the Gelabar Land of Oaks. Remember, all is not what it appears to be in the cave. The Cumbas have laid traps to make you turn back. You will have to be strong, courageous and determined. Well, it's time for me to be off. I wish you well."

Chelzy, Matthew and Tory stared upward as Melzabod disappeared from their sight. "I have a feeling that it is not going to get any easier," Chelzy grimaced.

"We can't waste any time standing around and talking," Matthew said. "Let's get moving. The cave awaits us. The sooner we get in there, the sooner we can get to the Sea of Weeping Willows and out of this crazy place. Weeping willows can't be as bad as oak trees, can they?"

"They sound kind of gentle to me. I guess that's what you call wishful thinking," Tory said in a saddened voice. "That's what my mom always says to me when I ask her for something really outrageous that I kind of know she won't say yes to. And you know what? I am missing my mom right about now."

"I hope our families are all right. What if they think we were abducted, and they have everyone in the town out looking for us?" Chelzy asked.

"I bet they even have an Amber Alert circulating in Pennsylvania and surrounding states, or maybe even in the entire country," Matthew said.

"We are really going to be in trouble when we get back, if we get back," Tory said.

* * * * * * * * *

"Believe in yourself, believe in yourself, believe in yourself," Chelzy kept whispering to herself as she and Tory followed Matthew down the path. She then thought to herself, "What's the worst that can happen? I can die. We can all die. How? Probably in these treacherous, horrifying lands; either at the hands of the Dark Queen or one of her evil creatures; or . . . a very hungry, mad oak. And we don't even know what we are going to have to face in the Sea of Weeping Willows. I shouldn't even be thinking about it. I can't quit or give up. I can't look or act scared no matter how much I am. I can't let everyone down. They can't know how I feel. I have to be brave. I have to believe in my abilities. We have to succeed."

CHAPTER 19

The Dark Cave

The Trio continued walking in the direction that Melzabod had pointed out to them. After escaping from two harrowing experiences with oak trees, they decided that each of them would have a job to do to help ensure their safety. Afraid that the Cumba trees or the young oaks would reappear, Matthew decided to take the lead so as to keep a brisk pace and keep an eye on what was ahead. Tory acted as a lookout to the right and left and above while Chelzy focused on looking through the trees for anything that resembled a cave.

"What if we don't find the cave? What if we're stuck here forever?" asked Tory.

"I don't think Melzabod would give us false information," Chelzy replied. "For one thing, she is our friend; and don't forget, she serves the Bright Queen."

"Let's just keep moving. It has to be here somewhere. Just keep looking," Matthew said in an attempt to encourage Chelzy and Tory.

"I don't see anything that resembles a cave. I wish we had Skeemor here with us. I bet he could find it fast," said Chelzy.

"You called? So, you are looking for a cave. Hmmm . . . now let me see . . . what can I do, what can I do?" Skeemor chimed in.

"Skeemor, you're here!" Chelzy shouted. "We should have known that you would not desert us, especially not now. This is your area of expertise, isn't it?"

"Yes, yes, of course I'm here, of course I'm here. Where do you think I'd be, at home making ankle bracelets out of acorns? Climbing trees to scout for caves is one of my finely developed skills among many. Now, now, let's find that cave. Follow me, follow me; and do so as fast as you can. I am beginning to feel the earth shake beneath my feet, so that means trouble cannot be far behind. This way, this way!"

"Skeemor, you're the best," Matthew declared. "I told everyone that you would show up to help us. Not that anyone doubted you, of course. Well, I mean, some of us may believe in you more than others but . . . All right, I'll shut up now. I know, too much talking."

"I beg your pardon, Bro. I believe it was me who was wishing for Skeemor to show up to help us. By the way, how do you know about ankle bracelets, Skeemor? You're a squirrel, and squirrels don't wear them. Well, at least not where I come from; then again, we are in a very strange place," Chelzy asked, partly growling at Matthew but mostly smiling at Skeemor.

"I don't live in a cave, you know. Well, maybe sometimes. Oh well, speaking of caves, stop lollygagging, stop lollygagging and look."

"Skeemor disappeared. Where'd he go so fast?" inquired Tory. "He was just here a second ago talking to us."

"Skeemor, where are you?" Chelzy shouted.

"I'm here in the cave, through the bushes. Follow my voice, follow my voice," Skeemor answered.

Upon hearing Skeemor's voice, Chelzy took the lead and ran into a clump of bushes. As she separated the thick brush, she saw Skeemor standing upright with his forearms crossed at the entrance of a cave.

"Well it's about time, about time. What took you so long? Oh yes, I keep forgetting. You three like to traipse around chatting all the time, all the time. I'll be on my way now. Be careful and remember what Melzabod told you. Things are not what they appear to be in this cave; and, Chelzy, listen to your inner voice. Gotta go, gotta go." And with that, Skeemor scampered out of sight in the blink of an eye. Before Chelzy had time to thank Skeemor for finding the cave for them, he had disappeared into the bushes, and Matthew and Tory had caught up to her.

"Yes, you found the cave! Or rather, Skeemor found it. Speaking of Skeemor, where did he go, Sis?"

"He disappeared in the bushes. He doesn't stick around once he accomplishes a task."

"But at least he led us here to the entrance of the cave. Did I ever tell anyone that I love adventures but I don't like caves because they are so small and dark," Tory announced. "I'm claustrophobic, which, you may already know, means I get really nervous when I am enclosed in small spaces. I don't even like elevators. I usually make my mom and dad walk the steps with me when we are at big malls or in any kind of tall building."

"Well, Chelzy doesn't like elevators either. Hey, Sis, do you remember the time the two of us had to take an elevator together in the hospital when we were visiting our neighbor, and I was jumping up and down to make it shake? Oh, and the time I pushed all the buttons so it had to stop on every floor," Matthew said while chuckling.

"It's okay, Tory, just ignore my brother. We'll always be right beside you; so don't worry, you'll be fine. Just don't think about it.

Pretend you are at the playground or at any other open area," Chelzy said in a reassuring manner.

"Who is going to go in first?" Matthew asked hesitantly.

"I'll do it. It's only a cave, and you'll be right behind me. I have to get over my fear sometime," remarked Tory. "I guess this is as good a time as any. And if we run fast enough, we should be able to get through it in no time."

"But we don't know how long this cave is, and even worse, we don't know what's in it," warned Chelzy. "But one thing is for certain, it comes out in the Sea of Weeping Willows, so I want to go first. Let's get going."

"Do you want to argue with her, Tory? I don't. I know when Chelz makes up her mind, there's no changing it."

"I think Chelzy just convinced herself that we don't have a choice in the matter; and if she wants to lead us in, that's cool with me," whispered Tory to Matthew.

"Nah, I think she is just following her instincts, just like the Bright Queen told her to do," Matthew whispered back.

Within seconds, Chelzy began running while curling her hair and yelling at the same time, "Hurry up, stay with me." Chelzy's pace slowed as the cave darkened. "I've reconsidered, Tory, you can lead the way now if you want to. I think I want you to take over as cave leader. You don't like small spaces and I don't particularly like dark spaces."

"It's still kinda light. I'm not afraid. Follow me," Tory said after giving out a loud sigh. "Chelzy, you hold on to me. Matthew, you hold on to Chelzy, just so we don't get separated."

The pace of The Trio grew slower as the cave narrowed and grew dimmer. Chelzy held on to Tory's shirt with her right hand as she anxiously curled her hair with her left hand.

"I thought it'd be a lot darker in here, but we can still see where we are going. Wow, it looks like there is some type of glitter in the walls," Chelzy commented.

The cave was not completely dark. There appeared to be a mysterious substance in the walls that radiated a small amount of light. Since the light from the gems in the Bright Queen's Kingdom also illuminated the Gelabar Land of Oaks, The Trio concluded that the Bright Queen had arranged for very small pieces of gems to be installed in the cave walls for travelers and visitors. It seemed to explain, to their satisfaction, the presence of light in the cave; and they were very pleased that she had done that.

But, all of a sudden, darkness surrounded The Trio, and Chelzy came to an abrupt halt and lost the grip on Tory's shirt. She also could not feel Matthew's hold on her shirt any longer. "Matthew, Tory, are you here?" There was no answer. "Where are you?" Chelzy's voice trembled as she began nervously curling her hair with her left hand and feeling her way through the dark with her right hand. "Is anybody there? Please, answer me. Matthew, Tory, say something."

Just then, Chelzy felt something soft but strange brush against her face. She heard a sound like a bird flapping its wings, and then she felt as if something had become entangled in her hair. Her entire body began wriggling and twitching. Then she heard a growly noise. She gave out loud shrieks, like a cat caterwauling in heat, while violently shaking her head back and forth. "No, no, stop it! Go away, leave me alone! Help! Someone help me!"

She ran screaming with all her might. Whatever was in her hair left her but she could feel more creatures fly past her while, at the same time, brushing up against her. She kept calling out to Matthew and Tory, but there were no responses. She reached into her pockets and pulled out her treasures. She held the black cloth in her right hand

and the card in her left hand. She extended both hands upward while saying, "Oh cloth, so colorful and bright, glow and protect us with all your might." Just then, the cave became lit.

"Chelzy, what are you doing? Why did you use your power?" asked Matthew.

"What do you mean, why? Didn't you feel the creatures? They were all around us, attacking us. One was even in my hair. I could feel them as they flew past me. I was really scared and I needed light from the black cloth; and nobody was answering my calls for help."

"What creatures? What are you talking about?" asked Tory.

"They were flying all around us. Now we're safe. The black cloth is protecting us."

Giving out a loud sigh, Matthew said, "Chelzy, the only thing we saw was you running around in circles with your hands pushing something away that wasn't there. You were calling out to us but we kept yelling that we were right here next to you, trying to hold on to you. And the only one you are protecting now is yourself, because you were moving your entire body around so violently, Tory and I had to let go of you. There is no danger here. You just wasted one of the black cloth's powers."

"I guess I am forgetting that Melzabod warned us that things are not as they appear in the cave," Chelzy said after giving off a big sigh. "Sorry, but why was I the only one seeing and feeling strange things? I know what I saw . . . I mean, what I felt. And I'm the one who is supposed to know what to do and when the right time is to do it. Now I'm really confused, and I feel terrible; but I truly felt that I was in danger. That is why my treasure and card worked."

"Maybe this is some sort of test, and the Bright Queen chose you to see if you could pass it," remarked Tory.

"But, why test me? Why now, when we are trying to get through this cave to reach the Sea of Weeping Willows? And anyway, I guess

I failed big time. I'm really sorry, guys," replied Chelzy, annoyed at herself.

"Look," Matthew interrupted. "Did you ever think that maybe the Bright Queen was preparing you for what's ahead?"

"What do you mean, Bro?"

"I mean," started Matthew after taking a big breath, "that you should have remembered what Melzabod told us, and then trusted the Bright Queen's words to you and not panicked like you did."

"Wait a minute, like you would not have panicked if it happened to you, Bro?"

"You know, I think I would have remained calm and cool," Matthew said with a smirk on his face.

"You know, Matthew, you're a cheesehead, just like the kind that has a lot of holes in it like your brain," said Chelzy with her hands on her hips, still holding her treasures. "And I'm sorry I let everyone down."

Not only was Chelzy aggravated by Matthew's obvious lack of confidence in her abilities but also by his over indulgent boasting of how he thought he would have reacted if he was in her place. She fought to keep tears from rolling down her cheek.

"All right, that's enough, you two. I don't think the Bright Queen wants us to spend our time arguing. Did you forget that we have a job to accomplish?" said Tory, looking back and forth between Chelzy and Matthew. "And, Chelzy, I think your brother is right. You need to stop and think, and not react so quickly, and trust those inner feelings, just like the Bright Queen told you to. And you didn't let us down. We both probably would have reacted the same way. Right, Matthew?"

"Hey, Sis. I'm sorry for acting like a cheesehead. Tory's right, I probably would have done the same thing."

"It's okay, Bro. All right, listen. Let's keep going and take advantage of the bright light from the black cloth," Chelzy said. "It should enable us to travel faster."

This time Chelzy led the way, followed by Tory and Matthew. When the light from the cloth had dimmed and the protective shield had diminished, Chelzy placed both her treasures in her pockets securely. The glitter in the cave walls continued to light their way. There was little conversation among them. Everyone was concentrating on reaching the end of the cave and the entrance to the Sea of Weeping Willows.

Curling her hair as she walked, Chelzy said, "I wonder what the Dark Queen's Earth is like. The Bright Queen mentioned dangerous creatures, but she never explained what they look like. What if the Dark Queen and her creatures capture us? What if we never see our moms and dads again?"

"Chelz, we're going to get home. We have our treasures to help us rescue the children and protect us. We will be okay," Matthew said, reassuring his sister.

"Promise, Bro?"

"Yeah, I promise."

All of a sudden, the light from the glitter on the cave walls darkened, and the cave became completely black. "Matthew, Tory, am I imagining that I can't see a thing?" Chelzy shrieked.

Reaching out and taking hold of Chelzy's shirt, Matthew responded, "No, it's really dark in here. Tory, where are you? Can you hear me?"

"I'm over here. Just follow my voice."

Chelzy began feeling her way with her hands against the cave walls. Matthew held on to her shirt tightly.

"Chelzy, Matthew, where are you? Please find me," said Tory with her one hand touching the cave wall and the other outstretched, searching for her friends. "Help me! Find me! I don't think I am imaging this."

"Do you feel anything in front of you? Chelzy says she feels something strange, like a soft wall. Try hard to feel what is around you, Tory. Stay calm. We're gonna help you," instructed Matthew.

"All right, I'll try," Tory said, "but I'm just so scared. Wait, I feel something. It's soft and squishy, but I can't get my hand through it. What do I do?"

"I feel it, too," said Matthew. "You must be on the other side of some type of wall. Bang on it, push on it, kick it, and Chelzy and I will do the same."

After a lot of punching and pushing, no one was able to break through the jellylike but thick wall that separated Tory from Chelzy and Matthew. Exhausted from their futile attempts, The Trio stood in complete darkness. Matthew still held on to Chelzy's shirt as they listened to Tory crying. "Matthew, we have to do something. We can't leave Tory. It's like she is trapped in a room surrounded by a squishy wall that we can't get through. What are we going to do? I don't think we can all be imagining it. What if I use my black cloth treasures again? Maybe if we can see her, we can find a way out for her."

"Chelzy, this will be the second time that you've used your treasures. That means you will only have one more time left, which you have to save to get home, and we aren't even near the Dark Queen's Earth," Matthew explained.

"Do you have any better ideas, Bro?" Chelzy quickly responded.

"No, unfortunately, I don't. Go ahead, Sis," Matthew said.

"No, no, don't cry Tory. That will just make the lights in the Bright Queen's Kingdom grow dimmer. I am taking out my black cloth and my card. I don't think any of this is a figment of our imaginations, and we have to get out of here. All right, here goes."

"Oh cloth, so colorful and bright, glow and protect us with —no, no, I am not going to do it! I am not going to use another power!" Chelzy shouted.

"But, Chelz, it's dark. We are not imagining it, and we have to get Tory back with us," yelled a nervous Matthew.

"Yes, we are! Things are not as they seem, don't you remember? Everybody's been warning us that in this cave, some things are imaginary. Everyone, just stand still, be calm, take a couple of deep breaths and clear your minds of what's happening here. Think of playing in my backyard or anything else that was fun and made you feel really happy. Think about it really hard," a determined Chelzy instructed.

Chelzy thought about a gymnastics competition last year that she participated in and won first place. It felt so good to receive the first-place ribbon in front of her parents and a few of her friends that came to watch her compete. Matthew kept thinking about his basketball friends from his former school and how much fun they had in the March Madness tournament. Tory found it harder to concentrate because she was trapped by some very strange material; but after hearing Chelzy's instructions over again, Tory closed her eyes and started thinking about a cheerleading camp that she went to last summer. There she made two new friends and learned new routines.

Chelzy was right and, once again, as everyone was concentrating real hard, light slowly filled the cave. One by one, they slowly opened their eyes. The Trio could not believe what they saw. Tory stood on the other side of a transparent wall made of a substance that felt like jelly. Once again, each tried to punch a hole through the wall, but could not. "We only imagined the darkness; but this wall is real and looks like sap, yet feels like gelatin. This wall must be a trap set by the Cumba trees," Chelzy said with a disappointed sigh.

"Chelzy, Matthew, I know what I have to do." Tory slowly put her hand in her pocket and lifted out the game piece that she had chosen when they started to play The Lost and Found Game.

"You're going to transform into a mountain lion? How is that going to help?" asked Chelzy.

"Don't mountain lions have long, powerful claws? I think this is our only hope of breaking me free from this trap. Stand back. I'm going to tear myself out of here."

Tory held her game piece tightly between her hands. She began thinking only of becoming a mountain lion, but nothing was happening.

"Tory, concentrate harder," Matthew encouraged.

"I'm trying to, but it's so hard when you are scared."

"You can do it!" yelled Chelzy.

Tory squeezed her hands even tighter around her game piece as she closed her eyes and concentrated. She envisioned herself as a big and powerful mountain lion with huge paws and retractable long, sharp claws. She took three deep breaths and kept saying to herself, "I am a mountain lion, I am a mountain lion, I am a mountain lion." Once again, she imagined a large, slender, powerful animal with green eyes, a long tail and a muscular build. She kept thinking, "I am a strong, fierce, brave mountain lion . . ." And then it happened: Tory's head was encircled by a yellow halo of light as she began to spin in a counterclockwise direction. She then transformed into a tall, ferocious looking mountain lion. She looked at Matthew and Chelzy, and gave out a huge roar, which caused both of them to take several steps backward and grab on to each other.

"I think we better step back even farther. Is that really you, Tory?" Matthew asked.

147

"Are we sure that this mountain lion is not going to hurt us, and it's really Tory controlling it?" asked Chelzy, who began once again to curl her hair and squeeze her brother's arm tightly.

The mountain lion stood on its hind legs and, with its claws extended, it tore into the wall until there was a hole large enough for it to run through. It ran to Chelzy and Matthew, who froze in their tracks, not knowing what to expect from the mountain lion. All of a sudden, it lowered itself to the ground and, with its head, motioned for Matthew and Chelzy to climb on its back. After exchanging glances, Chelzy got on first, followed by Matthew. The mountain lion took off with great speed while its passengers held on tightly.

"Look, I can see the end of the tunnel," Chelzy shouted.

"So can I. Let's go, Tory the mountain lion. Get us out of here," yelled Matthew.

With those words, the powerful animal rode with its two passengers clutching its mane, and all were equally happy to rid themselves of the menacing cave. They did not expect nor were they prepared for what was about to happen next.

CHAPTER 20

Tears to Rain

The view was breathtaking and, at first glance, the surroundings appeared to exude calmness in contrast to all the dangers The Trio had experienced in the Gelabar Land of Oaks. There was a mist coming from waterfalls that was scattered among a sea of weeping willow trees. The tiny water droplets felt cool but inviting to whatever object welcomed them. The atmosphere looked tranquil, except for low muffled sounds coming from the trees. In addition to the slight motion of a breeze and the unusual sounds that permeated the air, The Trio would soon discover that there existed something very unusual and foreboding about the area.

"Hey, get off my back!" shouted Tory as she attempted to stand upright. "You guys are heavy; and if you haven't noticed, I am not a mountain lion anymore." With one quick jerk, Chelzy and Matthew slid off Tory's back, and all three found themselves atop a hillside.

"Wow! That was really cool! Thanks, Tory, for getting us out of that cave. Who knows what would have happened next," said Chelzy. "It was so hard trying to figure out what was real and what wasn't."

"Yeah, but you really did a good job figuring out that the darkness was just a trick, probably to get us to use another one of our treasures, Sis. The creatures in alliance with the Dark Queen will try anything to get us to fail. We have to be careful. We each need one power of our treasures to get home."

"All right, it is time for a status report. Do you realize, Matthew, that you used only one of your treasures' powers?" Tory noted. "So, you still have one more that you can use, and one to save to get home. And Chelzy, you also only used your treasures once, and I have all three left, but we have a long way to go. If we are going to get back home, each of us has to save one power. And you both still haven't used your game pieces like I did."

"Look, down there. There's got to be a million weeping willow trees," Matthew observed.

"I don't think there's a million of them, but I also don't think I have ever seen so many trees of the same kind in one place," noted Chelzy. "It's really pretty, but I am somehow getting a feeling that there is more to this place than what we see on the surface."

After exiting the cave, The Trio had landed on a small hill overlooking the Sea of Weeping Willows. Unlike the Gelabar Land of Oaks, there appeared to be less movement by the trees, except for the swaying motion of their branches and leaves. This motion created a pleasant breeze in the air, which The Trio noticed immediately. They concluded that there seemed to be less light in this land, probably because of its proximity to the Dark Queen's Earth.

"Let's climb down this hill and find a path to walk through these trees. They look a lot friendlier than the oaks," Matthew said. "We have to find the main trail to lead us to you know where."

This time Tory led the procession down the hill. Just as they were about to enter what seemed to be a wide trail, Chelzy shouted, "Wait, look, all the trees ahead are surrounded by water. I don't see any dry land. Oh, wait a minute. That's why it is called the Sea of Weeping Willows. I thought *Sea* meant lots of trees, not lots of water. How are we supposed to walk through this place if there is no dry land, just water? Where is all this water coming from? It's not raining, and it doesn't look like it's running down from the hills, because we are on a hill and it is bone dry."

Tory stopped and took off her sneakers and began to wade in the water. In a shallow end, she walked up to a tree and inspected it closely. It was then that Tory made a discovery. "The water is dripping from the leaves of the weeping willow trees. It's like they're crying. That's the sound that we've been hearing."

"Well, don't blame us. It's the Dark Queen's fault," a voice came from a nearby tree.

"Of course, these trees talk. Why wouldn't they? I just hope they are friendlier than the oaks that tried to make us their next meal," Matthew whispered to Chelzy and Tory as one particular weeping willow tree caught his attention.

"Hi, my name is Chelzy and this is my brother, Matthew, and our friend, Tory. We have been sent by the Bright Queen to—"

The willow tree interrupted, "We know. We know all about your quest. News travels fast through these lands. By the way, my name is *Salix arbuscula* 436, but you all can call me Salix or 436 for short."

"Not to be insulting or anything, but that is a strange name," responded Matthew.

"That is my scientific name in Latin. You see, all living creatures have a Latin name; the first word stands for its genus, and the second word for its species. We are all mountain weeping willows, so we all have the same name. The only thing that distinguishes us is the number after the name."

"I remember my teacher, Mrs. Simms, telling us about scientific names when we were studying classification in science class. We had to look up the scientific name for humans for her. Let me think . . . now I remember. It is *Homo sapiens*," Matthew noted with great pride in his recall ability.

"Now who's the brainy one, Bro? I'm shocked! I thought you slept through most of your classes."

"I did not, Chelz! Anyway, if you were caught sleeping in Mrs. Simms class, she would write a note and send it home to your parents, requesting that the napping student be put to bed an hour earlier each night for a week. And that was no fun."

"How would you know if it didn't happen to you, Bro?"

"Okay, stop it you two. If you haven't already noticed, we have a problem. How are we supposed to get through this land if there's water everywhere? And why is there so much of it?" Tory asked.

"The sadness of the captured children causes us to cry. Willow trees like us are very sensitive to the emotions of other creatures, especially humans. That is why our branches bend downward and we are called weeping willows. If you don't rescue these children in time, we will drown in our own tears," said 436 as he wiped tears rolling down his bark with one of his branches.

"Our survival depends upon your success. Therefore, we will help you as you travel across our land. However, we must warn you that dangers lurk even here in the Sea of Weeping Willows. Some of the Dark Queen's creatures travel onto our land from time to time. News travels quickly, and they already know that you have arrived. They will stop at nothing to try to capture you, so you must be careful. Our ability to protect you is limited, so you must use all your resources to survive."

"I guess the Dark Queen's creatures," sighed Tory, "really do exist and they are here. That's really scary."

"Well, lucky for you," said 436, "the boys and I have been working on a plan since we heard of your arrival and your quest. We have been collecting light hollow logs. And, as you probably know, if you weren't sleeping in science class, we trees give off oxygen. We have been busy sealing the logs at both ends with a special sap, and then filling them with oxygen through a hollow reed. You can use these logs to breath underwater."

"Wow, just like oxygen tanks. Do you think it will work?" asked Chelzy.

"Why can't we just use my silver feather to transport us out of here to the Dark Queen's Earth?" asked Tory.

"I would much rather that you save the feather's powers for when we are in immediate danger," replied Matthew. "And anyway, we wouldn't be sure where we would be transported, and we might land near her evil creatures. I don't think we should make a dramatic entrance into the Dark Queen's Earth."

"I guess you have a point. We still have a long way to go, don't we?" Tory responded.

"But the point is that we still have some powers left if we need them. We can do it," Chelzy said emphatically. "Remember, the Bright Queen believes in us. Those children need to get home to their family, and we need to get home to ours. I just keep thinking how terrible I would feel if I was taken away from my family. My instinct keeps telling me that if we believe in ourselves, we can accomplish anything, including this quest."

"This time I agree with you, Sis, but there is another problem. What happens when our treasures get wet? Will their powers still work? Won't they fall apart, especially the cards?"

Each of The Trio took their cards out of their pockets and inspected them. Their treasures appeared intact and showed no damage from the adventure so far. Tory gently placed her feather in her right pocket and the silver feather nugget card in the left. Matthew rubbed the black onyx stone against his shirt before placing it in his right pocket. He did the same with the black dust card before placing it in his left pocket. Chelzy just stared at her black cloth and her card as she caressed them in her hands.

"What's wrong, Chelzy?" asked Tory.

"I'm just afraid that I won't know when will be the right time to use another power," Chelzy replied. "And it will be the last one that I can use to protect us. What if I use it at the wrong time? I don't want to waste it. I know I have to keep one power to get back home. The voice in my head seems to know when it's logical, but only my heart truly knows when the right time to use it will be. Do I listen to my head or my heart?" Chelzy then gently placed her treasures in their proper places in her pockets.

"Sis, listen to the one that told you that the darkness in the cave was not real. You were right then."

"Will try to do, Bro, but I'm still worried. How are we going to keep everything dry?"

"I can't believe the three of you for a minute. Do you not trust the Bright Queen? Do you not trust the Bright Queen? She made sure that you were well equipped for your journey. Your treasures are protected from the elements of fire and water but not from the evil spells of the Dark Queen. So, beware, beware! Keep them out of sight. You will not know who is watching, you will not know who is watching," warned Skeemor, who was using his squirrel-like abilities to balance himself on a tree limb.

"Skeemor, you're here! And people say that dogs make great pets because they are faithful companions. You're the best! And you're going to help us again, right?" shouted Chelzy.

"No, actually I came to take a bubble bath in all this water. Of course I came to help! I thought that was obvious, I thought that was obvious," remarked Skeemor as he ruffled his tail, which got wet when he nearly fell into a waterfall while hopping from tree to tree. "And, excuse me, I am not yours or anybody else's pet, and I take offense to being compared to a dog. They are not bad creatures, but I am in a class of my own; and I would appreciate it if you would not include me in any future analogies, future analogies."

"Oh, I didn't say that to insult you. I just meant that you are loyal and devoted to the Bright Queen and to us too; and I just didn't think that you would come all this way, knowing how dangerous it is getting," remarked Chelzy.

Taking a deep breath, Skeemor said, "Let me give you a refresher course called silver to gold, silver to gold. Now do you understand? But remember, my help is also limited. I must go now, go now. Remember, Chelzy, listen to your instincts." With those words, Skeemor jumped from tree to tree until he was finally out of sight, at least, for the present.

CHAPTER 21

Encounter with the Malutes

Salix 436 had given The Trio berries and special greens to eat that grew in the Sea of Weeping Willows. The Trio sat atop a nearby hill, which was dry and served as a good lookout perch. Water from the willow trees was pure and pleasant, and helped wash down the sweet tasting food that The Trio found much more enjoyable than broccoli, spinach and other vegetables that their moms always told them to eat. Salix 436 introduced Salix 214 and Salix 708 to The Trio, explaining that these willow trees were instrumental in designing the oxygen logs. Chelzy thanked the trees for their help and asked 436 if all the weeping willow trees were as friendly and helpful as they were.

"Most of the trees in the Sea of Weeping Willows are our allies and can be trusted. However, there are some willows that are afraid that they may not survive the floods that will be created by the tears and sorrows, and have pledged their allegiance to the other side," 436 explained. "She has vowed to help them survive if they help her stop you and, of course, they believe her."

"I presume by 'the other side,' you mean the Dark Queen," said Matthew.

"Precisely, and therefore, you will need to be extra cautious. I can give you a clue as to how you will be able to know who is on your side and who is out to harm you," said 436. "You see, all willow trees in this land have been given an even-numbered name. Those willows who have deserted us and teamed up with the Dark Queen have added a one to their name in defiance of our code of conduct. That means their names are all odd-numbered. If I had teamed up with the Dark Queen, my name would be Salix 437. They are only concerned with saving themselves, and their loyalty is only to the evil queen. Listen when they call out to one another. If you hear an odd number in their name, get away from them as quickly as possible."

Willow trees 708 and 214 fitted Chelzy, Matthew and Tory for their oxygen logs, and 436 instructed them on how to carefully use their equipment. They were getting ready to embark upon their journey when Chelzy had one final question for 436. "Why can't we build a raft or a boat to travel across your land, 436? It seems like such a long distance to walk or swim, even underwater with oxygen logs."

"My dear Chelzy, there will be areas where the land rises above the water and you will be able to just walk. Where the water is deep, there are currents, which run in many different directions, and these would carry your boat off track. We will point you in the right direction and the willows will guide you along your way. They will hold out their branches, which you will need to grab on to, and they will pull you along, keeping you on course. You will have to walk and swim for now, but there will be places where you can stop and rest a bit."

Continuing, 436 said, "Remember, if you start walking or swimming in the wrong direction, we will grab your hands with our branches and redirect you."

"Boy, am I ever glad mom and dad took us for swimming lessons. Tory, will you be okay in the water?" Chelzy asked, curling her hair one last time before getting it wet.

"No problem, Chelz. My dad tells me I'm part fish in water."

"Good, let's do this. Who wants to lead the way?" asked Chelzy.

"I'll do it. I was on a swim team in camp last summer, so I really am a pretty good swimmer. I'll try not to go too fast," Tory said.

"Okay, Tory, but walk as much as you can so we don't get too tired," remarked Matthew. "I'm also a good swimmer, so when you get tired, I'll take the lead."

"So, I guess I'm in the middle as usual; but I'm getting used to it. Lead on, Tory the adventurer," Chelzy said, motioning ahead with her right hand and curling her hair with her left hand.

They each strapped on their oxygen logs and entered the water. "This water feels so warm, just like the ocean water when we are on vacation at the shore every August," Chelzy remarked. Matthew then began describing their yearly trips to the shore with their family to Tory. It was better than thinking about what dangers they might run into next.

At first, the water was only knee deep; then the depth increased to a point where the water came up to their waists. "This isn't bad at all," Chelzy said, just before Tory stepped into an area that took her several feet underwater. Chelzy quickly put the hollow reed in her mouth seconds before stepping into what appeared to be the deep end of a swimming pool. Matthew, who also prepared for the change in depth, followed Chelzy. At that point, Tory had already started to breathe through the reed attached to her oxygen log.

The Trio walked for quite a distance until the deep water required that they start swimming. Tory began, and Chelzy and Matthew followed. Like three scuba divers, The Trio swam through a forest of trees, helped periodically by branches of willow trees to correct their direction. When the three began tiring, the branches gently embraced each hand, pulled them forward, and passed them off to yet another branch, as The Trio glided through the water like graceful ballet dancers. Since the willows had made makeshift goggles for them, The Trio was able to enjoy the beauty of the landscape from a totally different perspective. Then it happened.

When Tory grabbed the next branch, she immediately knew something was different. Instead of the branch pulling her forward, it pushed her down deeper into the water. She immediately tried to pry her hand from the branch, but it would not let go. Chelzy saw what was happening and started to swim upward when she felt something tug at her leg. Matthew quickly grabbed the branch with both hands and tried to force open its grip on Chelzy's foot while, at the same time, he was evading two branches that were trying to grab him. There was a massive struggle between The Trio and several willow trees that were determined to stop them from advancing. Finally, Tory was able to break loose and swam to the surface yelling, "Help! Help! Someone help us."

All of a sudden, a blue unicorn flew over her head. "Melzabod, Melzabod, help us," shouted Tory.

"Swim to that small island while I distract the willows," Melzabod responded.

"I can't leave Chelzy and Matthew. The willows are holding on to them," yelled Tory.

"Go back underwater and have Chelzy and Matthew hold on to you, then use your silver feather to transport all of you to that island," instructed Melzabod.

After hearing Melzabod's directives, Tory swam down and grabbed on to Chelzy's sleeve and Matthew's legs, being careful not to be grabbed by a willow. At that point, she realized she would have to free her hands in order to take her treasures out of her pockets, so she tried to motion to Chelzy and Matthew to hold on to her instead.

Focused on trying to escape the grips of the willows, neither understood what Tory was trying to tell them, so she let go of them and carefully removed the silver feather from her right pocket and the silver feather card from her left, and began bringing them together, hoping that Chelzy and Matthew would understand her movements. Just then, Matthew pried himself loose of the willow branches and grabbed Tory's arm. He saw that Chelzy was being pulled away so he freed himself from Tory and, using all his strength, he swam down as close to Chelzy as he could.

Chelzy outstretched her two arms and tried to grab her brother's hand. They were only inches away. When all seemed hopeless, the willow branch that was holding Chelzy's leg loosened its grip and Chelzy grabbed Matthew's hand. Matthew pulled Chelzy in Tory's direction and then latched on to Tory's arm once again. Holding the silver feather in her right hand and the silver feather card in her left hand while concentrating on the small island that Melzabod had pointed to, Tory said these words after inhaling oxygen from her log, "Silver feather, bright and light, transport us to a safe place with all your might."

The silver feather grew in size, and within seconds, Chelzy, Matthew and Tory found themselves sitting comfortably on its cushioned surface. As they glided above the water, they heard a willow tree shout out, "957, how could you let them get away? The Dark Queen is not going to be happy about this."

The silver feather traveled to the nearby island and gently placed The Trio down on the ground. It then returned to its normal size and floated upward and then downward; and as Tory extended her arm out, it gracefully lowered itself gently on the palm of her hand. She then safely returned it to her right pocket.

"My heart is still racing a hundred miles an hour. I didn't think we were going to get out of the water alive," said Chelzy, still panting from her harrowing experience. "Tory, you were great using your silver feather."

"You can thank Melzabod for that," replied Tory. "If she hadn't showed up and told me what to do, I probably would have been frozen in fear. I couldn't even reason straight. All I kept thinking was that a disgusting, wicked willow was going to pull me down into the deep water and keep me there until I ran out of oxygen and drowned."

"Yep, that was a close call; but we should be safe for a little while. Now, the big question is, where do we go from here and how?" Matthew asked. "What if there are more odd-numbered willows out to get us?"

"Hurry, run, incoming malutes!" screamed Pelamar with his beaver tail acting as a radar device pointed toward the sky. "Quickly, you must run and hide now!"

"How are we supposed to run? There's no oxygen left in our logs and there's not much land to run on." Chelzy said as she nervously curled her hair, even though it was dripping with water.

Tory grabbed Chelzy, who grabbed Matthew, and all three ran to the end of the island and toward the water. Three large black birds, known as the Dark Queen's malutes, came diving down toward The Trio with speeds comparable to jet planes. Chelzy, Matthew and Tory ran with all their might, zigzagging to avoid capture by the flying creatures. Just as they were approaching the edge of the land leading to water, one of the malutes dove down and grabbed Chelzy with his two large talons. As they quickly rose into the air, Tory began screaming, "Matthew, Matthew, look, it's Chelzy! They have Chelzy!"

Matthew looked upward toward the sky and saw Chelzy in the grips of a very large black bird. The other two malutes were getting ready to dive again, this time to capture Tory and him. He looked in all directions but there was no help in sight. Melzabod was nowhere to be seen; neither was Pelamar. Matthew knew that if Chelzy was to be saved from being killed by the malute or taken to the Dark Queen, it was up to him to do it. He had to act now.

He put his hand in his pocket and removed his Lost and Found game piece, an eagle. "I always wanted to know what it would be like to fly. Here goes." Holding it tightly in his hand and concentrating on becoming an eagle, Matthew closed his eyes and kept saying to himself, "I am an eagle, I can fly, I am an eagle, I am strong and mighty and fearless and I can soar, I can fly, I am an eagle . . ." A yellow halo of light encircled Matthew's head. Within seconds, Matthew began spinning counterclockwise. Matthew's transformation drew Tory's attention as she stepped backward. A beautiful eagle, much larger than normal size, arose out of the yellow light and immediately took flight, rising high into the sky.

Chelzy was screaming loudly but tried not to move too much for fear of falling from the clutches of the malute. At this high distance, she knew she would surely not survive the plummet to the ground. The eagle's wingspan was quite a bit larger than that of the malutes', but the malutes did not appear to be intimidated by the eagle. Instead, one bird started to dive toward Tory while a second took Chelzy higher in the sky. The third malute was headed right for the eagle.

Matthew knew that if he attacked while the malute flew over dry land, Chelzy would fall from the bird's claws and be seriously hurt or killed; but if he waited too long, then the malute might fly out of sight and he would no longer be able to rescue his sister. And then there was Tory, who was running around frantically trying to evade the malute that was targeting her from the sky. Matthew, the eagle, had to make a decision.

Without hesitation, he flew in the direction of the malute that had Chelzy in his clutches. However, he made sure that he did not catch up to him until he saw they were flying over water. Then he made his attack. After flapping his wings to give himself sufficient air speed, the eagle soared upward and then began a steep dive. This caused the malute holding on to Chelzy to also dive down to a lower altitude. With his wings expanded to their full length, the eagle glided on top of the malute and then repeatedly struck the malute's body with his piercing talons. The malute, unable to escape the eagle's attack, released Chelzy.

Chelzy was dropped into an area of water between willows that was deep enough for her to survive the fall unharmed. Immediately, a friendly willow threw a hollow log to Chelzy.

In the meantime, the eagle flapped its powerful wings and flew back toward the island. When it arrived, a malute was on its final approach toward Tory. She was running in a zigzag fashion along the edge of the water, trying to desperately escape the Dark Queen's evil creature. It was a race to see who would get to Tory first, the malute or the eagle.

With all his might, the eagle drew his powerful wings up and down until he was gaining distance over the black bird. With only seconds separating the two birds from their destination, the eagle reached his target first and quickly scooped Tory up with his powerful talons. The eagle now focused on out-flying the malute and depositing Tory in the vicinity of Chelzy. Using his keen eyesight, the eagle honed in on an area of water where he saw Chelzy holding on to a huge log. He dove down right above the water and gently deposited Tory close to Chelzy.

Just then, the water reversed its direction and became very turbulent. It began moving upward. The water was creating large waves that were pulling the two girls in an ascending waterfall. All three malutes began attacking the eagle, which was now flying over Chelzy and Tory. Chelzy began waving and shouting, "Matthew, Mathew, down here. Hurry!"

Right before the malutes reached the eagle, it began to alter itself. The huge wings retracted and changed back into arms. The tail feather and talons became legs, and Matthew's head arose from that of the eagle's. Just as the transformation was complete, Matthew fell into the water a short distance from Chelzy and Tory. He swam and reached the log just in time. The water continued to rush upward at a great speed, carrying the log and its passengers along the way.

"What's happening? We're moving backwards and upwards! Where are we going?" Tory screamed.

"Hold on. Whatever you do, don't let go," Matthew shouted.

Chelzy was holding tightly on to a branch that extended from the log. The water was rushing so quickly past her face that she could no longer see anything in front of her. "Bro, where are you? I can't see a thing."

"Sis, just hold on tight. We'll be okay, just hold—" But, before Matthew could say anymore, the log, along with The Trio, traveled up a tall waterfall, hitting the top with great force. When the rapid motion of the water had subsided, all that was left in a shallow pond was the log, floating peacefully along. Along the edge of the pond lay Chelzy, Matthew and Tory. The weeping willows were gone as were the rivers of water made from tears. The skies were dark, and the earth's greenery had turned to deep rust and brown colored grass and shrubs. Chelzy, Matthew and Tory had arrived in a land of the malevolent and the wicked.

CHAPTER 22

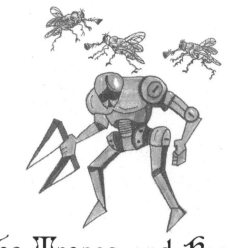

The Trones and Kreons

"Oh, my head hurts," groaned Chelzy as she rubbed the back of her head.

"Are you all right, Sis? Tory, where's Tory?"

Before Chelzy had an opportunity to reply, the terrain caught her attention. Except for a small pond, the waterfall was gone. The land was covered with a variety of plant life, none of which was green. Everything was dark and dreary; not fall colors, but colors that seemed to radiate a sense of gloom and doom. The pond was shallow with waves that mysteriously came from nowhere.

"Where are we and where is Tory?" asked Chelzy as she stood up, massaging her head and walking over to her brother who was standing on the water's edge. "And why are we dry when we just came from falling backwards into a pond from a waterfall? And where did the waterfall go? And how did we even survive the fall?"

"I guess I always have to provide the answers, don't I, don't I?"

"Skeemor, you're here. How did you get here?" asked Chelzy. Did you go up and over that waterfall too? And how is water able to fall upwards? Of course, what am I thinking? It's magic; but it was more like a roller coaster ride."

"Have you seen Tory, Skeemor?" inquired Matthew of his friend.

"One question at a time, one question at a time. First of all, I don't swim up and over waterfalls. I skillfully balance myself on a log and travel in style, as all squirrels are known to do. Actually, you were all holding on to a branch from a friendly willow, not on to just any old log. The willow cushioned your upward fall. I believe his name was . . . let me think now, let me think now . . . oh that's it, Salix arbuscula 436. I never forget a name; and I am especially proud that, in this case, I actually remembered, I actually remembered a willow's name. They can be quite unusual and confusing, you know, you know, with all the numbers.

"In any event, Tory left you two to rest while she went off in that direction to look around. She is quite the adventurer, you know. I told her that I'd keep an eye on the two of you in the meantime, in the meantime. Remember, just like in your earlier travels, many things are not what they seem to be, not what they seem to be. Be careful. You must continue to distinguish between what is real and what is imaginary," explained Skeemor.

"And how are we supposed to do that? It's getting harder," Matthew muttered.

"The Bright Queen told you that this would not be an easy quest to accomplish, but she also believes that Chelzy has very sharp abilities, very sharp abilities. Actually, almost as good as mine; so, it is important that you listen to her. And, Chelzy, you must continue to listen to what your heart tells you to do, not just your brain, not just your brain. That is instinct, and you will need it to rescue the children and get home."

"Is everyone all right?" asked Tory, emerging from a dark, wooded area.

"Tory, you're okay! Where were you?" Chelzy exclaimed.

"I have been scouting around to see if I can figure out where we are. I think I have come to a conclusion, and I don't know if you are going to like what I am about to say. And I think Skeemor already knows exactly what this place is."

"We're in the Dark Queen's Earth, aren't we, Skeemor?" Tory inquired.

"Yes, you are; yes, you are, and I am here to warn you about the Dark Queen's creatures. By now, she has become aware that you have survived the Sea of Weeping Willows and that you have arrived in her kingdom. She has probably already sent out her scouts to locate you and to capture you. Kreons are the Dark Queen's robots that have the ability to transform into familiar animals. They will try to confuse you, try to confuse you. And if they succeed, they will trap you and bring you to the Dark Queen."

"You mean they can change into Tibbit, Pelamar, or even you?" Chelzy asked, taking a big gulp of air and feverishly curling her hair.

"Yes, yes, this is possible. But you, Chelzy, will be able to figure out what is real and what is not. And beware! Trones appear as flies buzzing around you, but they are actually very small creatures that have one eye with an appendage that extends outward. At the tip of this appendage is a suction cup that allows the trone to attach to you. Once attached, it transforms into a large, three-legged mutant animal that is capable of running very fast. If it captures you in this way, you will more than likely not be able to escape its grip, and it will transport you to the Dark Queen very quickly, where you will become another one of her servants. The three of you must be very careful, must be very careful," explained Skeemor.

Pacing back and forth in deep thought, Matthew stammered, "H—how are we supposed to hide from these kreons and trones, especially since some of them could look like you, Skeemor, or one of our other friends? We're never going to be able to rescue the children, let alone save ourselves and get home."

"Well, we can't turn back; and the only way we can move is forward," Chelzy explained, "because that's the only way we can get home. We each have two powers left, and we each have to save one to return home; and I also have the ability to turn into my game piece, a deer. So, we have our treasures and ourselves to get us through all this. I'd say that we are still pretty well equipped."

"I hope that all this is enough, Sis," Matthew remarked.

Skeemor, perched atop a large black rock, replied, "Save the power of your treasures until you are sure that the danger is real and there is no other way to escape. Chelzy's instincts will serve you well. Time to go now, time to go now." Skeemor then disappeared into some thick brush.

The Trio sat on a large boulder, looking in three different directions. Matthew was the first to make an obvious comment that all three were thinking, "Are we ever going to get home? Or are we going to become servants and live here the rest of our lives, waiting for someone to rescue us? Or, worst of all, will we even survive this place and the Dark Queen?"

Chelzy slid across the boulder and sat close to her brother. She put her hand on his shoulder, "Bro, we're together and we are going to stay together, and we are going to get home. Better yet, we are going to meet the Bright Queen's challenge and rescue the three children, because you're good at figuring things out, Tory is a good adventurer

. . . and me . . . well, I have that smart voice in my head and my heart telling us what to do. Right?"

"She's right, Matthew. We are a team, and we are going to out-smart the Dark Queen," Tory added.

"You know what, Sis? I'll never call you birdbrain again . . . well, maybe never. Okay, now in which direction are we supposed to go?"

"We have to find the Dark Queen's castle. If she is using the children as her servants, they will be working for her somewhere either in the castle or on the grounds," said Chelzy. "But how do we locate it? I was hoping Skeemor would have told us."

"That's the way to the Dark Queen's castle," Pelamar said while pointing. Well, while you three were busy chatting as usual, I climbed a nearby hill and, being such a well-equipped beaver, the radar in my tail indicated a large structure in that direction. It's a distance from here, so I suggest you get started."

"Wait, we can't just start walking into a land that has so many dangers. The Dark Queen could have laid traps all around us. And what about her trones and kreons? We have to have a plan," warned Matthew.

"Bro, listen. We can't just stay here. We are probably safer if we keep moving. They always say that a moving target is harder to hit, so how about if we start walking and I keep looking ahead of us. Tory, you keep a lookout to the right and left; and, Bro, you look behind us. I'll take the lead."

As The Trio embarked on the next part of their journey, they started walking in the direction that Pelamar had pointed out to them. Nervously curling her hair, Chelzy continued, "We have already used some of our treasures' powers. Let's hope that we don't have too many encounters with the Dark Queen's creatures."

"I prefer we don't have any encounters with them," added Tory.

"All right, everybody stay close together and keep a sharp eye for anything unusual. Let's walk kind of slow. Ready? Let's start," Chelzy said in a voice resembling a drill sergeant while, at the same time, trying to camouflage the tremor of fright in her voice.

"Sounds like a plan to me," admitted Tory. "I'm kinda glad I'm in the middle this time."

With low-hanging, foreboding clouds and only a limited amount of light to guide them along their way, Chelzy, Matthew and Tory began the end of their long journey but the start of their quest. As they walked through the dismal forest, each placed their hands in their pockets. As they focused their attention on their surroundings, they snugly held on to their treasures and cards. It was only a matter of time before they would have to call upon their powers.

The challenge of their quest weighed heavily on their minds. They knew they had to move through the Dark Queen's Earth, deal with her trones and kreons and the evil Queen herself, find the imprisoned children, and release them. Then they had to get back to the Candesia Land of Pines and still conserve the last power of each treasure in order to return home. They realized that if they used the last power of each treasure, they would be trapped in the Dark Queen's Earth forever.

CHAPTER 23

The Dark Queen's Earth

The murky woods that lay before The Trio were anything but inviting. The landscape was gloomy and drab with little or no personality to it. It appeared as though an artist painted all the trees, bushes and other plants using only gray, black and brown paints. "The Dark Queen herself is probably the only one who could get pleasure from living in this morbid, depressing place," thought Chelzy. "I bet the Dark Queen has a calendar with pictures of this place hanging in her kitchen; that is, if she actually has a kitchen. She probably has her kreons hunt for her, and the imprisoned children cook and clean for her."

Each step that Chelzy, Matthew and Tory took was careful and deliberate. They walked as if they were marching through a field strewn with mines and traps. They took nothing for granted because they knew their safety was at stake.

"I wish I had more than one set of eyes. This place is really creepy," muttered Matthew as he walked backwards on the stone path so as to be able to keep an eye on what was happening behind them. He periodically turned his head to make sure he was walking in the same direction as Chelzy and Tory.

"Eerie is more the word. It's so strange that there are no normal looking animals or any signs of life, except these scary looking trees and what looks like mutated snakes," added Tory.

The trees consisted of crookedly shaped branches that radiated out in every direction. Some had black leaves on them while others were just bare. The tree trunks were twisted and many had holes in them that you could see through. Their bark reeked a stink of hopelessness that filled the air with a repugnant smell. There were long jet-black snakes, some of which had more than one head, wrapped around tree branches. There was a gray fog that hugged the ground and covered areas of what appeared to be marshes.

"It looks like there was a battle here and the trees lost," said Matthew, "but at least they are not walking around, trying to stomp on us or catch us for food." Matthew then approached a tree and said, "Hi there," but nothing happened.

"What are you doing, Matthew? Are you crazy?" hissed a very angry Chelzy. "Maybe they're just sleeping, and why would you want to wake them up? Do you really think for a second that the trees in the Dark Queen's Earth would be friendly? And what about the snakes? They don't look any friendlier than the trees to me. I have been inspecting the area and I think danger surrounds us, so let's not tempt the trees or snakes or anything else just in case we irritate them and they decide to attack. Right now, I am just happy they are not being aggressive towards us."

"Sorry, Sis. I'll try to behave. I guess my curiosity just got the best of me."

Tory, moving her head from side to side, scrutinized the area to the right and left of The Trio. "I sure miss the colors back at the

Bright Queen's Kingdom. I hope we see them again soon. I don't think I'll ever take colors for granted again. This would make a great haunted forest on Halloween night."

"I have an idea!" whispered Chelzy. "Let's find something we can use as a fly swatter. We need to protect ourselves against the trones. If they attach themselves to us and turn into those three-legged creatures, we won't have a chance to escape, let alone rescue the children."

"Good idea, Chelz. Let's look for some branches with leaves attached. Stop here! I'm going to break a branch off this tree." And with one quick motion, Matthew reached up and pulled on a nearby branch.

"Hey! What do you think you are doing? There's a hands-off policy here. Get lost before I decide to catapult you directly into the Dark Queen's courtyard!" yelled the unfriendly tree.

"O—Oh, I—I'm so sorry. It won't happen again," Matthew stammered as he motioned for Chelzy and Tory to start walking again. Matthew whispered to them, "What happened? I thought they were like normal trees, you know, the non-talking, non-moving variety like we have back home."

"What did I tell you, Matthew? But, as usual, you wouldn't listen to me. Now what, Bro? Do you have any other brilliant ideas? So much for trees that don't talk."

"I would normally allow you to use my tail, but you see there's only one of me and three of you, so let me see. Oh yes, I packed these for just this occasion," Pelamar said excitedly as he began unpacking a brown sack that was attached to his tail. "Actually, it will really be a relief not having to drag these behind me anymore. They were slowing me down."

"Pelamar, are we ever happy to see you! What do you have in that bag?" Chelzy inquired of their friend.

"My dear young ones, you will recognize them instantly. Oh, no you won't. That's right. You never had to work in the Bright Queen's garden. Anyway, the Bright Queen grows many colorful herbs and medicinal plants in her kingdom. This one, which you won't find in your world, is called the *Cumonious erborfius*. You see, it is usually used to ward off fevers of any kind; but, in this case, these leaves will come in handy for you to use as fly swatters. These large, broad leaves are usually yellow in color; but, unfortunately, everything turns dark in this land. I'm beginning to tarnish myself. I happen to have packed one for each of you."

Pelamar handed a Cumonious leaf to each of The Trio. "Now I must move on." Turning his head as he scampered off, Pelamar warned, "The radar in my tail is sensing some activity ahead and it could be dangerous. Be careful, children." He then disappeared into the bushes.

"Activity? What kind of activity do you think he is sensing?" Tory whispered, almost not wanting to be heard.

"There's a problem. If we hold the Cumonious leaf with one hand, we won't be able to hold on to our treasures; and what if we need them in a hurry?" asked Chelzy.

"Well, Chelzy, what do your instincts tell us? What should we do? This is important. We need to be free to defend ourselves against the trones, but how can we do that and, at the same time, be prepared to use our treasures?" Tory asked, shrugging her shoulders.

"I think Tory is right. This is a tough decision. If we hold the leaves and we are put in grave danger, we may not have enough time to throw the leaves down, put our hands in our pockets and say the magic words." After pausing to think about what he just said, Matthew continued, "Wait, maybe one of us should keep both of our hands free. Who wants to do that and be prepared to use a treasure just in case?"

"I'll do it," Tory offered. "Chelzy, you are a fast mover and, Matthew, you are pretty strong, but I'm good at whipping my treasures out of my pockets quickly and saying the magic words."

"Or maybe we should just all be prepared to use our treasures and not even bother with the Cumonious leaves Pelamar brought us," said Matthew.

Chelzy stood with her two hands now on her hips as she emphatically announced, "Look, I don't think Pelamar would have gone through all the trouble of dragging a bag of large, bulky leaves all this way if he didn't think they were important to us. Our basketball coach always told us that the best offense is a good defense . . . or, did he say, the best defense is a good offense? Oh well, anyway, I think each of us should have a leaf to defend ourselves because we are not even sure what treasure we may need to use until the time comes, if it comes. And what if we get separated?"

"Well, Sis, I just hope that you are better at fighting the Dark Queen's creatures than you are at playing basketball. Anyway, I don't know if you are right, but I do think we should go along with what you just said. It makes sense."

Each took their positions, Chelzy leading the way, Tory in the middle and Matthew at the end, scanning the area as they began their journey once again. Each held a Cumonious leaf tightly in a hand, ready to swat any incoming trones. They took the main trail, which they were fairly sure would lead them to the Dark Queen's castle, and it was in the direction that Pelamar pointed out. They were trying to imagine what it might look like but decided that it was probably as dark, dreary and lusterless as her earth.

"When we get to the Dark Queen's castle, we don't even know where to begin looking for the captured children. And what do we do when we find them? And that is, if we find them, how are the three of us supposed to be able to fight off her creatures? Even Quercus and his oaks were not able to succeed, so what makes anybody think we can do this?" asked Chelzy.

Matthew stopped walking for a moment and said after giving off a big sigh, "Well, evidently, someone does believe that we can. Remember, she wears a crown of gems? Listen, we can do this just because we can. All we have to do is believe in ourselves, in each other and especially in your judgment, Chelz. The Bright Queen must think we are pretty special, and I don't want to let her down or those three kids. We're all they have right now. If we don't make this happen, the Bright Queen's Kingdom may grow dark before she can find someone else to try to rescue them; and then her kingdom will be gone for eternity along with all her creatures, some of which are now our friends. They will either die or be taken prisoners by the Dark Queen. Is that what you want to happen? And anyway, you were the one talking about a good offense or defense, remember? Are you with us, Chelz?"

"Of course I am, Bro. I don't want anything to happen to our new friends. I was just making sure that you weren't getting cold feet or something. That was a pretty cool speech. Why don't you ever talk like that when we are home?"

"I hope you enjoyed it, because I am never going to talk to you like that again because you usually don't take me seriously when I am trying to be sincere about something."

"Calm down, Bro. At home, I never know when you are being honest or pulling my leg. I was only kidding. What you said actually makes me feel better. I think you are smart even though I will never admit to ever having said that. But you know what? After this experience, I don't think I will ever call you a cheesehead again. I mean, especially if you promise to never call me birdbrain again. Deal?"

"Deal, Sis!"

The woods became darker and even more ominous. An unearthly feeling infected each member of The Trio. A fog started to encompass their path, making the trail almost impossible to follow. This forced each of them to shuffle their feet in order to make sure they were still on the stone-covered trail. The dark clouds hovered so low that, at one point, Chelzy tried to hit them with her leaf. The silence was almost foreboding. Each of The Trio became too frightened to speak. They huddled closer to each other as they walked, daring not even to squirm an inch.

The air became thickened with a strange odor. The trees along the trail moved for the first time. Each began moving away from the path while, at the same time, bending their branches forward as if they were bowing. Chelzy slowed down. Sensing an impending assault by something evil and menacing, she immediately stopped in her tracks. Tory bumped into Chelzy while Matthew stopped before walking into Tory. What was about to happen quickly drew The Trio's attention.

The trees along the path stood up straight and then lifted their branches, forming a kind of honor guard. The Trio heard caterwauling in the near distance and became not only speechless, but frozen in place, only able to stare ahead. Feeling the presence of something wicked and sinister, they knew the honor guard was not for them. Their bodies stiffened, their breathing became shallow and their eyes widened as they awaited their first villainous encounter in the Dark Queen's Earth.

CHAPTER 24

The Dark Queen

Skeemor, Tibbit and Pelamar were congregated in a huge, hollow tree trunk, keeping close to The Trio but far enough away so as not to be detected by the Dark Queen or any of her creatures. Chelzy, Matthew and Tory were huddled together, frozen in terror.

"What should we do?" Tory whispered, shivering from fear. "What's happening?"

Before either Chelzy or Matthew could respond, a cloud, thicker, taller and darker than the fog, appeared a short distance down the path. The cloud positioned itself very near the ground; then, all of a sudden, it began spinning rapidly, creating a strong wind. A loud guffaw suddenly erupted, shattering the silent, dense atmosphere. The Trio held on to each other while Skeemor, who was close by and watching, grabbed on to a nearby branch. The maelstrom grew larger and larger. The cloud was blacker than night and the winds as strong as a cyclone. Chelzy, Matthew and Tory were holding on to each other precariously, trying to see beyond the dirt and debris that filled the air around them.

Loud shrilling laughter emerged from the cloud followed by a bloodcurdling voice that said, "My little children, how nice of you to come to my earth. I've been expecting you." The laughter continued as the cloud took on a shape. The Dark Queen materialized, dressed in a long black robe decorated with black stones and sequins. She stood very tall and erect, and a black tiara made of onyx stones adorned her head. Her eyes were as big and black as her onyx stones. Her hands were clenched in tight fists. Her narrow face was defined by her accentuated cheekbones and thick black eyebrows. Her jet-black, long, straggly hair lay lifeless on her chest. Her appearance was so dreadful to The Trio that she made the scariest Halloween witch look like Cinderella.

Petrified and huddled together, The Trio tightly held on to their Cumonious leaves. "Go away, leave us alone," shrieked Chelzy.

An even louder, bloodcurdling laughter erupted, "Hahaha! Leave you alone? Is it not you who are trespassing? I must do what I must do to protect my land from you brazen children. But first, what type of host am I if I do not send someone to officially greet you?" And with those alarming words and more of her menacing laughter, the Dark Queen opened her right hand. Three flies emerged and started to fly in the direction of The Trio.

Matthew shouted, "They're trones! Everyone, start swinging your leaves! Protect yourselves!"

The Cumonious leaves were drawn to duty like weapons on a battlefield. The flies, able to fly at a high rate of speed, attacked The Trio from all directions. It seemed as if there was an army of them instead of only three. Every time a Cumonious leaf struck a fly, the fly would retreat for only a few seconds before it would circle around for yet another attack. Chelzy, Matthew and Tory had to use both their hands to hold on to and swing their large leaves. "My arm is getting sore. I don't know how much longer I can do this," shouted Tory.

"We can't stop. We can't let them attach themselves to us," yelled Matthew. "Chelzy, what are you doing?"

Chelzy threw her Cumonious leaf on the ground. "Matthew, Tory, protect me."

Chelzy put both her hands in her pockets and pulled out her treasures. She held the black cloth in her right hand and the black cloth card in her left hand. She stretched out both arms in the air, hoping a fly would not attach itself to her. "Quick, hold on to me." Matthew and Tory kept swinging at the trones with one hand holding the leaf, and they each took hold of Chelzy with the other hand. She then said the words, "Oh cloth, so colorful and bright, glow and protect us with all your might."

Immediately, the black cloth started radiating gold, red and black light. With Matthew holding on to Chelzy's arm and Tory on to Chelzy's pants pocket, the light from the black cloth encircled The Trio, forming a protective barrier around them. Every time a fly tried advancing toward them, it was repelled by the black cloth's force field.

"My eyes, my eyes, away with you, you dastardly children!" screamed the Dark Queen as she shielded her eyes with both her hands from the bright lights coming from the black cloth. "I will get you! This is not the end, just the beginning! You will not escape me!" With those words, the Dark Queen, followed by her trones, turned into a black cloud that twisted until it rose into the sky and out of sight.

Chelzy gave out a loud sigh. "Wow! That was too close. The Dark Queen is really scary and evil. I don't want to ever see her or her trones again!"

"The Bright Queen was right. You knew exactly when to use your treasures. If you hadn't used the black cloth, the trones would be dragging us off to the Dark Queen's castle right about now. But, we are not out of the woods or, in this case, out of this nightmarish place yet, and we are going to have to deal with her again if we plan on rescuing the children," said a very tired Tory as she tried to catch her breath and rubbed her right arm, which was sore from swinging her Cumonious leaf.

"I have to agree with Tory, Sis. You really did great."

All three were somewhat relaxed now that they were surrounded by the black cloth's light that was also protecting them from anyone or anything intruding upon their space. They walked quickly and cautiously, knowing that the power of the cloth would wear off at any time. They kept silent even as each was enveloped in his or her own thoughts. Matthew was envisioning this as a video game with the Bright Queen fighting the Dark Queen, each having their followers fighting in mortal combat. He had a hard time, though, imagining Skeemor, Pelamar and Tibbit fighting the trones and kreons. He decided that he would prefer playing the video game rather than be part of it.

Having been gone so long, Tory was worried about what her mom and dad were thinking about now. "Maybe they have investigated our disappearance, and have spoken to Chelzy and Matthew's grandfather and found out about the stories of Sycamore Street. That will make them even more concerned and upset," Tory thought.

Chelzy, on the other hand, kept wondering why the Bright Queen felt she had such good instincts. She was the youngest of the three, and even though she considered herself pretty cool, she didn't think of herself as the smartest or the most talented of the three. However, she believed in the Bright Queen and knew it was important not to doubt her own abilities, especially after what had just happened.

"The Dark Queen gave up pretty easily. I bet she knows about the powers of our treasures, but I don't think she knows that I cannot use the black cloth again and that I have to save one of its powers to get home," Chelzy mussed. "At least, I hope she doesn't."

"You know, we better start walking faster while we still have the force field to protect us," added Matthew. "The Dark Queen is smart and may decide not to use her trones again soon because, like you said, Sis, she'll think you can still keep using the black cloth; but we're forgetting her other evil forces, the kreons. I have this feeling that we are going to be meeting them sometime very soon."

This time, Matthew's instincts proved to be true.

CHAPTER 25

Doubt Yourselves
and You Will Fail

The Trio continued their journey along the dark stone path toward a castle in the distance. Within several minutes, the magical light and protective force field discharging from the black cloth had disappeared. Chelzy carefully put the black cloth back in her pocket. The path began to wind through the gloomy and shadowy forest. The children's heartbeats could be heard echoing in the eerie stillness. "The only small sign of any life," Tory thought, "are the trees with their black, wrinkled leaves, not like those of the fall, but almost of a dreadful season that doesn't even exist in reality. If such a season did exist, I wonder what it would be called. Even the ugly two- and three-headed snakes are gone."

"This place is gruesome. If we had a season at home when the trees looked like this, I would call it Sad Season, because all the trees look like they are dying, or the Ugly Season, because everything looks so dark and grotesque," remarked Tory. "I would not want to live in a place with a season like this."

"Tory, I think they are like this all the time. I don't think seasons can exist where there isn't a sun," remarked Chelzy. "I wonder, though, if they were once green and pretty and full of life just like the trees we have back home; or do you think they grew like this from their beginnings?"

"I have a feeling that as long as the Dark Queen has existed, this place has always been morbid looking, Sis. All right, let's figure out what powers we have left."

The Trio realized that each of them had one power left that they could use and still get home. Matthew could use his onyx stone one more time to make them invisible and Tory could use her silver feather to transport them. Chelzy was the only one who did not use her game piece yet. Each then would still have one power to get them home.

"I am already a really fast runner; can you imagine how fast I can run as a deer?"

"We are counting on that, Sis. We may need to hop on you and get away from trouble at any time."

"Hop on me? I don't think deer are that strong, and I don't think I'll be able to run that fast with both of you on my back. But, I guess I will worry about that when the time comes."

All of a sudden, they approached an area where there were squirrels, rabbits, mice and birds trudging along the forest floor. The squirrels were not climbing trees and the birds only walked on the ground, looking for worms under the fallen, black leaves. There were no birds flying or even perched in the trees. The rabbits were not hopping from place to place. Instead, they were all meandering about, looking for something edible. All the animals were shades of black, gray or brown, none having a trace of white or any other color on their bodies, and they were all of normal size, not like that of Skeemor, Tibbit and Pelamar.

As they were cautiously walking along, Chelzy suddenly stopped in her tracks. "I just thought of something awful again. What if the kreons turn into Skeemor, Tibbit or Pelamar? How will we know if they are real or not? How will we know if we can trust them?" asked a very concerned Chelzy. "We're just lucky it hasn't happened yet, or at least, I don't think it has."

Tory quickly responded, "Don't you remember Skeemor telling you to just trust, you know, that voice inside your head? We all believe in you. Chelzy, just don't forget the words of the Bright Queen. You won't let us down. I just know it."

"Okay, no pressure, no pressure. Oh, great! Now I'm beginning to sound like Skeemor," a nervous Chelzy said.

"Here's another problem that we keep bringing up but no one has answered. Once we get to the Dark Queen's castle, how will we know where the captured children are?" asked Matthew. "I don't think that we are going to have a lot of time to go looking for them once we are actually inside the castle, if we get that far. And how are we supposed to rescue them if we get caught? We will need rescuing ourselves."

"I beg your pardon!" interrupted Tibbit. "Has not the Bright Queen given all three of you what you need to be successful in your quest? Has she not given you me, the very handsome, talented, resourceful and cunning rabbit? Oh, did I leave out humble?" Tibbit stopped to brush off his fur in an attempt to make himself look extra presentable. "Or have you forgotten? You all give real meaning to the term 'short memories.' It is true, dangers do lie ahead, but the powers you possess are stronger than the dangers if used wisely. Emily, James and Nathan need you, and they are in the dungeon. Once you enter the castle, you will see a tall, winding staircase on the right. Do not, under any circumstances, go up that staircase. Instead, go straight down a long narrow hallway that is located to the left of the staircase. At the end of this hallway is a staircase that leads down to the dungeon."

"Dungeon? What dungeon? You want us to go down into a dungeon?" scoffed Chelzy.

"If you are to rescue the children and complete your quest, dear Miss Chelzy, then yes, you must proceed down into the castle's dungeon. There you will find the children. And there is no need to yell at me. I can hear perfectly fine. Did you say something, Matthew? I think I do have to adjust my rabbit ears after all," said Tibbit, pointing his ears in Matthew's direction.

"I said, I can use my black dust card and onyx stone to make us disappear once we are in the castle so we can get to the dungeon before we are discovered." Matthew did have to repeat himself because it seemed Tibbit was somewhat annoyed with both Chelzy and his ears.

"And I can use my silver feather treasures to transport us out of there once we have . . . what were their names?" asked Tory.

"Slow down, slow down," warned Tibbit. "Powers? You may have to use the powers of your treasures just to get near the castle. Remember, you have a distance to go and there still may be dangers and traps ahead."

"Tibbit, do you think we used our treasures too soon? Maybe we should have kept them until we were closer to the Dark Queen's castle," Matthew questioned.

"What do you mean you may have used your treasures too soon? How many times—" When he heard rustling in the bushes, Tibbit immediately ran out of sight.

"Did anyone else notice that Tibbit did not look well?" Chelzy remarked. "I mean, his gold finish was sort of dull. He didn't shine like when we first met him."

"Sis, look around. Nothing shines in this horrible place."

"Doubt yourselves now and you will fail. Doubt yourselves now and you will fail," a voice seemed to come from a cluster of nearby bushes.

"Is that you, Skeemor? Where are you? I can't see you," yelled Chelzy.

The silver squirrel darted out from a nearby bush, muttering the same words over and over again as he circled The Trio. "Doubt yourselves now and you will fail. Doubt yourselves now and you will fail."

"We are just scared, Skeemor. And can you please stop for just a minute so we can talk to you? You are making me dizzy," said a wobbly Chelzy as she tried to regain her balance.

"Follow your instincts, Chelzy, and you will all be successful in your quest, and then so will I. Things to do, things to do. I have to run, have to run."

"Why did Tibbit leave so quickly?" asked Tory.

"I don't know, but I dread to think what is going to happen next," Matthew groaned.

"We're not sure if we just saw the real Tibbit or the real Skeemor. Did anybody think of that?" Chelzy warned.

But before anyone could say anything else, Skeemor had also disappeared into the woods. Chelzy, Matthew and Tory just stood quietly for a few moments, looking around for any sign of their friends. Chelzy sat down on a large rock. Once again, the mood among The Trio had changed. Panic began to invade the minds of the once adventurous, daring threesome. Matthew turned to his sister and, for the first time since their journey began, he saw a tear roll down her cheek.

CHAPTER 26

The Black Tiger

"Sis, we are going to be all right, and we will get home," Matthew said as he put his hand on his sister's shoulder, trying to comfort her.

"How can you be so sure, Bro? I am just a kid and I am not a good leader. And everyone keeps telling me to just follow my intuition or feelings, or whatever you want to call it, but I am not sure I even know what that voice in my head sounds like or if I would recognize my instincts even if they hit me in the face. Anyway, I don't want to let everyone down. It's not only you and Tory that I am worried about but also Emily, James and Nathan. They are probably three kids just like us, and they are probably as scared and as tired as we are."

"Chelz, do you know when you want to do something that you know you shouldn't because you are not supposed to and something inside of you tells you to not do it because it is wrong, and you decide to listen to that voice from inside?" Matthew asked while shuffling his feet on the dirt.

"Yeah, I guess so."

"Well, I think that's kinda like instinct. And from past experiences, I think you listen to that voice a lot better than I do. Mom and dad always tell me to use more common sense when I do things I shouldn't; and I think that is kinda like instinct. I think that is why the Bright Queen chose you to give us advice."

"Chelzy, if you ask my mom and dad, they will tell you that there are a lot of times that I don't listen to that voice either. So see, you are the best person for the job," added a confident Tory.

Tory barely finished her sentence when a loud rustling sound came from between two black bushes. "I sense trouble ahead. Beware!" warned Pelamar. "As you walk forward from here, there will be many junctions in the path where you can walk straight or walk to the right or walk to the left. There is another path to the Dark Queen's castle, and it will be a safer path because the Dark Queen will not know that you have taken it. It is a secret path that only she and a few of her trones know about and, of course, me. Take twenty giant steps ahead, and when you come to the nearest junction, take the path to the left. Hurry! Go now!"

Before anyone had the opportunity to thank Pelamar, he was gone. Chelzy quickly rose to her feet, and The Trio stood side by side. Having observed that there were many places where the path gave two or three choices, they had to decide who should count the twenty giant steps. Each one's steps would probably lead them to a different place, and Pelamar said that there was only one safer path to the Dark Queen's castle.

Giving a big sigh, Tory said, "Okay, Chelzy, which one of us should take the giant steps?"

After only a few minutes of thought, she replied, "I think Matthew's would be too big and mine too small; but I think yours, Tory, would be just right. After all, you are the adventurer."

"Let's do it quickly. The Dark Queen is probably planning her next attack on us right now," warned Matthew. "Wait! How can we be sure that was the real Pelamar? What if it was one of the Dark Queen's kreons and the impostor is sending us into a trap?"

"Bro, that voice inside my head is telling me it was the real Pelamar and not an impostor. So, let's do what he said."

"I'm in. Let's do it," Matthew said with eagerness and no hesitation.

The Trio formed a straight line with Tory in front, Chelzy in the middle and Matthew in the back. After taking a deep breath, Tory began taking giant steps while counting, "One, two, three, four—"

"GROWWWWWWWL! ROARRRRRRR!"

The Trio stopped dead in their tracks. Tory, being in front of the line, looked ahead until she saw something that caused her to put her hands to her face and start screaming. A short distance ahead of them was a huge tree that looked like something out of a scary Halloween picture. It was black and bare of leaves. It had crooked branches that looked like a witch's hands with long curved fingers and nails extending from them. Close to the top of the tree was perched a large cat that appeared to be a black tiger with gray stripes. As soon as it saw The Trio, it began its descent to the ground. With its long claws extended to grasp the limbs and bark of the tree, the cat slowly and carefully planned its attack as it came closer and closer to the ground. The branches of the tree were actually assisting the tiger in its descent as it stalked its prey.

"I don't want to be eaten by a ferocious cat! Run!" exclaimed Matthew as he turned and started running in the opposite direction.

Chelzy and Tory immediately followed. By the time The Trio was well beyond where they had started to count Tory's paces, the black tiger was out of the tree and in fast pursuit.

"We are not going to make it!" yelled Chelzy. "He is getting closer."

The Trio was running as fast as they could, but the black tiger was quickly gaining on them. His dark green eyes radiated a sinister glare that seemed to reach out and touch them. They could hear his loud panting as he continued his chase. "What do we do?" yelled Tory. "There's no place to hide."

"Just don't look back! Keep running forward!" screeched Matthew.

"Help! Help! Somebody please help us!" cried Chelzy.

At that point, a loud noise appeared to come out of nowhere. It was like a freight train in a hurry to make a deadline.

"Now what is happening? What is that noise?" hollered a panting Tory.

"My normal swishing noise is not very distracting to any predator, so I decided to improvise, thanks to the Bright Queen!" shouted the blue unicorn as she swooped over their heads.

"Melzabod, you're here!" Chelzy shouted.

After flying past The Trio, Melzabod quickly set her sights on the attacking cat. Around her neck was a net that that could be released with a quick pull on a string. As Melzabod began her descent, she carefully lined up her flight path so it would be between Matthew, the last in line, and the black tiger. Melzabod knew that she would have to be very precise in dropping the net so as to capture the tiger and not Matthew. If she failed, she knew that the tiger would overtake The Trio. After deciding that her flight plan was not precise enough, Melzabod pulled up at the last possible moment.

After circling the area one more time, she began her dive. She gently put her mouth around the string. She knew that she didn't have a lot of power in the Dark Queen's Earth, and she wasn't even sure that she would have enough strength to lift the black tiger. So, once she trapped the cat in the net, Melzabod knew she would have to use whatever energy she had to take the tiger as far away from Chelzy, Matthew and Tory as possible. Like a jetliner coming in for a landing on a runway, Melzabod lined up her flight course with the tiger's attack path.

"Everybody, duck quickly! Melzabod is flying really low and is headed our way," shouted Chelzy.

Within seconds, Melzabod flew over the heads of The Trio, dropped the net and then scooped up the black tiger, which was now only a short distance from them. As she flew away, she bellowed, "Don't stop! Keep going! You must get to the Dark Queen's castle!"

Matthew fell against a tree, Tory lay flat on the ground and Chelzy sat on a tree stump, all totally exhausted.

"I guess that was the real Melzabod! If it wasn't, that net would have been thrown over us," said Chelzy.

"I want to go home. I'm scared and I don't want to be here anymore. I really want to go home," a very tired Tory cried.

Matthew tried to calm Tory down as best he could. "Tory, the only way home is in the Candesia Land of Pines. And to get there, we have to go through the Dark Queen's Earth. And anyway, do you really want to give up on rescuing those kids when we've come so close?" asked Matthew. "We're all scared but we still have each other and a few more powers and magic up our sleeves. The Bright Queen believes in us and so do our friends, Skeemor, Tibbit, Pelamar and Melzabod. They have always been close by and have come to our rescue when we needed them the most. And, don't forget Chelzy's special ability to think problems and situations through and come to right decisions. What about Skeemor? If we don't go through with this quest and let him help us, he'll never turn to gold."

Suddenly, Matthew noticed that Chelzy was very quiet and preoccupied in her thoughts. She wasn't even paying attention to Matthew's speech to Tory. "Hey, Sis, what's wrong? You're very quiet."

"I just realized, Bro, that we are never going to get to the Dark Queen's castle."

"Why not?" interrupted Tory, who stopped crying after hearing Chelzy's comment to her brother.

"Because Pelamar said there is only one safe path to the castle, and it is exactly twenty paces from where we were. The only problem is," continued Chelzy, "where were we before we started to run? When we ran away from the tiger, we ran past our starting point, and we'll never figure out where to start counting twenty paces again."

"I can figure it out," said Matthew. "Well, you see . . . ummm . . . I was afraid to say anything, but when I saw the cat stalking us from the tree and getting ready to attack us, I took the onyx stone out of my pocket to get it ready to use. You know, just in case, but it kinda of—of—fell on the ground."

Tory quickly asked, "Where is it now? Did you pick it up?"

"No, I couldn't; there was no time. Anyway, I figure if we keep walking back on this path, we should find it; and it will mark the exact spot where I was standing, and then we can figure out where you were standing, Chelzy, and then we'll know where you took your last pace, Tory. What number was your last pace?" asked Mathew.

"It was four. I counted up to four paces. So, then we can continue from that spot," Tory reported.

The Trio began their walk back along the path. Their eyes were glued to the ground in search of the black onyx stone. It was decided that Tory would be the lookout for any lurking creatures that might jump out at them from behind the trees or bushes. She walked back-wards and looked alternately right and left for impending danger. Chelzy and Matthew walked slowly, side by side, examining the stones and dirt below them. Since there were a lot of dark colored rocks along the path, it was difficult to distinguish anything out of the ordinary like an onyx stone.

"I don't want to rush you two, but the sooner we get out of here, the better. Any luck?" asked Tory.

"It has to be here somewhere, but where?" whispered Matthew. "Wait, over there, I see something shining."

Matthew ran ahead until he stopped abruptly. Looking down, he was happy and disappointed at the same time. The black onyx stone had disappeared, but in its place was glittering black dust. It looked the same way as it did when he had first found it on their walk home from Grandma and Grandpa Stone's house.

"This is it! This is it!" Matthew shouted.

"Where? I don't see the stone; I only see some shiny dust. Oh, no! It's the glittering black dust. Why do you think it transformed, Bro?"

"Because I think it wanted to help us find the area quicker." Turning around, Matthew instructed the girls to get in the same po-sitions as they were before their encounter with the black tiger. "Tory, you go first, but be careful not to step on the black dust."

Matthew turned back around and looked down. The glittering black dust had disappeared, and in its place was the black onyx stone. Afraid that it might turn to dust again, he gently picked it up and placed it in his pocket.

"It's as if it just knew that we had to find it. I guess it is all part of its magic," said Matthew.

"Do you not have a quest to accomplish? Why are we standing around chatting about the mysteries of the universe? You all have sixteen more paces to take and a path to find. If you stay here any longer, the Dark Queen's demons, you know, the trones and kreons, will surely find and attack you again. Hurry! Hurry! Move along, move along," Skeemor instructed in a somewhat annoying tone. "At this rate, I may never turn gold, never turn to gold."

"Skeemor, you won't believe what just happened. The black onyx stone turned to—" started Chelzy.

"Yes, yes, yes, I know, I know. Have to go, have to go; so should you, so should you. Things to do, things to do." It seemed that whenever Skeemor got really nervous, he repeated himself even more.

Before Chelzy could say anything else, Skeemor had disappeared into the bushes. Tory took her position first in line, followed by Chelzy, then Matthew.

"Five, six, seven . . .," counted Tory, until she finished all twenty paces. "All right, here we are, and here's the path that Pelamar told us to take."

Without even a hesitation, The Trio was glad to be off the main trail and on the path that their beaver friend had told them would be safer. They knew that eventually the Dark Queen would find out that they had taken a new path and she would send her demons after them, so they decided that they had to travel as fast as they could.

Even though their friend informed them that they would be on a less dangerous course of travel, The Trio remained extremely cautious and apprehensive. Once again, they came upon a variety of mutated snakes. As they skulked along the new trail, Tory pointed out a large one slithering along a tall branch of a tree. Matthew pointed out several other snakes that appeared to be aware of their presence but not wanting to have anything to do with The Trio. Some had one head while others had two or three heads along with multiple tails. He wondered if they were the Dark Queen's spies.

Farther along, Chelzy pointed to several large black birds perched in trees along the path. She wondered if these were the same birds that had captured Emily, Nathan and James, and also if they were the ones that came after them in the Sea of Weeping Willows. Upon seeing the birds, Matthew clutched the onyx stone in his pocket, making sure it did not turn to black dust.

There was a thick fog that hugged the ground, making it difficult at times for The Trio to see where they were going. The trees appeared to be bent over in pain as a low groaning sound permeated the air. The three were walking at a brisk pace while, at the same time, huddling together for security. They began to see creatures that were unlike any animals they had known. One gray creature had large black eyes, a long, thin body and ears that were pointed like a serrated knife. Another had a small body, large head and a very long tail that was wrapped around its body many times. Even though the creatures examined Chelzy, Matthew and Tory as they walked by, none posed a threat to them.

"I am glad that Pelamar said that this would be a safer path, but I don't feel so safe with all these repulsive-looking creatures staring at us," Chelzy said, taking a hard gulp.

"How do we know that one of them is not a kreon?" asked Tory.

"We don't, but we would have been attacked by now if one of them was a transformed kreon. Look, we are getting closer to the Dark Queen's castle. You can see the top of it through the fog," Matthew said, pointing straight ahead and to a tall crooked tower atop a nearby hill.

"Do you think that by now the Dark Queen has discovered that we took this path?" asked Tory.

"She is very cunning and evil and smart, so I would really be surprised if she doesn't already have a plan in place. That is why we have to hurry. Just keep looking ahead. Try not to make eye contact with these creatures," whispered Matthew.

The Trio walked quickly through the shadowy forest of the Dark Queen's Earth. They held on to each other tightly, imagining what threats may lay ahead of them. Each step brought them closer to the Dark Queen's castle and to the next trap that the evil Queen had readied for them.

CHAPTER 27

The Beginning of the End

In the main chamber, or Great Hall, of her castle, the Dark Queen was pacing back and forth in an agitated fashion. She summoned her kreons and trones, although a few remained in the dark woods, searching for The Trio and strategizing ways to capture them. She demanded to know what path The Trio was taking. One of her kreons scouted their whereabouts on her orders. He brought back information that Chelzy, Matthew and Tory were taking the alternate path to the castle.

Enraged that the unwanted visitors were spared a confrontation with her trones and kreons, the Dark Queen bellowed, "How did the children discover the secret path? And why have you not captured these children and brought them to me yet?"

Karsorex, the head kreon, responded, "We have tried, Your Majesty; but as soon as one of them senses danger, they call upon the magic of one of their treasures to protect them. We are powerless against their treasures. When one of us posed as a tiger, their unicorn friend captured him before he could seize them."

"Powerless! You say you are powerless? I will not tolerate such incompetence! Do you not know that I am more powerful than all their treasures put together? You will do as I say. Go and transform into one of their friends. You have been spying on them, so you should know who they are and what form to take. Gain their trust, and then capture them and throw them into the containment room with the other children. And take their treasures away from them so they will be mine. Do I make myself clear? GO NOW, and do as I say or I will take each of you kreons apart one bolt at a time. As for you, my dear trones, I will pluck your wings and the one and only appendage you have and leave you helpless. NOW GO!"

The kreons and trones could not move fast enough to get away from the Dark Queen. Karsorex decided not to report that he had already transformed into one of their friends in the event that his plan did not work. He would rather take the credit if they are successful in capturing The Trio. As they were scampering away, they were still arguing among themselves as to whose fault it was that The Trio evaded them. "As usual, you trones are careless and don't know what you are doing half the time. You had the perfect opportunity to capture them, and you let them slip away," stated Karsorex bluntly, making sure that the insult was well directed.

"You may be bigger than we are, but if we ever wanted to, we could hook on to you and become ferocious animals that could devour you whole, except of course, as metal, you are not very appetizing," responded a trone. "Yuck! Just the thought of it gives me indigestion and a bad taste in my mouth."

As the trones and kreons were arguing among themselves, Chelzy, Matthew and Tory were concentrating on the trail ahead and trying not to look at the snakes, large birds or strange creatures that kept appearing in the woods. At the same time, the trones and kreons began to carry out the Dark Queen's commands. The Trio walked quietly while keeping a steady pace. All of a sudden, Chelzy screeched as softly as she could, "Look, I can see the castle clearly!"

It appeared as if the dismal fog was acting as a protective cloth, covering the castle; but, as The Trio got nearer, the fog drifted upward, unveiling its prized, malevolent possession. The palatial edifice appeared as no other they had ever seen. Instead of it being a big, beautiful and elegant building, it appeared as a morbid, almost prison-like structure with tall pillars that held statues of kreons and trones along with ferocious looking cats and snakes with several heads and tails. They stopped, looked up at the castle, and then looked at each other.

"It looks pretty big and spooky to me. It just reeks evil, and just the sight of it from here gives me goosebumps. I think I'm leaving. And anyway, if I'm not mistaken, that is a moat around it. How are we supposed to get across it? Now, I really think I'm leaving," declared Tory.

"To go where, Tory?" Matthew asked. "There is no turning back. We can only go forward. We are all scared, but that can't stop us now. We are so close, so let's just keep going. I am sure our friends will turn up to help us."

Chelzy added with a less than confident tone, "I hope you are right, Bro."

Without continuing the conversation, the three just continued walking as if some invisible force was drawing them in. When they arrived right outside the moat, a large drawbridge lowered itself. There was no one or nothing in sight. A thick gray fog seemed to hug the water in the moat surrounding the castle. The keep, or round tower, stood upright, piercing the fog as if conjuring up evil spirits.

"I thought castles are supposed to be impenetrable. This one looks too inviting to me," Matthew commented.

"I don't suppose that we are just going to walk on the drawbridge and onto the castle grounds. That would be way too easy, and surely a trap," remarked Tory.

"Listen to me. I agree with Matthew, there's no going back. I don't think we have a choice, Tory. How else are we supposed to get into the castle?" Chelzy replied.

"She's right. Tory, you and I have to be ready with our treasures, and use them only when we really need them. Chelz, you can't use the last power of your treasure because you have to save it to get home, but we are going to need you to help us decide when the right times are to use ours. If we are captured, we will be doomed here forever, and so will the children that we are supposed to rescue," Matthew warned.

With that advice having been said, Chelzy, Matthew and Tory stepped onto the wooden drawbridge to begin the end of their quest.

CHAPTER 28

Up or Down

The walk seemed very long. There was no conversation among The Trio, only sounds of shallow breaths and sighs could be heard from time to time. Each step they took was guarded as they each remained vigilant and focused on the venture at hand. Once across the drawbridge, Chelzy, Matthew and Tory stood motionless, looking up at the tall curtain, or wall, of the castle. Suddenly, they heard a loud noise. When they turned around, they saw the drawbridge being raised.

"Oh, great, now we are really trapped here," Matthew said in a low voice.

"What—what do we do now? How do we get inside?" Tory asked, her voice trembling.

"Look up at the towers. Have you ever seen a castle in a story that didn't have lookouts in the towers guarding it?" questioned Matthew as he pointed upward. "It looks deserted."

"No, on the contrary, I smell a trap," Tory said as she took a hard gulp and exchanged glances with Chelzy and Matthew.

The three kept walking until they approached the gatehouse, or door, of the castle. A portcullis was suspended above the doorway. The heavy, grilled door guarded the main entrance of the castle in the event of intruders or an attack. The Trio stared upward at the protruding iron spikes. Each was thinking the same thing.

"All right, this is beginning to look like a setup to me, too. What if we walk under it and it is released. We are gonna die," remarked Matthew.

"I saw something about castles on a cable channel once, and I think it comes down slowly, like with pulleys," Tory said.

"I don't think the Dark Queen wants to kill us. I think she wants to capture us alive so she can use our sadness like she does with Emily, Nathan and James," added Chelzy.

After a count of three, as decided by Chelzy, everyone ran under the portcullis and through the doorway. As soon as they had cleared the entranceway, they found themselves in a large courtyard. There were several entrances into the main part of the castle.

"They are waiting for us behind one of those doors or behind all the doors. The Dark Queen has a plan of attack, and she has readied her evil trones and kreons to help her. What are we going to do? This is not a game. We have to be right," warned Chelzy.

"Okay, concentrate, Chelz, which door do we go through? You can do this. Tory and I are prepared with our treasures, and you with your game piece. We still have their powers to get us through this. We can do this, Sis."

"Skeemor always tells us to take the middle path, so let's take that door," said Chelzy, pointing to the center door.

"All right, but I think we need to walk back to back so each of us is facing a different direction. This way, we will be ready for an attack," Matthew instructed.

Forming a triangle with their bodies and with their hands in their pockets, they slowly walked toward the middle door. Matthew pushed the door open with his head and foot, but only wide enough for the three of them to slide through. Once inside, the door swiftly slammed behind them. Tory screamed.

"SHHHH!" Matthew said in a loud whisper.

"This way! Don't you want to find the children? But you will have to hurry, have to hurry."

"Skeemor, are we ever glad to see you!" Matthew shouted.

"Now who is being the loud one?" Tory remarked.

"Follow me. The children are up there on the third floor in the last room on the left. We must go up the staircase on the right. Must go now, must go now! Must go quickly, must go quickly!" the squirrel said.

"Let's go. Let's follow Skeemor," said an excited Tory.

"No, wait! Tibbit told us under no circumstances should we go up that staircase," warned Matthew.

"You are right, the children are in the dungeon. Follow me quickly," said another squirrel.

"Skeemor, is that you? It can't be you! He's Skeemor! No, you're Skeemor! Okay, who's Skeemor?" said a confused Chelzy as she riveted her attention on the two Skeemors.

"Hurry, hurry, he's an imposter. Follow me upstairs. Time's a wasting, time's a wasting," said the first squirrel.

"It's a trap. I'm Skeemor; follow me before it is too late. Quickly, the Dark Queen is coming," warned the second squirrel.

The first squirrel ran in the direction of the staircase while the second squirrel ran straight toward the stairs leading down to the dungeon. "Chelz, quickly, tell us what to do. NOW would be a good time!" Matthew yelled.

"Follow me!" she immediately responded.

Running as fast as she could while following the first squirrel, Chelzy led Matthew and Tory up the staircase until they came to the third floor. Chelzy remembered that Skeemor told them that the children were being held in the last room on the left on this floor. She went up to the last door and yelled, "Is anyone in there? My name is Chelzy, and I am here to help you escape." Immediately, there was pounding on the door and voices could be heard pleading for help.

"Let us out! Let us out!" several voices were heard shouting from the room.

They quickly tried the doorknob, but discovered it was locked. "We don't have the key. How are we supposed to get them out?" Tory asked.

"Whatever we do, we better do it quickly, because I have a feeling the Dark Queen already knows that her kreon has failed at its attempt to trick us into going down to the dungeon. By the way, Sis, how did you know which squirrel was the real Skeemor? And how did you know that Tibbit was an impostor?"

"Later, Bro. Let's find the key fast. Look around. It has to be here somewhere."

As Chelzy, Matthew and Tory were frantically searching for the key to free the children, the Dark Queen had already observed in her magic window that the kreon had not been able to lure The Trio down into the dungeon. She was enraged with anger because, once again, her kreons had failed at achieving their task. She began shouting, "AGAIN! You have failed me again!" The robot that was trying to pass as Skeemor transformed back into himself and stood meekly in front of the Dark Queen with his head down and speechless. "Take him to the dungeon! I will deal with him later. The rest of you, follow me. I guess I will have to get the job done myself!"

Chelzy stopped searching for a moment and leaned against the tall, wooden door. She was ready to give up the hunt for the key when she was pleasantly surprised by the appearance of a friend.

"My tail is also a metal detector. I forgot to tell you. The Bright Queen had it installed just for this occasion. She figured that it might come in handy," Pelamar said, holding the key to the door in his two front paws.

"Pelamar, you're a life saver. You are Pelamar—I mean, you're not a kreon, are you?" asked Chelzy.

"You're not callin' me an old, ugly, squeaky, rusty robot, are you?"

"No, no; sorry, Pelamar."

Pelamar disappeared down the hall. The yelling and pounding on the door had stopped. It appeared that the captive children became skeptical about who was on the other side of the door and were too scared to trust anyone. Chelzy took the key and placed it in the keyhole. "Here goes." Afraid that this was just another one of the Dark Queen's tricks or traps, she slowly turned the key counterclockwise. Matthew and Tory held their breaths, waiting to see if the key would continue to move in the lock.

There was a loud click and the door became ajar. Matthew and Tory stepped back. Chelzy slowly took hold of the large metal door handle and swung the door open. Chelzy then put both of her hands to her mouth in disbelief.

CHAPTER 29

The Circle of Fear

The Dark Queen and all her evil companions gathered in the courtyard. The trones were all buzzing around her as the kreons just stood listening. Karsorex, having second thoughts about not reporting details regarding his encounter with The Trio while posing as one of their allies, stated, "Your Majesty Dark Queen, when I masqueraded as one of their friends on their journey here, I heard one of them say something interesting about their treasures. It appears that they can only use their treasures a certain number of times and then they are powerless."

"Very fascinating, indeed; but did you find out the details? Do we know who has powers left and who does not? And do we know what those powers are?" the Dark Queen demanded.

"Well, I—ah . . . ah—didn't stick around because one of their friends was coming, and if it was the real Tibbit, I would have blown my cover; but I did misinform them by giving the wrong directions to where they could find our captives. I gave them directions to the dungeon, Your Majesty."

The Dark Queen crossed her arms, stood at attention and yelled, "What is this? I have to endure yet more ineptitude! You stupid robot, you have not provided me with any valuable information that I can use! And how is it they didn't follow your directions? You see, they have climbed the staircase and are right now with our three captives. Take him to the dungeon! We can use him for spare parts."

The remaining trones and kreons were frozen in fear of what the Dark Queen might do to them. She continued in a pernicious tone, "Listen carefully. As soon as they free our prisoners, one of those children will use magic to try to escape the castle; but we don't know who that will be. So, we have to be cunning and swift." Pointing to three of the trones, the Dark Queen said, "You, my evil insects, go now and hide upstairs. As soon as you see one of the children's treasures, capture it and bring it back to me. Keep them from using any of their powers. Fail, and I will have your heads on my dinner plate tonight. Stop lollygagging and go . . . NOW!"

The three trones immediately circled the Dark Queen three times and then flew up the winding staircase, arriving on the third floor. They each hid, one behind a vase, one behind a picture on the wall and one behind an unlit candle on a table.

"We are so glad to see you," said a drawn and tired James. "My name is James Owens and this is my sister, Emily, and my brother, Nathan. We have been here for what seems like forever, and we gave up all hope of someone coming to get us."

"You really are kids, just like us," said a surprised Chelzy.

"How long do you think you have been here?" asked Matthew.

"We don't know because there is really no night and day here, and we don't change," replied Emily, "or grow older. It has been so, so long, and we miss our mom and dad very much."

Nathan added, "We overheard the Dark Queen telling her subjects, I rather call them her evil creatures, all about you coming to try to rescue us. I really don't think she thought you would get this far; but we are certainly glad you did."

"Let's get outta here. We can talk later. Quick, everyone, hold on to each other and to us. Tory, we should be close enough now for you to transport us to the Candesia Land of Pines with your feather," instructed Matthew.

Matthew held on to Tory and made sure that everyone was somehow connected to her. Tory took out her silver feather with her right hand and the silver feather card with her left hand. She closed her eyes and slowly brought the feather and the card together so they were touching. "Silver feather, bright and light, transport us to a—"

All of a sudden, a trone, from behind the candle, flew out and seized the silver feather from Tory's right hand while another trone, hiding behind the picture, grabbed the card from Tory's other hand.

"NO, NO! Come back!" screamed Tory.

As he held the onyx stone tightly in his right hand and the card in his left hand, Matthew shouted, "Everyone, hold on to me, NOW!" Knowing what just happened to Tory, he moved quickly. The trone, hiding behind the vase, tried to grab the black dust card, but Chelzy quickly caught the trone off-guard and swatted it away with her free hand. Bringing both hands together and holding them close to his heart, he recited the magic words, "Black stone, so dark as night, make us invisible with all your might."

All six children became invisible. "I hear them coming," whispered Chelzy, "so we better get out of here fast."

"We can't go down the staircase because we may bump into them. We may be invisible, but we are still capable of bumping into things. We have to go up the stairs," murmured Matthew.

"But we will become visible in a few minutes. If we go up to the tower, how will we escape?" Tory said, terrified of even considering what the outcome might be.

"Bro, you're right. We don't have a choice. Let's go."

As the six children cautiously climbed the stone steps leading up to the tower, the trones transformed into their ugly, three-legged creature form. They ran down the staircase with one having his prized catch, the silver feather, attached to his suction cup, while another trone held on to the silver feather card. The Dark Queen, with the remaining army of trones and kreons, was on her way up the staircase. As soon as she saw the returning two trones, she stopped immediately.

"Bravo, bravo! My fly friends, you bring me treasures." The Dark Queen spoke slowly and meticulously, emphasizing every word as she inspected the treasure. "Why, it is a silver feather. What power does it have?"

"We don't know, Your Majesty, but we also brought you a card that appears to work magic with the feather. We were able to steal both before the girl was able to call upon its powers. I am pleased to say that she is powerless now."

This time the Dark Queen spoke with even greater evil and contempt in her voice. "I will ask you only one more time, what power does this feather possess?"

"We don't know, Your Majesty, but we are sure that we can make the children tell us once we capture them."

"What do you mean *once* we capture them? Where are they? Why haven't you done what I have sent you to do?"

"Your Majesty," the trone began, "as soon as we snatched the feather, the boy took objects out of his pockets, said some words, and they disappeared."

"Disappeared? Are you telling me that all six children are invisible?" shouted an angry Dark Queen. "Everyone, up the steps! Spread out and make sure they do not escape! I will deal with you two incompetents later."

All six children reached the top floor of the tower. Out of breath and tired, they sat on the floor against the wall as they slowly became visible again. Tory sat with both hands in her pockets, searching just in case her silver feather and card decided to reappear by some magic. They did not. Now that they were all out of powers, a somber mood befell The Trio.

"How did we become invisible, and what was that object you were holding, and do you have any other magic up your sleeves?" asked an inquisitive James. "Or should I say, in your pockets?"

"The treasures with magic powers were given to us by the Bright Queen through a game board that we were playing, but we kinda used them all up," replied Matthew.

"Who is the Bright Queen? Unfortunately, the only queen that we know is the Dark Queen, and she is sinister. She kidnapped us, treats us like slaves and won't let us go home. We are prisoners in this dark and ugly place. We cry all the time; and all we want to do is go home and be with our family," said a very sad Emily.

"That is why you are here," explained Tory. "Your sadness empowers the onyx stones to give off just the right amount of light for the Dark Queen and her land; but, at the same time, it travels to the Candesia Land of Pines and weakens the Bright Queen's gems, causing her kingdom to slowly grow dark. And it is important to the Dark Queen that only the dim light given off by her onyx stones exists in her kingdom. She and her creatures cannot exist in bright light."

"What does the bright light do to her?" asked Nathan.

Chelzy continued, "The light blinds her and gives her great pain. I actually saw it happen when I used my black cloth in her presence. Light also drains her of her evil powers. Your tears have been keeping her powerful and well."

"I hear them coming. They must be close by, what do we do? Sis, now's a good time for you to listen to that inner voice again," Matthew said in a loud whisper.

The Dark Queen and her evil companions were nearing the top floor after scouring the third floor and finding no one there. They had concluded that since they formed a straight line across the staircase as they climbed upward, the children could not have sneaked past them.

"I have an idea," Chelzy said in a low voice in fear that the Dark Queen might be approaching their floor and hear her. "Emily, James and Nathan, I'll explain later. I'll turn into a deer and lead the way. They will not be expecting a deer to come running down the steps, and all of you can hold on to each other and form a straight line behind me. Tory, you go first and hold on to my tail. Everybody else, hold on tightly behind her. Don't look back. Just look ahead, and whatever you do, don't stumble on the steps. Keep a fast and steady pace, or more like a run. Just keep up with me. Whatever you do, do not let go of anyone."

Chelzy held her game piece in her hands and concentrated on becoming a deer; hopefully, a fast running deer. Nothing happened at first. She closed her eyes, clutched her hands together and concentrated as hard as she could. "I am a deer, I am a deer, I am graceful, I am swift, I am a d—" Everyone else was very silent and barely breathing. A bright yellow halo encircled Chelzy's head and she began spinning counterclockwise. To both the amazement and delight of everyone, especially Nathan, Emily and James, she transformed into a tall, beautiful and confident deer with her head held high.

"All right, everyone, do as Chelzy says. Get in a line. Tory, you go first and grab her tail. Emily, you go next, then Nathan and James. I'll go last," said Matthew. "Go, Chelzy, as fast as you can and run them over if you have to. We'll be holding on tightly to you and to each other."

Chelzy, now transformed into a deer, turned around to look at the five individuals she was leading into battle. She knew that this was her last chance to help everyone escape the evil Dark Queen and return to the Candesia Land of Pines in order to get home. She knew that she could run pretty fast as a deer and, since she was on a track team in her former school, she knew her combined abilities could certainly bring everyone safely down the stairs. But, she also knew that if she ran too fast, the children behind her might trip and fall. She knew that she somehow had to lead them away from danger.

Almost as if she was the locomotive and they were the cars in a train, the deer took a deep breath, gathered all her strength and let loose. They were on the fifth floor of the tower, and it sounded as if their attackers were very near. The deer was counting on the element of surprise in order to catch them off their guard. She figured that the Dark Queen would be walking in the middle of the stairs, leading her evil ones, so she decided to run down the right side of the staircase.

The line of offense was thin because the Dark Queen, with her trones and kreons, barely spanned the width of a very wide staircase. The deer now focused on what she had to do. She ran confidently and steadily, and was able to sprint fast enough and hard enough into the Dark Queen's barricade to push a few kreons aside. This was rather easy to do because the robots had no real sense of balance and it was easy for them to be knocked over. In doing so, it had created a domino effect, causing all the kreons and trones, as well as the Dark Queen, to lose their balance and fall. The deer kept going and the children, holding hands, were able to keep the brisk pace the deer had set. By the time they had reached the landing on the third floor, the Dark Queen and her creatures had regained their composure and were upright.

"You, imbeciles! You didn't tell me they had animals up there with them."

"We didn't know, Your Majesty. You see, they didn't h—" one of the trones attempted to say.

"Never mind . . . AFTER THEM!"

The trones turned from three-legged mutants back to flies and were able to travel at a great speed down the staircase. By the time the deer and the children reached the second floor landing, the flies were right behind them.

"Don't let them touch you," Matthew screamed. "They have suction cups; and once they attach to you, they turn into mutant creatures, and you won't be able to escape!"

Instead of continuing the attack, the flies flew past them and down the stairs. It was as if the trones had received a message via text, or some other secret device, from the Dark Queen to alter the attack plan. And perhaps, because she was expending so much energy at one time, the deer began transforming back into Chelzy. By the time the six children had reached the bottom of the staircase, Chelzy was herself and the trones were waiting for them, flying in place and forming a barrier so the children could not escape.

They could hear the Dark Queen shouting and panting out of breath as she descended the last flight of steps, "If you try to run, they will use their suction devices and capture you in a fashion that is quite painful. And what kind of host would I be if we do not have a chat before my loyal subjects take you to your accommodations?" Then the Dark Queen finally arrived at the bottom of the staircase. "Now, I will ask the questions, and you will give me the answers. First question is for you, my dear child," the Dark Queen said, pointing to Chelzy with her thin, crooked finger, which held a large onyx ring. "What are these magical treasures that you have, and how do you use them?"

"I don't know what you are talking about," Chelzy replied.

"Really, my insolent child? You see, my patience is running thin, and I want an answer to my question . . . NOW!" the Dark Queen screamed in her sinister, raspy voice while her evil companions formed a circle around the children. The evil queen stayed inside the circle but her trones and kreons kept moving clockwise as if they were looking for something hidden on the children.

The Dark Queen continued in her stern voice, clearly enunciating each word, "If you do not give me the information I seek, I will take you, one by one, out of this circle of fear I have created and punish you. I will take you apart piece by piece, limb by limb, in the same fashion I intend to dismantle the trones that have failed me. Do I make myself clear?

"Now, dear children, I want you to give me your magical treasures and explain how they work. I already have the silver feather and the card that must go with it; so you see, I just need to simply know how to make it do magic." There was a pause. "I'M WAITING! HOW DO I MAKE IT DO MAGIC?"

When the Dark Queen shouted those words, the trones and kreons stopped moving in the circle. The children became very still, except when Chelzy looked at her pocket and then at Matthew. Matthew moved his head back and forth, signaling Chelzy not to do what he thought she might be thinking of doing.

"YOU, my dear boy," the Dark Queen pointed to Matthew, "I will take to the dungeon first; then perhaps the others will talk."

The Dark Queen grabbed Matthew, and Chelzy screamed, "Leave my brother alone!"

"Your brother? How very interesting this is! Then maybe you might want to save him from a horrible death. Come, brother, I will take care of you. I will personally take you apart, piece by piece."

A squirrel came running out of nowhere and started biting the Dark Queen's left ankle, and a beaver, with a very sharp front tooth, began gnawing her right ankle. "Ouch! Ouch! Get away you dirty rodents!" The trones, not sure what to do and waiting for a direct order from the Dark Queen, just hovered above her, while the kreons just stood frozen in their places.

While the Dark Queen was yelling in pain and trying to shake off Skeemor and Pelamar, who were both creating a splendid diversion, Chelzy yelled, "Matthew, hold on to me, and everyone grab him! NOW!" Chelzy then started reciting the magic words as she held the glittering black cloth in one hand and the black cloth card in the other. The ruckus made by their friends gave Chelzy just enough time, and within seconds, a protective force field formed around the six children.

"NO, Chelzy! NO! Don't do it," screamed Matthew, but it was too late. Chelzy had used the black cloth's third and last power, the power that would have taken her home.

"Sis, that power was your ticket home. Why did you do it?"

"Because I could not let anyone hurt you, Bro," replied Chelzy, "And anyway, we have to get out of this place or all of us will be thrown in the dungeon or worse."

With the force field intact, the group stayed close together as they walked out into the courtyard. Nothing was able to penetrate the force field, even though the trones and kreons tried hard. As soon as the

Dark Queen was able to free herself from Skeemor and Pelamar, she raced after the children. "Stop them! Put the gate down!" she screeched.

Now it became a race to see if the children could outrun their enemies. The kreons were not able to run quite as fast because, as robots, their metal parts weighed them down. It took them a few seconds more to reach the gatehouse, or door, than it did the children. The trones were flying around the force field but were not able to penetrate it. They eventually rejoined the kreons who, by the time they reached the gatehouse, found another kreon lowering the portcullis.

"Quickly, we have to get under the portcullis," shouted Matthew.

Chelzy was leading the way and was barely able to slither under the iron gate that was being lowered; but once she was under it, the force field stopped the portcullis from moving. "All right, I am going to stay here, and the rest of you walk around me and slide under the gate, but don't let go. When everyone is on the other side of me, I will run out."

Tory went first, followed by Emily, Nathan and James. Matthew went last because he was the one holding on to Chelzy and this enabled him to help his sister move quickly by pulling her arm. With Matthew's help, Chelzy lurched forward; and as soon as she was clear of the portcullis, it came crashing down.

"Wow, that was awfully close," said Tory, after giving off a big sigh of relief.

"We have another problem, and it's a big one," said Matthew. "Look, the drawbridge is up. How are we supposed to get across the moat?"

As the children discussed their new problem, the Dark Queen and her kreons and trones were busily trying to lift the portcullis. It appeared that when Chelzy jammed the gate, it damaged the mechanism and it was much harder to lift. A very angry Dark Queen kept reprimanding and hurrying her companions to lift the gate so as to pursue the children.

"Now what are we going to do?" asked Tory. "The force field won't last forever; so if we can't get across the moat, we are doomed."

"We can jump in the water, but swimming will drain too much energy from the force field. Also, it takes a lot of strength to lower the drawbridge, and I don't think we even have the time to figure out where or how to do it. We are not going to be able to solve this predicament on our own, and I don't know who can possibly help us," said Chelzy.

"Well, the one called Chelzy, you are lucky that I have been well trained in all the workings of a castle, which includes drawbridges. I will lower the drawbridge so that you may cross the moat; but do it quickly, because I sense that the Dark Queen has figured out how to fix the portcullis, and she and her evil ones will be here shortly," said the gold grizzly bear.

"Greeter, it's you. You came to help us too?" Tory shouted.

"Do I look like an apparition in a bear's costume, the one called Tory? I requested it of the Bright Queen. I had a feeling there might be a job that our smaller friends would not be able to accomplish; but do not tell them I said that. And so, as usual, I was right. It will only take me a minute to get to the drawbridge mechanism. As soon as you see the drawbridge down, get across as fast as you can." With those words, the gold bear disappeared from sight as he ran to accomplish his task. The children stood in silence, staring at the drawbridge as it slowly retreated from its housing. Within a short time, Greeter's loud growling voice yelled, "That's it, the drawbridge is down. Cross now, the one called Chelzy, the one called Matthew, the one called Tory, and the ones called friends."

Once the children were across the moat, Greeter, along with Skeemor and Pelamar, followed them and then disappeared into the woods. Having figured out how to repair and raise the iron gate, the enraged Dark Queen, with her trones and kreons, was not far behind.

CHAPTER 30

Showdown in the Woods

"This is not going to work. The force field is going to dissolve any minute," Tory warned, "and the Dark Queen and her disgusting creatures are not far behind us. I can hear them, and we don't even know if we are running in the right direction."

Grinding his hand across his forehead and into his hair, Matthew added, "No matter what trail we take, the trones or kreons will find us; and we don't have any more treasures to protect us. There's no one that can help us get back to the Candesia Land of Pines. And anyway, we have failed our quest. We rescued the three of you, but we don't have the ability to return you to your family. Chelzy, you used your last power that would have taken you home; and, Tory, the Dark Queen has both your feather and its card."

"So, what you are saying, Bro, is that we failed big time. I am sorry that we can't return you to your families. We really tri—wait a minute, there is still one treasure that has the power to take one of you home. Bro, it's yours, so you will have to accompany one of them in order for the treasure to work."

Chelzy barely got the last word of her sentence out of her mouth when Matthew quickly interjected, "No way, Sis! Are you crazy? That's not going to happen. I am not leaving you here. I won't even think about it."

"I really want to get home," Tory began, "but I don't think I could leave here either without you two. I just couldn't. We have got to find a way to either get my silver feather treasure and card back or at least get back to the Bright Queen and beg her to help us."

"That's final, one for all, and all for one. We are in this together, and together we'll stay." Matthew then turned to Emily, Nathan and James, "We are really sorry. I hope you guys understand."

"We know how much you tried to help us, and we thank you for that," Nathan said, "but no one is a match for the evil Dark Queen. And we would do the same thing if we were in your shoes. We would stick together, no matter what."

"Match? Did I hear match?" a voice came out from between two straggly tall bushes. "You must have been reading my mind. This feather absolutely clashes with my mane. It just is not my style, and it doesn't do a thing for me. I tried it behind my ear, and that didn't work. It makes me look silly, and I have to keep my stylish reputation, you know. Pelamar attached it to my tail, and that looked even worse. Would anyone be interested in having it?"

"Melzabod, is that you? Where are you?" said Chelzy, not realizing that the Dark Queen was nearby.

"Right here," said Melzabod, curtsying with her forelegs and head, "at your service. And since my favorite evil one is getting very close, I think it is time to hand this treasure back to you, Tory."

"How did you get it?" shouted an excited Tory as she reached her hand out to take the silver feather from Melzabod's mouth. "Why can't I grab it? I'm trying, but I can't."

"With the force field," explained Matthew, "nothing can come in or go out until it disappears, which I think is beginning to happen. It's amazing that it lasted so long."

"As I said, the feather doesn't match my mane; but it even looked worse in the Dark Queen's crown, where she proudly wore it," said Melzabod, "so I swooped down on her and snatched it right from her onyx crown. Quite ingenious of me, even if I have to say so myself. Hmmm . . . I think I will say so. I'm a genius!"

At that moment, the Dark Queen emerged from between two trees, along with her small army of trones and kreons. The protective force field was now gone. "Everyone, cause a commotion—start screaming, make ugly faces, do anything—NOW!" yelled Matthew.

The Dark Queen was about to grab the feather from Melzabod when all of a sudden she yelled, "Ouch! Stop it. Get away from me, you horrible creatures." Skeemor and Pelamar were biting the Dark Queen's legs again, which distracted her from the feather long enough for Tory to grab it and start running ahead. Pandemonium ensued with everyone screaming and moving about in an attempt to distract the Dark Queen and her creatures.

"Quick! Everyone hold hands, and someone hold on to me," Tory screamed.

Everyone ran after Tory. Emily grabbed on to her arm. Nathan and James tried to take hold of Emily, but were unable to because the trones were attempting to attach themselves to the children. Nathan and James were waving their hands in all directions, trying to protect Emily and Tory from the flies.

"Quickly, kreons, turn into tigers now and attack them," yelled the Dark Queen while pointing to the kreon nearest to her. While this was happening, a trone attached itself to Chelzy with a powerful suction cup as it turned into an ugly three-legged creature. It had a large head with one huge jet-black eye. Its skin resembled crumbled paper with more of a rubbery texture. Two wrinkled and flattened wings were attached to its body, and appeared to be held tightly in place with super glue, while three short, stubby, clawed legs protruded from its underside.

However, the most frightening piece of its anatomy was its one suction cup, which was positioned at the end of a flexible rod-like structure that protruded from its back. The size of the suction cup was almost as big as the creature's head, and it was surrounded with jagged stones, which began piercing Chelzy's back. Matthew was trying to free his sister from the trone, but the force of the suction cup was too strong for him. Chelzy started to call out in pain as the sharp edges of the stones dug into her back.

"I have captured one, Your Majesty! I have captured one!"

"Well done, my friend. And why are you tigers just standing here while the other children are getting away? ATTACK NOW!"

The kreons, which had transformed into tigers, stood frozen in their tracks and were not about to run after the children. Standing between the Dark Queen and the children was a very tall, ferocious grizzly bear that gave off one very loud roar. Greeter was not about to allow anyone to get near Tory, Emily, Nathan and James; and when the flies heard Greeter, they retreated into the woods. The tigers also decided that they did not want to take on the huge bear and they, too, headed for safer ground.

"The controls for this suction cup must be somewhere back here. Hmmm . . . let's try right about here," said Pelamar; and after taking one deep breath, he took a big bite into the trone's backside. Giving off a big groan, the trone released the suction cup from Chelzy, who fell to the ground. Matthew then grabbed his sister, and they immediately ran to join the other children. "Ugh! What a bitter taste. Anyone have mouthwash on them? I really have to get my teeth cleaned after this trip," commented Pelamar as he quickly disappeared into some nearby bushes. He yelled back, "You deserve it, you one-eyed diabolical creature! By the way, you're ugly too."

"Hurry up, everyone form a connection to me," screamed Tory. At the same time, the Dark Queen, limping from her wounds inflicted by Pelamar and Skeemor, who also disappeared in the bushes, started screaming at her kreons and trones to come back and capture the children before they all got away.

Greeter was keeping the Dark Queen at a safe distance for the time being, but the children knew that she was resourceful enough to find a way to pursue them. Tory only had a matter of a few minutes to call upon the magic of her treasure and card to transport them to the Candesia Land of Pines.

While Chelzy and Matthew were catching up to the others, Greeter left the area, and the Dark Queen convinced her evil companions to return. She then gave the order to attack again. At her command, the kreons attempted to turn into grizzly bears but, for some reason, they could not. They were then told to turn into mountain lions, which they did; and Greeter was nowhere to be seen.

The hunt was on. Just as the children had formed a connection to each other and to Tory, and had a head start, they could see the mountain lions running fast towards them. The Dark Queen, with her trones, was not far behind them.

Matthew shouted, "Keep the connection and run as fast as you can. Do not let go. Tory, say the magic words. Let's get out of here. Now is really a good time. Hurry!"

Tory put her left hand in her pocket and then remembered that a different trone had taken the silver feather card. "I don't have the card. I can't do this. We can't transport out of here."

Within seconds of hearing Tory's disturbing words, Matthew freed his hands. He then shouted to the others to form a connection to him, took the onyx stone and the card out of his pockets, and held them in both his hands. He drew them close to his heart and recited, "Black stone, so dark as night, make us invisible with all your might."

The mountain lions and flies, along with the Dark Queen, were only a few yards from the children when they disappeared. "NO, Matthew, NO!" shrieked Chelzy. "That was your last power."

"Sis, remember, I am not going home without you," Matthew responded. "If you are trapped here, so am I."

"Not again! They got away again. Spread out and find them, you imbeciles!" bellowed the Dark Queen. "Hmmm . . . did I hear one of them say they used up their last power and they are trapped here. Oh, how convenient for me."

The children were running as fast as they could. Even though they were invisible, they knew they could be caught if someone or something ran into them. They decided to take a trail that would take them back to the Dark Queen's castle because they figured the Dark Queen would never think that they would double back to where they came from. They were wrong.

"These nasty children are very cunning, so I want you all to split up. Half go forward, and half of you go back to the castle. Listen for their voices. They are probably plotting their getaway at this moment," said the Dark Queen.

"We only have a few minutes to be invisible. Chelzy, what should we do?" shouted a very terrified Tory. "I hear her. The Dark Queen is coming."

"Take the middle path, take the middle path. The treasure will be at the end. Things to do, things to do; I must go," said Skeemor in a low voice as he raced across their path. "I can't see you, but I certainly can hear you. If I can hear you, so can the Dark Queen, the Dark Queen. I would converse more quietly, more quietly."

"Skeemor, where are—"

"Never mind, Bro, let's jus—wait a minute, what middle path? Look, that wasn't there a minute ago. Run! Everyone follow me."

"Are you sure that was Skeemor?" asked Tory.

"I sure am. Let's go!" responded Chelzy.

The six children ran down a path that had appeared out of nowhere. A surprise was waiting for them at its end.

CHAPTER 31

The Elusive Treasure

The children ran as fast as they could through the extremely narrowed, middle path that Skeemor had told them to take. They knew the Dark Queen, with her mountain lions and flies, was not far behind them. The path was difficult to traverse because of its size and the low visibility. It was also lined with very tall trees that were giving off a foul odor and had only a few branches near the top. As they ran past a tree, it would bend over and almost touch them. Several were giving off a sound similar to that of an owl. It almost sounded as if they were saying "here." Since the Dark Queen's loud shrieking informed the children that she had found the path they were on, the children concluded that the trees were communicating with her.

"We're visible again. Now what?" shouted a very scared Tory.

"Skeemor would not let us down. If he said to go this way, there must be a good reason. Wait, I see something. It's an entrance to a cave. Let's get into it quickly!" yelled Chelzy. Everyone came to an abrupt halt behind Chelzy when she arrived at the entrance to the cave.

"We'll be trapped for sure in there. They will find us easily. I would rather keep running," said Nathan.

"NO, Skeemor said there is a treasure at the end of this path, so this cave, or something in the cave, must be the treasure. And if we turn around, we will surely run into the Dark Queen. My instincts tell me we need to get into the cave NOW!" said Chelzy, trying to reassure and, at the same time, rush her brother and friends into the cave.

Hesitantly, they all agreed to follow Chelzy's directions, and they moved forward. The opening was not very tall, and Matthew had to bend over slightly to enter it. There was very little light inside, but enough to be able to see the walls, and the floor of the cave was covered with a mist, almost like fog.

"Wait a minute. Look at the walls. There's drawings and writing on them," said James.

The Dark Queen stood outside the cave with her evil creatures. "So, my friends, what do we have here? It looks like the miserable little brats have taken refuge in a cave. How convenient and nice of them. It is so much easier to trap them all at once. Shall we call them out or should we just go in after them? Pat yourselves on the back. We did a good job finding them," boasted the Dark Queen.

"Bro, she's here, right outside the cave. I can hear her. Quick, everyone, look for the treasure."

"Come out, children; come out, children; wherever you are. I don't feel up to playing games. I can just come in and get you, but it will go a lot better for you if you come out on you own," shouted the Dark Queen.

All of a sudden, the earth shook. Everyone felt it, even the children inside the cave. Six huge oak trees emerged from the woods and stood between the Dark Queen and the entrance to the cave. They stood side by side, forming two rows, which made it impossible for anyone or anything to enter the cave.

"Don't even think of sending your flies past us because we are prepared to use our broad leaves as fly swatters and our branches as bats," said a confident Quercus.

The Dark Queen screamed, "Out of my way or I will send my mountain lions to climb you with their very sharp claws. They will slowly tear your bark, inch by inch!"

"If we swing our large branches, my friends and I are very capable of throwing your cats into oblivion," Quercus said adamantly.

Matthew stood watch right inside the cave entrance so he could prepare the others should the Dark Queen or her evil companions come near it. Inside the cave, the children were frantically looking for the treasure that Skeemor had told them would be there. Chelzy, on the other hand, was trying to decipher the drawings on the walls. "Over here! I think I figured it out. These are drawings of trees, but it all looks so familiar. Wait, I've got it! This looks like The Lost and Found Game we were, or maybe I should say, are playing. This is the Gelabar Land of Oaks, and here is the Sea of Weeping Willows and a waterfall."

Pointing to a particular place in the Dark Queen's Earth, Chelzy continued, "We are here in a cave where there are six stick figures; and right in front of us is a card. It's the silver feather card! That's the treasure! Skeemor must have grabbed it from the trone and brought it here for safe keeping for us. It's here in the cave, but because it is so small, we probably just can't see it because of the fog. Everyone, get on your hands and knees, and feel around for it."

Matthew came running inside the cave shouting, "You are not going to believe this!"

"Believe what, Bro?"

"Quercus and his friends are protecting the entrance to the cave so no one or nothing can enter it," Matthew explained. "He's the friendly oak tree that helped us in the Gelabar Land of Oaks, and he brought his friends with him to form a barrier right outside the cave. They are buying us some time, but I am not sure how much."

"I found it! I found it!" hollered Tory. "The card, it's the silver feather card."

"Okay, Tory, do it quickly. We have to get out of here fast, because I don't know how much longer Quercus and his friends can protect the entrance," said Chelzy. "Everyone, grab on to Tory!" Chelzy quickly grabbed Tory's shirt as did Matthew. Chelzy reached out to Emily and took hold of her hand while Nathan and James grasped Matthew's free arm.

Without hesitation, Tory put the silver feather in her right hand and the silver feather card in her left hand, and closing her eyes, she slowly brought the feather and the card together so they were touching and said, "Silver feather, bright and light, transport us to a safe place with all your might." She thought as hard as she could of the place where they first arrived in the Candesia Land of Pines. She kept thinking of the striking, vivid colors that greeted them when they arrived on their colored slides and all the oddly but beautifully colored grass, trees and bushes. Amidst tension and impending attack, Tory focused intently. Within seconds, all that was left in the cave were the drawings on the wall and the fog.

CHAPTER 32

The Gathering

All six children, holding on to one another, were transported to a very familiar spot in the Candesia Land of Pines, that is, familiar to three of them. It was the place where The Trio first arrived. The area, unlike the repugnant and hostile Dark Queen's Earth, was like a kaleidoscope of bright and picturesque colors. To a first-time visitor, it would appear as a delicately painted portrait radiating warmth and life. There wasn't any fog or mist in the air, only a light warm breeze that seemed to embrace all the creatures. As soon as The Trio and their friends were transported there, the trees started to hum a pleasant and captivating tune. It was as if the entire Candesia Land of Pines began celebrating a happy occasion.

"Where are we?" asked a concerned Emily.

"Don't worry, Emily, I think we are in a safe place," James said. "It just looks and feels right; and it's really beautiful, like the opposite of where we came from."

Chelzy and Matthew took a moment to gain their composure. Tory, on the other hand, could not contain her happiness at seeing the place where they arrived at the beginning of their quest and shouted, "We did it! We're here; now we can go ho— Oh, I'm sorry. No, I'm really so sorry. Chelzy and Matthew, you both used your last power that would have taken you home; but you did it to save all of us. Don't worry, I won't leave you. I can't. We said one for all and all for one. But, what do you think is going to happen to all of us now?"

"No, Tory," Chelzy replied, "you have to take Emily, James or Nathan home with you. It's not right for everyone to stay here when two of you can return home. Anyway, how bad could it be to be trapped in the Candesia Land of Pines with the Bright Queen? Now that our new friends are here and the Dark Queen's Earth will no longer exist, this land should stay bright and safe."

At that point, the Bright Queen appeared with a beautiful rainbow behind her. She glowed from the gold and diamond tiara on her head to her delicately sapphire-lined slippers; and it was refreshing to the six children, especially Emily, Nathan and James, to finally see something bright and colorful again. Greeter appeared from the woods as tall and grizzly as ever a bear can be, except of course, he was now a radiant gold, having just been buffed from head to toe. The Bright Queen had given him swift running abilities as a reward for his loyal service to her before he left to help The Trio. This ability enabled him to return to the Candesia Land of Pines so quickly.

"Bright Queen, it is so good to see you. It was a terrible journey," explained Chelzy. "You were right. There were many traps and hidden dangers; but we made it back, well kind of. And if it wasn't for Pelamar, Tibbit, Melzabod, Greeter, Quercus and especially Skeemor, we would have all been captured and imprisoned by the Dark Queen or, even worse, we could have been killed."

"I know Chelzy," said the Bright Queen. "I received word of all the dangers that you had encountered on your journey and all the challenges that you had to overcome. You all acted admirably."

"Did I hear my name? No, I did not hear my name. Yes, it was my name that was said." Pelamar appeared with a toothbrush sticking out of his mouth, saying, "I just can't seem to get rid of the sour taste of the Dark Queen from my mouth. Yuck! I am still looking for mouthwash. Anybody have any? I'll take any flavor. Anything has to taste better than her."

Tibbit, who before his trip to the Dark Queen's Earth was transitioning to gold, was now completely gold and admiring himself in a mirror he was holding as he ran out from between two bushes. "Well, if I have to say so myself, I look marvelous! Gold makes me look even slimmer and more handsome, don't you think?"

Melzabod, on the other hand, made a very dramatic entrance as she swooped down, barely missing several tall pine trees that bent when they saw her coming. "Excuse me. I am not looking my best. I need a good grooming of sorts. All that traveling, trapping a tiger and rescuing a feather messed up my mane. I hope the groomers at the palace have an opening today."

"Pelamar, Tibbit, how did you get here so fast?" asked Matthew.

Before either one could respond, Melzabod answered, "Why of course, with me. We left when you first entered the cave because we knew Quercus would help you stay safe; and Skeemor told you where to find the silver card, so our jobs were done."

"Speaking of Skeemor, where is he?" asked Tory.

"Did someone call me? Did someone call me?"

"Skeemor, you're here too. But, your tail and the tips of your ears are turning gold. How can that happen, Bright Queen?" Chelzy asked. "We failed our quest. We rescued Emily, Nathan and James but we can't take them home unless Tory's treasure can transport all of them. You see, Matthew and I had to use all the powers of our treasures when we were in real danger. We were not able to save the last one to take us back home. I guess we'll have to stay here with you if you'll have us. But if we failed our mission, so did Skeemor. So why is he turning gold?"

"First, you are right, Chelzy, you are unable to return home, and Tory's treasure has the power to transport her and only one child. You see, each of your treasures had the power to transport home its owner and one of the rescued children, but Tory was the only one who saved a power from her treasure. Tory, you will have to choose who will return home to their family. Are you prepared to do that?" the Bright Queen asked.

"I know I said one for all and all for one, and I'd rather stay here with my friends, but if I do that, then no one will be able to return home; and that's not fair to them. Somebody should return to their family, but I do not want to make the decision who goes with me and who stays. Can you do that, Bright Queen?"

"I am afraid I cannot do that. You, Tory, must decide who returns to their family."

Nathan stepped forward, saying, "Listen, everybody. Emily, James and I have spent a long time in the Dark Queen's Earth. We really don't know how long for sure, but we figure it has been quite a while. Even though we really want to go home to our family, we're happy that we are at least in this beautiful place; and Chelzy, Matthew and Tory have sacrificed a lot for us and have kept us safe. I mean, look, Chelzy and Matthew used their treasures so we could escape the Dark Queen, knowing that they could never return home. That's pretty cool, so we are staying too. Anyway, we had a lot of time to talk when we were imprisoned, and we all agreed that no matter what, we would not allow anything or anyone to separate us. We think our parents would want us to stick together, too."

The happy mood of the Candesia Land of Pines was quickly diminishing and being replaced by one that was more somber. Chelzy, who was curling her hair, now stopped and began crying. "I'll never see my mom and dad or my Grandpa and Grandma or my house or my friends ever again."

Matthew walked over to his sister, put his arm around her and wiped her tears with his fingers. "It's all right, Sis. We knew when we came that we were taking a chance. And look at the bright side, no pun intended, we get to stay in the Candesia Land of Pines with the Bright Queen and our new friends, if she'll let us."

Emily walked up to the Bright Queen and explained, "I don't know if this means anything and I know it was kind of wrong to do, maybe wrong like in stealing, but I took something from the Dark Queen's castle. First, I hid it in the dungeon, where we were kept most of the time; then when they moved us, I took it with me and hid it again in the room where they found us. When Chelzy, Matthew and Tory came for us, I quickly grabbed it and hid it in my shoe. Boy, was it ever hard running with this in my shoe."

After a slight hesitation, Emily continued, "You see, one of the many chores that Nathan, James and I had to do was to polish the Dark Queen's onyx stones. One of her kreons had to count the stones every day to make sure none were missing. I noticed that he didn't know how to count very well. He kept missing one number. So, when the Dark Queen put a different kreon in charge of the counting, I took one onyx stone, knowing that it wouldn't be missed. I'm sorry if it was wrong. I know it is dishonest to steal, but I was hoping that somehow we could use it to escape someday." She held out her closed right hand and slowly opened it. In her palm was resting a black onyx stone. She held it so tightly that the stone left indentations in her soft skin.

"Under the circumstances, dear Emily, you have earned the stone. You did the right thing. You were trying to save your brothers. May I have it?"

Emily gently placed the black onyx stone in the Bright Queen's hand. The Bright Queen closed her hand, turned around and asked the rainbow behind her to come and hold it. The rainbow shrunk in size and the Bright Queen was able to place the stone in its colorful arms that emerged from its arch. She then took out her wand and gently placed it on the stone. She then proceeded to recite an incantation. A multitude of brilliant colors were discharged into the air. It looked like a multitude of Fourth of July fireworks going off at the same time. Within several seconds, the stone returned to its normal, shining, black onyx state.

"There," she said, "this black onyx stone now has one power to take you home, Matthew."

"I can't believe it! Thank you, Emily, and thank you, Bright Queen, but what about Chelzy?"

"I'm afraid that only a piece of the Dark Queen's black robe empowered with magic can take you home, Chelzy; and the one I gave you was the only one I had," said the Bright Queen.

"You mean my black cloth was a piece of the Dark Queen's robe?"

"Yes, Chelzy, that's right. I put a magic spell on it so it was able to protect you and light your way when you were in grave danger," replied the Bright Queen.

"Skeemor, you're turning more gold!" shouted a very confused Chelzy.

"Well, more isn't good enough. I want to be all gold, I want to be all gold. This should do it."

Skeemor ran back into the bushes, and upon returning, he ran up to the Bright Queen with something hanging out of his mouth. The Bright Queen gently took it out of his mouth and held it up for everyone to see.

"What is it?" asked Tory.

"Well, when I was chomping on the Dark Queen's leg, yuck, in case you're interested, in case you're interested, I tore off a piece of her robe because, you see, her leg was getting too hard to chew on," explained Skeemor. "I thought it might come in handy, I thought it might come in handy. She didn't even notice, didn't even notice. It doesn't taste much better than she does."

"Skeemor, my friend, you did a wonderful thing," said Chelzy, "and because you have completed your quest, I can go home too." A tear rolled down Chelzy's cheek; however, it was one of happiness, not sadness.

The Bright Queen once again called upon her rainbow, but this time, to hold the black cloth. The rainbow came closer, bowed down before the Bright Queen and extended its arms out to her. With the power of her magic wand, sparkles of gold, red and black radiated from the black cloth high in the sky. Once again, it reminded Chelzy of Fourth of July fireworks, only bigger and brighter, much brighter. The colored sparkles danced in the air, at times, making vibrant designs of different shapes. Once it had settled down, the Bright Queen handed it to Chelzy. "I believe you know what to do with this."

With everyone present at the gathering, Greeter, Pelamar, Melzabod, Tibbit and, of course, Skeemor, the Bright Queen clapped her hands three times and said, "It is time. Matthew and Tory, you have been brave and have completed a very challenging quest. Well done, children. Emily, Nathan and James, you have endured great hardship; but, because of your new friends, you will finally return to your home, in your own time, and you will not remember any of this, for only the holders of the treasures will have the ability to remember. All of you have proven to be unselfish and willing to sacrifice greatly for each other.

"Chelzy, I think that you have learned many things. Being the youngest in a family does not mean you are less important, or less creative, or less smart. It only means that you are the youngest and have your own special gifts, and you are a very important part of your family. You have also learned that you have the ability to be very courageous and that if you listen to that inner voice, your instincts, you can accomplish great things. You are a great leader and you did a wonderful job, my child."

At that moment, three large pine trees came forward. "Eulb, it's you!" exclaimed Chelzy.

"Yes, and I brought Der and Reppoc along so we could all say goodbye to you. Since we welcomed you to the Bright Queen's Kingdom, we wanted to be here for your departure as well."

Quercus then appeared from nearby bushes along with several of his friends. Winston and a few other young oaks were right behind them. "We came to thank you for not only rescuing the children, but for saving our land from the Dark Queen's evil plans," said Quercus.

"You saved us too, Quercus, and we will never forget you," Chelzy responded.

"We couldn't have done it without the three of you," Quercus said, extending two branches out to them like open arms.

Smiling and elated with joy, Matthew and Tory each gave their thanks and said their farewells to Greeter, Skeemor, Pelamar, Tibbit, Melzabod, Eulb, Der, Reppoc, Quercus, Winston and their friends. Chelzy did the same, except for when it came to Skeemor. She knelt down in front of him, and holding his front paws in her hands, she said, "I will never ever forget you, my friend. If it was not for you, I would not be going home, and neither would any of us. You are my hero; and you are going to look really cool when you are all gold. I wish I could see you then." This time a tear of sadness ran down Chelzy's cheek. Skeemor gently wiped it away with his paw and gave her a hug.

"I, too, will never forget you, will never forget you. Every time I buff my gold finish, I will buff it extra shiny for you," Skeemor responded softly.

"Each of you came on a slide of a certain color, and you must return in the same fashion," said the Bright Queen. I am going to give each of you the gift of your special color. Whenever you see that color and touch it and close your eyes, you will be able to see my kingdom as well as all the friends that you have made here and all the love they have grown to have for you.

"Turn around, my children. There are three white tree stumps behind you. They are quite tall so, Chelzy and Emily, Eulb will help you up on the first one; Matthew and Nathan, Reppoc will lift you on the next one; and, Tory and James, Der will raise you both up on the last one," explained the Bright Queen. "Emily, you must then hold on to Chelzy; Nathan, you must hold on to Matthew; and, James, you must also do the same with Tory. All right, my pine friends, place the children on the stumps."

The tall and colorful pine trees gently placed the children on the tree stumps. The Bright Queen, Pelamar, Melzabod, Tibbit, Eulb, Reppoc, Der, Quercus and Winston, along with many other animals, all in colors ranging from shades of white, bronze, silver and gold, formed a circle around the tree stumps. Skeemor sat inside the circle and directly in front of Chelzy's stump. The Bright Queen laughed and said, "Chelzy, I believe if Skeemor could go with you, he would."

He stood up on his hind legs and waved to his friend for the last time, and she waved back.

"Now, Chelzy, Matthew and Tory, hold your treasures in your right hand, your treasure cards in your left hand, cross your hands and hold them close to your chest and your heart. Close your eyes. I want each of you to think about where you were before you rode down to the Candesia Land of Pines. Keep thinking . . . keep thinking . . . keep th—"

"Wait, Bright Queen," interrupted Chelzy, "I know we will be able to see our friends through the special color you gave to each of us, but will we remember everything else?"

"Unlike Emily, James and Nathan, you three will remember your quest and your friends; but you will have to decide if you wish to share your experience with anyone," the Bright Queen responded. "Is everyone ready? Concentrate, concentrate, concentrate . . ."

The children all nodded. Chelzy, Matthew and Tory followed the Bright Queen's directions and held their magical treasures and cards close to their hearts. With eyes closed, they each thought of the huge tree stump that they were standing on and the ladder from Tory's yard that they used to climb onto it. All of a sudden, Chelzy's tree stump turned yellow, Matthew's turned orange and Tory's turned red. Colorful twisting slides emerged from the stumps and the children began riding the slides backward, going upward.

Chelzy's slide, once again, was making melodic sounds while Matthew's orange slide was whistling a happy tune. Tory's red slide was emanating quick notes. Together, the sounds formed a loud, but pleasant, happy melody. The slides were traveling at a high rate of speed and formed a triple helix, which enabled the children to pass one another from time to time. The children traveled at a speed that was even faster than when they traveled down the slide to the Candesia Land of Pines.

All of a sudden, Matthew could be heard yelling, "Nathan, he's gone!"

The slides began to break away from the triple helix formation, and Chelzy, Matthew and Tory were now moving upward but alongside each other. Nathan, along with Emily and James, had disappeared, and each of The Trio was alone on a slide. All of a sudden, the slides traveled through a thick, white, puffy cloud. As they were moving through the cloud, they noticed that all the sounds had stopped. They began to slow down until they came to a complete halt.

CHAPTER 33

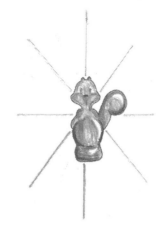

The Last Game Piece

"We're here! We're back home!" Chelzy exclaimed. "Look! This is the tree stump we climbed using your ladder, Tory. But my black cloth is gone. So is the card." The Trio found themselves sitting on the same tree stump where they had first started their journey.

Matthew added, "My treasures are gone too, and it looks like yours have disappeared also, Tory." Tory nodded in agreement. They looked in their pockets and all around them, but they could not find them anywhere.

"I guess they served their purpose and the Bright Queen figured that we don't need them anymore," Matthew said, letting out a big sigh. "After all, with no sadness in her earth, the Dark Queen's onyx stones will no longer keep her inhabitants alive, and she too will die; and the children of Sycamore Street will be forever safe from her."

"Do you think that Emily, James and Nathan are back with their family in the time they were abducted?" Chelzy asked.

Sitting next to his sister and leaning backward, looking up into the sky, Matthew responded, "Yeah, I do. Somehow, the sky looks a lot brighter than when we left, as if it's happier or something."

"I can see my ladder," Tory announced. "It's right there where we left it."

All three children were sitting on the huge tree stump that they had found in the woods behind Sycamore Street and in the place where they had first started their quest. Nothing seemed to change. The weather was the same as when they had left and it appeared that they had arrived near the same time of day as when they had first embarked on their journey. However, they were not sure when they had left in relation to the present. There was no night and day in any of the territories that they had traveled through, so they weren't sure if they traveled back in time, forward in time, or nowhere in time.

Chelzy, Matthew and Tory stood up straight and looked at themselves and each other. "We look the same. We have the same clothes on and we don't look older," Matthew remarked.

"Bro, I don't think we were gone that long, but probably long enough to be in trouble. How are we going to explain being gone so long to mom and dad?"

"Are you kidding? I am going to be grounded for life. My parents, most likely, won't let me hang out with you two anymore," added Tory.

Suddenly, the stump they were standing on began to vibrate. "Oh no, now what's happening?" yelled Tory.

"Everybody, quick, hold on to each other," bellowed Matthew.

Unexpectedly, the enormous stump began to shrink. The Trio formed a circle by grabbing the other person's hand and standing precariously as close to the center of the stump as possible. Now it became a matter of trying to balance themselves so that they would not fall. The stump continued to shrink until its size was that of a normal tree stump. In the center, Chelzy, Matthew and Tory stood motionless and speechless for a few moments.

"For a second, I thought maybe we were going to travel back down to the Candesia Land of Pines. But I guess without our treasures, that would never be possible," Chelzy surmised. "Anyway, our job is done and we accomplished our quest; that is, with a lot of help from our new friends."

"Well, we better get home," Matthew said. "Maybe we can just say we got lost because we really did. Wait a minute, Tory, this all happened because of your Lost and Found Game. I wonder what we will find when we get to our house. Do you think our treasure cards will be missing?"

"I don't know if I even want to see that game again. I think I might want to pack it up and give it back to my uncle," Tory responded.

"I agree. I don't think I want to play it again," said Chelzy.

No longer needing the ladder, The Trio jumped down from the stump. They located the ladder on the ground. Matthew took hold of the front with Chelzy and Tory lifting the back rung. They began walking the trail that would lead them out of the Magic Woods. They decided the name was very appropriate, but they were not sure that they would go near that particular tree stump ever again. They also decided that they would tell the truth—they got lost in the woods—but they would not tell about the adventures that came alive in The Lost and Found Game.

Even if they wanted to tell someone that they traveled through a portal into a mysterious land and rescued the three abducted children from 1982, with the giant tree stump gone, there was no proof that anything unusual ever existed or happened. They concluded that no one would believe them, with the possible exception of Grandpa Stone. But even if they confided in him and he didn't believe them, they would run the risk that he might tell their parents or, worse yet, he might stop telling interesting stories about the past to them.

"How long do you think we were gone?" asked Tory.

Matthew replied, "Hard to tell. I would say at least a day, maybe a lot longer. What do you think, Sis?"

"I think that we've been gone long enough to be in really big trouble. But did you notice that we were never really hungry or thirsty? It must have been something that the Bright Queen gave us when we ate and drank in her castle."

"Chelz, I have a question?"

"What, Bro?"

"When we were in the Dark Queen's castle and there were two Skeemors, how did you know which one was the real one?"

"Well, our Skeemor always repeated himself, and the other Skeemor did not. But more than anything, I used my instincts because that could have been a trick, too. And don't forget that when we were in the Dark Queen's Earth, an impostor of Tibbit tried to hoodwink us into thinking that Nathan, Emily and James were being held captive in the dungeon. I didn't realize it until we actually found them upstairs. He was very convincing."

"Well, I guess I should stop calling you a birdbrain, Sis. Well, maybe."

When they arrived at Matthew and Chelzy's backyard, they decided that they would leave the ladder near the back porch and return it to Tory's yard later. Everyone stopped for a minute and looked up at the porch. Chelzy started thinking about when she first discovered the glowing black cloth. Tory felt a little sad not having her feather in her pocket, and Matthew wondered if he could buy an onyx stone in a store to keep as a remembrance of his quest.

"I wonder if they sent out a search party looking for us," Tory said.

"It seems pretty quiet and doesn't look like anyone is trying to find us. Okay, here goes. I'll go first," Matthew said.

"No, wait! Do you remember that the playground down the street was built and dedicated to Nathan, Emily and James?" asked Chelzy.

"Yeah, so what, Sis?"

"So what? Just think about it. If Nathan, Emily and James returned to their families back in time right before they were abducted, then the playground should not be there. Right?"

"Wow, Chelzy, that makes a lot of sense. But maybe if it's there, it is because they built one anyway for the kids in the town," offered Tory.

"Yeah, but if that's the case, then there won't be a dedication stone with their names on it at the entrance. Anyway, we have to know for certain that this was not just some kind of dream, you know, like we all fell asleep and—" Chelzy paused and gave out a big sigh, "That would be ridiculous, wouldn't it? Why would we all fall asleep at the same time, and how could we all experience the same things in our dreams?"

Matthew quickly added, "What are we waiting for? Why don't we just go and look for the playground now before someone sees us and then we have to explain why we were gone so long, or worse, where we were? The playground may tell us if everything was just a figment of our imaginations or if it all really happened."

The Trio exchanged glances and then began running, first around to the front of the house, and then down the street. Huffing and puffing, Chelzy said, "So far, it looks all the same to me." When they came to the end of the street, they crossed, but they abruptly stopped running.

"This is it, isn't it?" Tory shuddered. "The playground is, or used to be, down this street. I'm not sure if I want it to be there or not. I mean, I want to know that Nathan, Emily and James were able to go back in time and be with their family, but that means that everything I did, or we did, was real. And that's insane!"

"It is kinda scary but we have to know for sure, so let's keep going," added Matthew.

"Yeah, but could—could we walk this time?" stammered Chelzy.

The Trio groped along as if traveling in uncharted territory. Matthew surveyed the road just in case some black dust or an onyx stone appeared; Tory kept scrutinizing the sky even though she knew the Dark Queen was dead by now as were her large black birds; and Chelzy kept looking ahead and anticipating what she would see very soon.

"It's down there, right past that gray, stone house," muttered Chelzy. Their pace slowed as they all centered their attention on the row of houses that lay ahead. Then, all of a sudden, they stopped dead in their tracks. There it was—the area where the playground once stood.

"It really did happen. It's gone, the playground is gone," Chelzy said slowly and deliberately. In its place stood an office building with a sign on the front that read: Law Offices of Dugan, Kelly and Owens. The Trio became silent for a few moments. "Everything that happened was real. We're not crazy."

"Owens? Isn't that James, Emily and Nathan's last name?" gasped Matthew.

"Yep, it is. You thinking what I'm thinking?" Tory queried.

At that moment, a gentleman wearing a three-piece pinstriped suit and carrying a leather attaché case in his left hand exited from the front door. He checked his wristwatch and began walking down the front steps. With car keys in his right hand, he began to walk to the parking lot adjacent to the building.

"Wait! Wait! Stop!" Chelzy blurted out in a loud scream.

"Sis, what are you doing?"

"I have to ask him something. He resembles James, but all grown up. We have to know for sure, and this is the only way we'll ever be certain, Bro."

The man suddenly stopped and turned his attention to The Trio, who were now walking toward him. "What can I do for you children?"

"Well, we were just wondering, what's your name?" Chelzy asked after taking a slow nervous gulp. "My name is Chelzy, that's my brother, Matthew, and that's our friend, Tory. We are new in the neighborhood and we just want to get to know as many people as possible. Are you Mr. Owens?"

"As a matter of fact, I am. How did you know that, or was it just a lucky guess?"

"It was sort of a lucky guess. I saw the sign on the building. What's your first name? I mean, we won't call you by it, but I was just wondering. And do you have any brothers or sisters?" continued Chelzy.

"Well now, aren't you a curious one. My name is Attorney James Owens, and I am glad to meet the three of you. Welcome to the neighborhood. I have an appointment, so I have to move along now. And by the way, yes, I have one brother, Nathan, and a sister, Emily. And the three of you do look sort of familiar, but I don't think we have met before. I hope you enjoy living in Simonsville. Maybe we will meet again soon." With that, Attorney Owens got into his car and drove away. Chelzy, Matthew and Tory stood there almost in shock.

"It all happened. That was James. Wow, I guess in a sense we are heroes because we saved them, and now they're alive and they're adults, which makes perfect sense," Chelzy concluded. Matthew and Tory were at a loss for words. Just as they started to turn to walk back home, something else drew their attention.

Another gentleman, much older than Attorney Owens, started to emerge from the front door. Wearing business attire and a black top hat, he was somewhat hunched over and walked slowly with a wooden cane. A white sedan pulled up in front of the office building, and a well-dressed petite, young woman got out of the car and began helping him down the steps.

Matthew gave Chelzy a quick glance and said, "Are you thinking what I'm thinking? Come on, let's go talk to him quickly before he leaves."

The Trio ran in front of the building and watched the woman help the elderly man reach the bottom of the steps. "Excuse us. Can we talk to you for a minute, please?" Chelzy inquired cautiously. She didn't want to seem too forward, although that did not stop her from talking with Attorney Owens.

"What can I do for you?" the young woman asked.

"Well, you see, we live a block down the street and we're kind of new to the neighborhood, and we were just trying to get to meet new people. I'm Chelzy and this is my brother, Matthew, and our friend, Tory."

"Well, it is very nice to meet all of you. My name is Amy Carmon, and this is my grandfather, John Avis Windsor."

With that introduction, Mr. Windsor tipped his top hat to The Trio and said, "It's very kind of you to take the trouble of introducing yourselves to us. I see many children playing, biking and running up and down the street, but no one stops to talk to an old man like me."

"My grandfather is an attorney and worked in this law office before he retired," Amy explained. "Now, he just likes to come and visit his former associates and the office staff. It really makes him feel good, and they always look forward to seeing him." As she continued to give her grandfather support by holding his left arm as they walked to the car, Attorney Windsor turned around and looked at the children several times. It appeared that he whispered something to his granddaughter but not loud enough to be heard by The Trio.

Chelzy, Matthew and Tory were speechless and motionless as they watched Amy help him into the car. After saying their goodbyes, Amy and her grandfather drove off.

Matthew shared his thoughts openly, "Just think how many people would not have been helped if James did not return home and become an attorney; and how about Mr. Windsor? I guess he lived a normal life and not one in a psychiatric hospital; and maybe Nathan and Emily both have families and are doing neat stuff. It's mind boggling!"

"I think you are right on the mark with this one, Bro. We did good, real good, but not without a lot of help. I'll never forget all the friends that we made, especially Skeemor."

"I really have to get home. Can I go with you first and check on my Lost and Found Game? I think I may want to just pack it up and give it back to my uncle," Tory said.

"Sure, let's run. I can't wait to see if our cards reappeared or not," exclaimed Matthew. The Trio was intrigued and overwhelmed with emotion by the events that transpired so far. As they hurried home, they kept thinking about the game and what they would find. They arrived at the Stone's house and ran to the back.

Chelzy climbed the steps first, followed by Matthew and then Tory. They stood on the porch, and after taking deep breaths, Chelzy opened the kitchen door. The three of them walked into the kitchen where Mrs. Stone was washing dishes in the kitchen sink. An unexpected visitor also awaited them. They stopped dead in their tracks and stood at attention not knowing what to expect.

"Well, you are a little late, but I'm not going to complain about ten minutes. Did you have a good time exploring the woods?" asked Mrs. Stone.

"Hello young'uns, I imagine you all had a very exciting visit in that special area with all the trees," said Grandpa Stone as he sat at the kitchen table, sipping a cup of coffee. With a sparkle in his eyes and a big grin, he winked at the children. "Good job, my young'uns. Good job. I mean getting home, you know, basically, on time." He gave a chuckle, winked again and then returned to sipping his coffee.

"Yeah, Mom, we had a great time. Thanks, Grandpa." Chelzy responded, after exchanging glances with Matthew and Tory, and taking a moment to absorb what her mom and especially her grandfather had just said.

Since it was evident that they were not in trouble with Mrs. Stone, they immediately walked past the dining room and into the living room. "Mom, what happened to the game we were playing? Where did you put it?" Chelzy shouted.

"What game?" Mrs. Stone yelled back from the kitchen.

Matthew quickly responded, "The Lost and Found board game we were playing right before we went outside; you know, the one Tory's uncle gave her."

Mrs. Stone emerged with a dish towel in her hand, "All right, guys, stop making things up. I don't know what you are talking about. Don't you remember? The only thing the three of you were playing was a video game. Chelzy and Matthew, you haven't played a board game in ages; and, Tory, you did not bring a board game here. Maybe your imaginations are playing tricks on you, like it does with Grandpa Stone from time to time."

Mrs. Stone returned to the kitchen and The Trio just stood perfectly still. "We know that we didn't imagine the game," Tory said. "What am I going to tell my uncle?"

"And how could we only have been gone an hour and ten minutes? It seemed a lot longer than that," Chelzy added.

"Did you hear what Grandpa Stone said to us? It's like he knew where we were but he couldn't say it," Matthew said. "Do you think his stories will change now since the abductions never occurred? Well, they did, but we just sort of undid them."

At that moment, something protruding out from under the sofa caught Chelzy's eye. "Wait, there's something on the floor under the couch."

"Listen, Sis, this is all sort of ridiculous, and even though we aren't going to tell anyone what happened, even if we did, no one would believe us anyway. Well, maybe Grandpa Stone would. Or maybe we are just imagining that he knows everything that happened to us. Everyone would just think we are crazy, and maybe we are."

As Matthew was trying to explain their situation, Chelzy slowly knelt down on both knees and put her hand under the sofa. She carefully removed an object, holding it securely in her hand.

"What is it, Chelzy?" Tory asked. "What did you find? Is it part of the game?"

Chelzy slowly opened her right hand. In her palm lay a small game piece about the same size as her deer game piece. But this time, it was not a deer, nor was it an eagle, or even a lion. It was a squirrel. With a big smile, Chelzy said, "This is a happy remembrance of The Lost and Found Game and of Skeemor. He must have placed it here for me to find with the help of the Bright Queen's magic." The game piece finished turning gold as Chelzy held it gently in her hand. "Told you, it really happened. I bet Skeemor is really pleased with being completely gold now." She then placed her prized possession in her right pocket.

"Wow, that's awesome!" Tory said.

"By the way," Mrs. Stone shouted from the kitchen, "your mom called a little while ago, Tory. She asked me to tell you that your Uncle Tony found an old board game when he went antiquing yesterday. He thought you might be interested in it and wants to know when you want him to bring it over. If she calls back, what do you want me to tell her?"

The Trio's bodies stiffened, jaws hung open, and nothing moved except Chelzy, who was curling her hair with her left hand.

Finally, Tory asked frantically, "Did she know the name of the game, Mrs. Stone?"

"Oh, something like *The Chest* or *The Box*, and it had the word 'magic' in there somewhere," Mrs. Stone yelled back to Tory.

Hearing that, Chelzy, Matthew and Tory exchanged glances, shook their heads, and decided that they were not ready to play another board game. At least, not anytime soon, not anytime soon.

About the Author

Lucille Procopio was inspired to write *Chelzy Stone's Mystical Quest in The Lost and Found Game* by her childhood experiences while playing in a wooded area behind the house in which she grew up. She is a former science teacher and elementary school principal, and continues to share her knowledge by tutoring students. She has two grown children and lives in Wilkes-Barre, Pennsylvania, with her husband and calico cat, aptly named Princess. She continues to write using themes centered on fantasy and magic for children.

For more information on Lucille as well as her other books, visit www.LucilleProcopio.com

Made in the USA
Charleston, SC
19 November 2013